ON THIN ICE

Rochelle Dowman

On Thin Ice
Published by Rochelle Dowman
New Zealand

© 2018 Rochelle Dowman

ISBN 978-0-473-43897-5 (Softcover)
ISBN 978-0-473-43898-2 (ePUB)
ISBN 978-0-473-43899-9 (Kindle)

Editing & Production:
Andrew Killick
andrew@safelittleworld.co.nz

Cover Design:
Paul Smith

This story is inspired by true events
and based on the author's memories of these events.
The characters' names have been changed
to protect and respect the identity and privacy of individuals.

ON THIN ICE

This book is dedicated to:

My Knight in Shining Armour, my wonderful,
amazing husband, Alan, for his undying support and
unconditional love – you are my soul mate,
the yang to my yin, TMD.

My beautiful, awesome sons, Andrew and Hamish –
I love you more than all the stars in the sky.

My step-children, André and Michele –
for your love, acceptance and respect.

Granny, without you, this book wouldn't have been possible.
Thank you.

'Some by birth, some by luck, all by love.'

CONTENTS

Chapter One

NICE HOLIDAY IN MEXICO?

Sophie ran like her life depended on it. Her long, honey-blonde hair streamed out behind her from under an enormous black and silver sombrero. Her heavily loaded backpack awkwardly jolted up and down with every stride. In each hand she gripped a suitcase extension handle as two trolley cases bounced along behind her, trying to keep up.

Leaving behind the nervous, hour-long wait she'd endured at the Los Angeles International Airport border after arriving behind schedule from Mexico City, she had 10 minutes to get to her connecting flight. As late as she was, there was no way on earth she was going to miss it now.

Sophie's cases were checked, x-rayed, stickered and carted off to the plane in record time. As she reached the final checkpoint and her boarding pass was being scanned, she breathlessly thanked the female border agent and vented her predicament.

'Okay, you'd better follow me!' said Sophie's latest heroine with a wide grin as she accepted the challenge. Then the border agent ran, carrying Sophie along in her slipstream, clearing a path through the crowd, and updating the status of the missing passenger on her walkie-talkie as they flew along. The agent's gesture of kindness was the only thing that held Sophie together and prevented her collapsing in a flood of tears.

'Nice holiday in Mexico?' the flight attendant asked sarcastically with forced politeness as she led Sophie into the plane and down the aisle. Sophie gave a strained smile in return as they arrived at her seat, but didn't answer. It occurred to her that she probably looked like just another late tourist, complete with her over-loaded backpack and ridiculously huge sombrero.

Just another tourist. And the last one to get on the flight. The whole plane had been waiting. For her.

She apologised as she squeezed past the tall man in the aisle seat, then past the spare centre seat, and tried to sit down beside the window. The enormity of her last three weeks was finally taking its toll and she realised she had absent-mindedly tried to sit down with her backpack and sombrero still on.

'You'll have to put them in the overhead locker,' said the flight attendant with a surly tone and a furrowed scowl.

'No, they're fine here,' Sophie replied meekly. She was scrunched over forwards like a half-shut pocket knife, with her backpack firmly pressed up against the back of the seat. 'I'll just keep them at my feet.' She felt exhausted and couldn't have stood up, let alone negotiate climbing over or squeezing past the poor guy on the aisle seat again.

'Okay, fine,' the flight attendant hissed at her, 'and please fasten your seatbelt.' Sophie sighed with relief as the woman abruptly turned with a whip of her head and proceeded to the intercom at the front of the plane. Twenty minutes after the final checks had been completed, the pilot was advised the plane was ready for take-off.

Avoiding eye-contact with the other passengers, Sophie leant further forward and shimmied off her backpack, placing it under the seat in front of her. She placed the sombrero on her lap, tilted over her knees, as she fastened her seatbelt.

Funny, she thought, how she always liked the window seat on

these long-haul flights. Of course she did like the view, but it was more because she loved being able to curl up and sleep against the cabin wall. But even though her body was exhausted, there wasn't a snowball's chance in hell she could go to sleep anywhere right now. Her mind was in a whirlwind as the events of the last three weeks spun round like a tornado.

The plane's engines purred louder and louder. Sophie felt like she was teetering on the edge of a cliff, wobbling, spent, every ounce of her just holding it together. After what seemed like an eternity, the plane backed out, then slowly rolled towards the runway. It turned the corner, then its engines roared as it sped down the runway.

Front wheels up. Back wheels up. Sophie was in the air. Lifting away from the continents of North and South America and all they had put her through.

Sophie let out a breath, realising she had been holding it since the plane had begun accelerating for take-off. She was a breath-holder and a lip-biter. These were her 'tells' when she was under stress. She closed her eyes and bowed her head a little, gripping the rim of the sombrero with her fingers, consciously trying to breathe normally. Sophie accepted she was finally losing the battle of holding it together. She bounced from the breath-hold to breathing more often and more deeply, as the plane rose higher into the clouds.

Exhaustion.

Relief.

Tears welled up and started to slowly spill down her cheeks until she was sobbing quietly as her body shook. With the sound of the wheels tucking up into the plane, the floodgates opened. The sheer relief of finally feeling like she might actually make it home alive had overwhelmed her.

'Hey!' A man's gentle voice interrupted Sophie's thoughts. A hand reached across the spare seat in the middle and gently touched her left shoulder. As one of her sobs finished, she took a deep breath and looked around. 'Are you okay?'

He's Australian, thought Sophie.

Aisle-seat guy looked genuinely concerned. Another smaller sob and a deeper breath. She had to admit it was comforting to hear a familiar accent.

'Yes,' she answered. Then another deep breath, and a quiet, controlled sigh. 'I am now.' She nodded, affirming this to herself as well as to the man.

How embarrassing, she thought. She hoped no one else had noticed her crying – she'd caused enough of a scene as it was.

Sophie wiped her eyes with her finger tips, thinking for sure her mascara must be smudged half way down her face by now. *Mascara raccoon eyes*, she thought.

'Tough saying goodbye, huh?' It seemed like more of a statement than a question.

Sophie was inspecting her finger tips to see just how much mascara was on them and remembered she wasn't wearing her wedding rings. Before going to Mexico, she had been advised to take off all her gold jewellery so she didn't get mugged. Aussie aisle-seat guy probably assumed she had left a boyfriend at LAX.

'Oh no, it's not that.' She didn't even want to begin to try and explain to a stranger the real reasons for her mini emotional meltdown. 'I'm just happy to be leaving this place behind.'

'Wow!' Aussie aisle-seat guy was nodding and smiling to himself now. 'So, messy break-up then!'

This was the conclusion he had jumped to? Now Sophie was smiling as well – at his preposterous imagination.

'Actually, I just had the trip from hell, and I've never been so relieved to get on a plane in all my life,' Sophie answered quietly, as she stared down at the sombrero over her knees. She looked at him briefly and smiled politely again, hoping he would understand she really didn't want to talk about it.

'Wanna talk about it?' he asked enthusiastically.

Oh no, she thought. This flight from Los Angeles to Melbourne, Australia, en route to Auckland, New Zealand, was nearly 16 hours long. The last thing she wanted to do was relive the terror of the last few weeks by telling her story.

'I'm Josh,' he said cheerfully as he held out his right hand across the spare seat to shake Sophie's. 'And I'm a really good listener.' He was bolder and braver than she was – there was no way she would ever dream of striking up a conversation with a stranger on a plane. She preferred to have quiet and solitude and keep to herself – read a book, watch a movie and sleep.

About that sleep, she thought.

She shook his hand gently. He looked to be in his early thirties, clean shaven, with short, spiky, styled brown hair. But there was something about his brown eyes and cheeky, daredevil grin that conveyed a kind heart and a gentle soul.

'I'm Sophie, and trust me, you really don't want to be bored with it all,' she said shaking her head. 'Suffice to say, we survived a fiasco in Mexico. Hence my relief to not only get on this plane, but to actually have it take off, and with no signs of it turning back.'

Sophie hoped her précis would quell Josh's curiosity. She smiled politely at him again and looked out the plane window for the first time. She found it reassuring to see only ocean below them and know that the flight was definitely headed for its destination. She sighed a long, loud sigh this time, as if to say 'Full stop' and 'Don't ask me anything more.'

'Come on!' said Josh, laughing. 'You can't tell me that, then leave me hanging! What happened to you? You say 'we.' Who is 'we'? Hey, did you get in trouble with the police or something?'

'Ah, yes! Actually, a couple of times!' Sophie laughed. 'It's a really, really long story,' she assured him and turned back to the window.

'Is 16 hours long enough?' Josh chuckled.

Even if she *did* feel like telling Josh the details, he probably wouldn't believe any of it anyway. The whole thing had been totally absurd.

On the other hand, she thought, *maybe it would be good therapy to get it off my chest so I can get some sleep.* He was a complete stranger, a good listener – or so he claimed – and she would probably never see him again. And anyway, he seemed like he wasn't going to let it go.

'Okay,' Sophie sighed, resigned to giving him the whole lot. 'But I have to warn you – it's a crazy story.' Sophie looked a little distracted, frowning down at her sombrero. Then she looked Josh straight in the eye. 'But it all happened. It's all absolutely true.'

'Right!' Josh hesitated. 'Well, try me!' he added with a challenge in his tone and the final coercion Sophie needed.

Chapter Two

ICE PASSION

Anton was 15 years old, turning 16 in two months' time. He was already 188 centimetres tall (or 6' 2" in the old measurement), and wasn't finished growing yet. With his shaggy, shoulder-length brown hair, slightly olive-toned skin and well-shaped shoulder and arm muscles, he had the athletic look of a tall, lean surfer. He was naturally happy – bubbly and chatty around his friends and at home – but slightly shy by nature, much like Sophie, his mother.

Anton tried his hand at all kinds of sports – cricket, rugby, basketball, softball – but it was ice hockey that had captured his imagination.

'Look Mum, I'm skating!' he would say when he was a little boy, with a huge, impish grin on his face, clomping around the house. He loved trying on Sophie's black Bauer hockey skates, complete with blade protectors, his tiny ankles wobbling to and fro. Those skates had a special spot in Sophie's closet and a special place in her heart. They would always remind her of Chad.

It had been teenage love – she had met Chad at the local ice rink. He was an ice hockey player, and she had fallen for him completely – him and a pair of beautiful white figure skates in the window of the rink shop! She was 17, and in her first year of nursing college, so she saved up money from her weekend nursing-home job to buy the skates.

The problem was, as Chad pointed out, she skated less like a figure skater and more like a hockey player. After several skating sessions when Sophie repeatedly humiliated herself by tripping over the toe-picks of her beautiful white figure skates, she reluctantly admitted he was right. So instead she bought a pair of very cool black Bauer hockey skates that Chad picked out for her, and never looked back.

Some weeks later, riding his motorbike en route to collect Sophie for a date, Chad was hit by a car and killed. He left her suddenly bereft, heartbroken. Three pieces of beautiful poetry he had written, and her hockey skates, were her only tangible memories of him.

A long time after Chad was taken from her, Sophie came across a little pearl of wisdom: if you lose your virginity to a man who breaks your heart, you will eventually move on; if you find true love with a man who then breaks your heart, you will also eventually move on. But if you lose your virginity to the man who is also your first true love, and if he is suddenly torn from you, breaking your heart, you will carry that scar forever. Sure, life goes on, and there had been lots of other joyous moments, but there was always a tiny void that rendered Sophie's life not quite complete. Even now, when she heard Paul Young's song 'Every Time You Go Away' she would quietly shed a few tears in Chad's memory.

At 19 she had met Charles Harding.

'Hi, I'm Charlie,' he said, coming out of nowhere and introducing himself with an outstretched hand. By then, she was in her last year of nursing college. She had stayed connected with people from the ice rink, who had rallied around her when Chad had died. But Charlie was from a different social circle. In fact, at 25 years old, it was like he came from a whole different generation. He'd bought a house, had a real job as a sales rep, and drove a flashy new company car with a dashboard like the inside of a cockpit, while Sophie and most of her friends only had part-time jobs and huge student loans.

She was young and impressionable, and he had impressed the socks off her.

But Charlie couldn't skate, and didn't want to. 'I can't see the point of skating round in circles,' he said. He didn't get along with her ice rink friends. So, as her relationship with him grew more serious, she unwittingly drifted away from the ice. Even now, several years into marriage and two children later, she still regretted that she hadn't kept up her passion for ice skating.

'Mum,' Anton had innocently asked when he was eight years old, while holding her treasured hockey skates, 'would I be allowed to have your skates when you grow out of them?'

Sophie giggled. Such a sweet, innocent boy. 'I'm sorry darling, but I won't ever grow out of them now because my feet will always be the same size,' she explained as she tied them onto his feet. He looked so disappointed. 'But would you like me to take you ice skating one day?'

'Oh, yes please!' He jumped up and down in the skates, then stomped off around the house to practise his 'skating'.

Anton had just finished a term of playing rugby. With his father's encouragement, he had been willing to give the sport a go but quickly discovered he hated it; and Sophie had been lumbered with the job of dragging him along every Saturday for the rest of the season. He had no other sporting ambitions in mind, so Sophie made plans for the two of them to go ice skating every second Saturday afternoon.

As they arrived at the old ice rink, Sophie was secretly pleased to have an excuse to get back into her old Bauers, and delighted to find some of the old crew were still there – almost as if time had stood still. They welcomed her back like the long-lost friends they were.

Anton was a natural. He simply stepped onto the ice in his hired hockey skates, and skated off like he was born with them on his feet.

Sophie taught him some basic skills and challenged him to learn a few tricks.

Less than a year later, she had taught him to stop in all directions – one foot, two feet, inside and outside blade edges. He could skate forwards and backwards, do fancy side steps, spin in circles in both directions and perform simple jumps. Sophie even taught him how to get a speed skating start then strike a hockey-style, ballet arabesque pose for the entire length of the rink.

Before long, Sophie and Anton were skating every Saturday, then doing two back to back public sessions as well. Anton was always the last kid off the ice and always disappointed when it was time to leave. Sophie felt the same – her love for the sport was alive and well.

Then one day, as Sophie and Anton were taking off their skates, Anton spied Kent, an Auckland Ice Hockey representative player, putting his gear on in the grandstand below them. The public skating session was well over and they were the last ones in the rink. An ice hockey game was scheduled for later that day, but Kent had arrived early to warm up because of a niggly old groin injury.

Anton was mesmerised, as Kent, a Canadian by birth, went through his warm-up routine on the ice. While watching intently, Anton tapped his mother on the arm, pointed at Kent with wide open eyes and said, 'Mum, I want to do that!'

A warm glow came over Sophie. Her son wanted to play a sport that was close to her heart, and he had come to this decision without the influence of either of his parents. She was rapt.

When Anton turned nine, Sophie enrolled him in hockey school, then bought him his first pair of hockey skates and a starter kit of ice hockey gear.

He had found his niche – the sport he was passionate about. He worked his way up through the ranks of peewees, midgets and juniors. Now, at just under 16 years old, he had been playing above his age group for a few years, qualifying for various regional and national rep teams along the way.

His younger brother, Hayden, had followed Anton's passion, also taking up the sport at nine years old. Hayden quickly found his own niche as a goal tender. There's something incredible about a kid who can stare down a speeding puck flying mid-air towards him, then put his little body between that projectile and the net behind him. He was two and a half years younger, but not at all in his big brother's shadow. Hayden had also been in several rep teams and, like Anton, was playing above his age group.

Sophie was fiercely proud of her boys and her world revolved around them. She frequently told them she loved them more than her own life. She would do everything within her power to make their dreams come true. God knows she was sacrificing a lot to offer them every opportunity to succeed.

Exhausting and expensive as it was, she wouldn't have traded any of it for the world.

With the commitment and dedication of a finely tuned military operation, she happily spent most of her non-working hours facilitating up to 14 different games and trainings per week. Often the boys had games scheduled for the same time in different parts of Auckland, and Sophie would cart van-loads of kids, including team mates and gear bags, back and forth across the city. Then there were plane trips up and down the country each year for national tournaments. No mean feat for a working mum.

The previous night, after Anton's under-19 ice hockey training session, he had appeared out of the change room with his colossal hockey gear bag over his shoulder, hockey stick in hand and a sheepish grin on his face. His wavy locks had been tousled and squashed into the unwashed 'helmet hair' fashion Sophie had grown so fond of. Little tufts – dubbed 'helmet horns' – were sticking up where the aeration holes had shaped them. Sophie was met with that familiar, stinky, stale hockey gear smell, as she hugged her towering son. He had developed a habit of resting his chin on the top of her head.

'Poo, you smell,' she grinned up at him as she embraced him tightly. It was part of their routine – she always said this to her boys at the end of their ice sessions. Sophie had been waiting in the grandstand during the team talk after training, and she hoped she was correctly interpreting what Anton's sheepish grin might mean. As they stood face to face, he humbly and quietly confirmed her hopes – he had been selected for the New Zealand under-18 ice hockey team, the Junior Ice Blacks, and would be going to the World Division III Championships the following year. In Mexico!

It would be a big moment in the lives of the New Zealand boys. In addition to the host nation, they would face down South Africa, Mongolia and Chinese Taipei, and the Junior Ice Blacks (named for the traditional colour worn by New Zealand sports teams) would enter the tournament as the number one ranked side.

True to character, Anton was mindful that there were other players around who hadn't been selected, despite the same amount of hard work and training. So he and Sophie kept a lid on their excitement until they were loaded into the van.

'That's fantastic! Well done, my darling. I'm so proud of you!' Sophie had a lump of pride in her throat as they drove out of the parking lot. During the 50-minute journey home they discussed the upcoming months and the schedule they were both now committed to. The team would commence their tournament build-up the following week, meeting four nights a week – two nights of on-ice training and two nights of off-ice training.

Sophie digested what it all meant for her. She would need to drive Anton to every session – firstly, because he was still on his restricted driver's licence and wasn't allowed to drive in the late evening, and secondly, because she assumed the management and coaching team would expect her to be there. That detail was usually taken as a given.

Sophie was a trained emergency nurse. She had a wealth of experience with trauma and sports injuries, and post-graduate diplomas in paediatrics (children up to 16 years old) and orthopaedics (bones) – handy qualifications for this age group, and for this sport! She worked full-time shifts at a private accident and emergency centre and had become close friends with her charge nurse, Bella, who allowed her to negotiate her roster to fit around hockey commitments.

Sophie was one of a handful of volunteers who helped keep the ice hockey club ticking along. Like the other volunteers, she was well aware that without her help certain things within the club just wouldn't happen.

Since Anton had started playing, she had managed several teams, and had completed a coaching course. This meant she could help coach on the players' bench during games and cover on-ice training sessions when the main coaches were away. Training usually took place at the hideous hour of seven o'clock on a Sunday morning. Understandably, the young coaches hated this time slot and every so often ditched their coaching duties in favour of partying. Someone had to coach the kids, and at least Sophie could skate proficiently and knew how the game worked.

But her most important role had become rink-side first aid, taking care of the triage and treatment of injured players. She had undergone the proper accreditation process so was able to refer players for x-ray, suture open wounds, make provisional diagnoses, plan treatments and then refer players on for appropriate care. She was an officially-approved independent authorised accident care provider, enabling her to fulfil her role without overstepping professional boundaries. By being this highly qualified and experienced – not to mention eternally helpful – she had quickly become the go-to first aid person for all premier, national and international tournaments. It was a specialised role, and she did it all for love, out of the goodness of her heart. 'Someone has to look after our boys,' she would say.

Having volunteered, things quickly morphed into a situation where management and coaches automatically knew she would find the schedule at the start of each season and write the important games in her diary. Occasionally, she would get a courtesy phone call a few days before a tournament, apparently made as a last minute afterthought or in a moment of panic, 'just checking' she would be there. But more often than not, everyone correctly assumed she just would be.

The world championships would be no exception.

Chapter Three

BUT IT'S MEXICO!

Mexico! Oh boy.

How could they afford it? Sophie would find the money – come hell or high water. She would make sure Anton got there, but if she went as well, that would add another NZ$3800.

Charlie had been made redundant twice in the last five years and had been without a job for long periods both times. The family had struggled through on Sophie's meagre wages, and by taking a holiday from their mortgage repayments.

Their finances had just recovered from the NZ$13,000 expense of an under-13 hockey trip to Vancouver and Kelowna in Canada the year before. Hayden had been selected as the goalie, and Anton as the assistant coach. Sophie had acted as the tour director and had given up huge amounts of time organising logistics and the itinerary. The team shared the cost of funding the senior coach, but everyone else had to pay their own way.

'But this is World Champs, and it's Mexico!' Sophie pleaded with Charlie in the kitchen the following evening, after Anton had gone to bed. 'I don't like what I've heard about the medical care there and no one on the team speaks Spanish. If I don't go, the boys won't have a medical person. And I've thought it through. We have loads of airline reward points, so maybe I can try and coordinate my flights using the points, and that way it won't cost much at all.

Plus, Bella will let me pick up some extra shifts at work, and I've got plenty of annual leave, so I can even get paid while I'm away. The only thing you would have to do is organise getting Hayden to school and hockey.'

'Fine,' Charlie had finally agreed, in one blunt word, and walked away. He wasn't happy about the cost, but if he was honest, he felt more comfortable about the trip knowing that one of them would be there to keep an eye out for his son. And with her medical skills, Sophie was the obvious choice.

It was only early November, and the 'Worlds' (as the championship was commonly referred to for short) were still four and a half months away. But Sophie knew if she was relying on booking flights with her reward points, she should get onto it as early as possible.

So the next day, she spent two hours on the phone with the airline. The first part of the tour would be a 10-day training camp in Utah. The team needed to train at altitude in Salt Lake City at 4,300 feet to prepare their bodies for competing in Mexico City at 7,350 feet. The American stop-over would be crucial preparation if the team wanted a real shot at gold medals.

The airline consultant patiently worked through Sophie's itinerary, working backwards from a flight that landed in Salt Lake City a few hours later but on the same day as the team. Using airpoints, Sophie could get to her destination by taking four different flights, totalling 36 hours from start to finish. She would fly in the 'wrong' direction to Melbourne, and wait four hours. Then fly direct to Los Angeles, and wait for six hours. Then fly well past Salt Lake City to Fort Worth, Dallas, waiting for two hours, before catching her final flight back to Salt Lake City.

After the training camp, she would leave Salt Lake City five hours earlier than the team and fly the same last two flights in reverse back to LA. She would stop there for three hours, then reach Mexico City half an hour earlier than the team, at the same airport, but at another terminal.

The whole travel plan was completely illogical and tedious, but it was the only way to use her air mileage points, and get to training camp on time. Sophie reserved window seats all the way. This meant she could curl up and sleep on the flights, enabling her to cope with the long journey.

Whew, she thought. *This is doable*. It was a lot of connecting flights and it was going to be long and exhausting. But it meant she could go on the tour. And she could make sure her son was safe.

Chapter Four

THE LINE IN THE SAND

At 39, Sophie had kept herself in pretty good shape. She was 170 centimetres (5' 7") tall, with a slender figure of 57 kilograms (125 lb). She definitely looked younger than her age, and got a kick out of shocking people when she told them her oldest son was nearly 16.

She thought of herself as an average-looking duckling that grew into an okay-looking swan. She wasn't supermodel gorgeous, but her mother insisted she had a natural, basic beauty. Like most women, Sophie couldn't see it. Sure, her features were pleasant enough and she did well with her figure. And she did have beautifully deep green eyes. But she always thought she was insipidly pale, and her hair had a mind of its own. There was no doubt where Anton had gotten his waves from. Sophie's hair was long – naturally a little wavy and fly-away – and warm, honey-blonde. She wore it with a heavy fringe. 'Rock bangs,' her Brazilian ballet teacher called it, while incessantly trying to convince Sophie to grow it out. Sophie would subconsciously bow her head a little in public because she preferred to hide under her fringe. Like Princess Diana had.

Sophie's friends insisted, and many strangers had said the same, that she looked remarkably like Phoebe from the American sitcom *Friends*. Sophie reluctantly admitted she could see the similarity. She was flattered, but mainly she was embarrassed by the attention this observation frequently drew to her.

Most of Sophie's wages disappeared on her sons' hockey costs. But the one luxury she allowed herself was a regular visit to a good hairstylist to keep her mane well cared for. She had found Ingrid years earlier, when Hayden was just a toddler, and then loyally followed her around four Auckland salons. Eventually Ingrid invited Sophie to her home for private appointments. It had developed into a social visit for them both, and Ingrid had become a close friend. Sophie would often arrive with take-out coffees and they would have a good old chin-wag as Ingrid dealt to Sophie's hair. Sophie tried to make every day a 'good hair day', always allowing a little extra time to get ready in the mornings. Nothing annoyed her more than when her boys tried to tousle it up, knowing full-well that it made her mad.

'You *never* mess with a woman and her hair!' she would tell them crossly.

From six years old, ballet had been Sophie's passion. She had danced until she was 16, when she felt she had achieved as high a level as her natural ability could take her – just two grades down from Prima Ballerina. But her pirouettes weren't perfect and nothing less than perfect would ever get her into the Royal New Zealand Ballet. So she had put this dream aside and taken up ice skating instead.

Anton was 12 when Sophie had confided in Charlie that she wanted to audition for a spot in an adult ballet class at the Auckland Performing Arts Centre. It was an Advanced class – the same level she had left at – but purely for those who wanted to dance for pleasure. She didn't know if she would be good enough but she wanted to give it a shot.

In Charlie's usual, unsupportive way, he had laughed raucously at this notion. And then snorted while saying, 'I can just imagine it – a bunch of fat, middle-aged, baby elephants jumping around!'

A typical snide response. Belittling and sarcastic. And this was rich from Charlie, who had gained quite a bit of weight himself since they had married. Sophie had stayed quite petite.

In spite of Charlie's less than encouraging response, Sophie conjured up the courage to audition anyway. She just wanted to dance again. She had to try. To see for herself. At the end of the class, the ballet mistress made a beeline in Sophie's direction and invited her to permanently join the class. She complimented Sophie on her good technique. The audition had been a total success!

Charlie couldn't have been more wrong, and when she got home, Sophie couldn't wait to tell him that she had made the cut. The only thing he had to say was 'Hmmm,' and carried on reading the newspaper.

Sophie's dancing helped her maintain her tone and strength. She also loved to walk in the surrounding sports fields, listening to her iPod, while her boys were in off-ice training.

The time she spent dancing and walking was the only time she had to herself. It kept her fit, but it also kept her sane, allowing her a chance to gather her thoughts. It gave her the strength to stay in a marriage that left her feeling neglected, invisible, taken for granted and completely unappreciated.

She had no doubt that Charlie loved her in his own weird way – like you love a comfortable pair of old shoes that you know you won't wear again but can't bear to throw out. She couldn't be sure he would notice if she went missing for a few days – except that his dinner wouldn't be ready on time.

Four years earlier, in an attempt to reach out to him, she had given him her little red diary to read. All her deepest, darkest thoughts and secrets. Her heart was poured out into it. And in it, she begged for him to listen to her. He just scoffed and laughed at her, throwing it back in her face saying, 'That's your problem!'

Any time she tried to talk to him about their marriage after that, he would roll his eyes and say, 'Oh God, not the stupid red diary again!'

Their relationship was a low priority to him. And now it had become that way for her too.

Sophie had come to the cold, hard realisation that she had outgrown the marriage. She certainly didn't hate Charlie. But the opposite of love isn't necessarily hate – sometimes it's just indifference. He had soaked up her love and attention back in their early days, and simply not appreciated it. She had received less and less back in return as time went on. God only knew, she had tried her best to keep the relationship alive, but it was more work than one person alone could achieve.

She had confided in Maree, her best friend, who summed it up beautifully. 'Honey, it's like you're flogging a dead horse, only that dead horse is now ashes, and the ashes were swept under the carpet a long time ago. There's nothing left to revive.'

Since then, Sophie had given up trying to resuscitate the horse. Her boys were the reason she stayed. But one day she knew they would grow wings and fly the coop. Until then, she would just have to get through each day the best she could.

The year before, Sophie had been approached in the supermarket by a woman from a modelling agency. The woman gave her a voucher for a free photo shoot and offered to help her put together a professional portfolio. It sounded too good to be true, but it also sounded like loads of fun! She didn't bother telling Charlie because she knew he would just laugh at the idea and tell her it was a preposterous and ridiculous waste of her time. She arranged to go along on her next rostered morning off. Charlie was at work and the boys were at school, and she was working a late shift, so no one would need to know.

Sophie felt flattered as the professional hair and make-up team fussed over her, making her look and feel like a star. The photographer said several times that she was a natural in front of the camera, but she shrugged it off – they probably said that to everyone.

Before she went home from work that evening, she was careful to take off the extra make-up so Charlie and the boys wouldn't ask questions. Usually a little mascara and lip gloss was all she applied. She preferred a cleaner, more natural look.

Soon after, the agency offered her a contract for some catalogue modelling. She quickly turned the offer down – it would have been too difficult to fit in with her boys and their training schedules. Plus, what would people think? That she thought she was beautiful enough to be a model? How ridiculous! How embarrassing!

Some weeks later, Sophie collected her portfolio from the studio, and after looking it over that afternoon before collecting Anton and Hayden from school, she placed it carefully in the back corner of the closet.

Charlie would never see it.

At their annual family New Year's Eve party, amidst Anton's frantic training schedule for the Worlds, and surrounded by her children, her parents and her closest friends, Sophie looked around with a genuinely happy smile, and decided her life was nearly perfect.

Except for one thing.

This party always symbolised new beginnings. Another year had flown by. But Charlie hadn't changed. Things were getting worse. He was rude, derogatory and sometimes just plain nasty. He hadn't been careful with their relationship and now he'd run out of time.

Individually, each of Sophie's three best friends had taken her aside and told her they hated how he spoke to her. They told her she should stand up to him. But standing up to him had never achieved anything. She and Charlie spent very little time together now and, sadly, Sophie was grateful for this. And besides, what would she even say to him if she tried?

Despite all that, here she was. Another year down the track. Another New Year's Eve party. Another new year beginning. With him.

Sophie suddenly felt overwhelmed. The thought of being stuck with this man for another year, or several years, let alone a lifetime, was unbearable. He wasn't the same man she married. He had killed off any feelings she once had for him.

Her mind searched frantically for the light at the end of the tunnel. She knew, and knew it with all her heart, that the day would come when she would definitely leave. But Hayden was only 13, and what if he stayed at home until he was 25? That would mean 12 more years!

Another single year, and she would lose herself. She would shrivel up and disappear into nothingness. She couldn't do one more year, let alone 12! Let alone the lifetime!

No! she vowed to herself, with sudden resolve. *I can't do it. I won't do it.*

This was the line in the sand.

She had put her life on hold for too long, waiting for something big to happen. Now she knew it was up to her – *she* needed to make something big happen.

She needed to make the change.

That night, she silently made herself a New Year's resolution – this year she would stop pretending everything was okay, and when the chance came up she would tell Charlie the truth.

She simply didn't love him any more.

Chapter Five

HERE WE GO!

With preparation for the Worlds, the first two months of the year flew past. One moment Sophie and Anton had been discussing plans in the van that November night when the team was named, then five minutes later (it seemed) they were at the airport saying their goodbyes. They would be away 20 days altogether, and it was by far the longest Sophie had ever been apart from Hayden.

Sophie didn't have a firm plan for what to do about Charlie. First she needed to tell him she didn't love him any more. Then, eventually, she would gain the courage to ask him for a divorce. She knew for sure it would be the hardest thing she would ever do in her life. She couldn't bear the thought that it might hurt Anton and Hayden. But there was always a reason not to leave. She was all too familiar with the rationalising that went on in her head. *Now is not the right time because…* Eventually she would have to just make it the right time.

She decided she couldn't do anything about it now, just as she was about to go away for nearly three weeks. Abandoning her youngest son, so soon after such a life-changing upheaval, wasn't something she was prepared to do.

The weeks between New Year's and her departure had been an emotional rollercoaster, and Sophie spent a lot of energy trying to keep her marriage problems at the back of her mind.

Anton had turned 16. And, in the midst of his busy training schedule, two weeks before leaving, he'd had one free weekend with no training sessions. Anton's childhood friend, Finley, had invited him to stay at his family's beach house, and the two boys planned to spend the days surfing. Sophie drove the two-hour trek to the beach with Anton and Hayden that Friday afternoon after work. It was a great distraction from everything that was going on in her life.

The trio always had a blast on their road trips together. Sophie subscribed to living by the immortal words of Aerosmith, 'Life's a journey, not a destination', and the journey had to be fun. At least most of the time. So they played loud rock music and laughed and sang at the top of their lungs.

Sophie had introduced the boys to the bands of her youth: Guns N' Roses, Van Halen, Bon Jovi and AC/DC, to name a few. Later they would find their own style, Sophie had no doubt. But for now they thought Mum's music and their road trips were *awesome*.

One day Hayden had said, 'People must get such a surprise when they first hear the loud rock music, then they look around and see this beaten up old van, and then they see you!' Sophie had laughed, appreciating the absolute compliment her son had intended it to be.

The journey went quickly and, sooner than expected, they reached the beach and unloaded Anton. Sophie enjoyed the view and sipped coffee while chatting with Finley's mother, Katie, another of her best friends, before returning to Auckland. On the trip back, Sophie and Hayden cranked up the music again and laughed and sang all the way.

Safely home, after offering a cursory greeting to Charlie, who was sitting watching TV, Sophie phoned Anton to make sure he had settled in okay and had found the sunblock and mosquito repellent she packed for him. 'Bye darling, love you,' she said, as she always did, then ended the call.

'Humph! You never say that to me when we talk on the phone!' Charlie had obviously been listening and was now complaining like a spoilt child.

When she thought about it later, Sophie couldn't figure out what had come over her in that moment. Perhaps she'd been caught off-guard, still a bit dreamy from the afternoon spent with her boys. She immediately laughed at Charlie's ludicrous complaint, and before she could stop herself the words had already left her mouth: 'Yes, well, 'Bye, tolerate you' doesn't quite have the same ring, does it!' She was still laughing as the realisation came over her that she had said the retort out loud.

Oops! she thought, as she walked out of the lounge to go and pack the dishwasher.

Charlie didn't speak to her for three days. Three peaceful, blissful days.

Now, here they were, at the airport. Anton and Hayden had gone to buy a snack, leaving Sophie and Charlie sitting opposite each other, sipping coffee. It felt awkward. They didn't talk to each other. They didn't look at each other.

They just sat. Waiting. Sipping.

Charlie had a captive audience. He pounced.

'What did you mean by that?' he asked, reminding her of the comment she had made two weeks earlier. It was the first time either of them had mentioned her 'faux pas'.

Sophie's New Year's resolution immediately flashed through her mind. *Don't lie to him*, she thought to herself. *You promised yourself.*

She quietly sipped her coffee, took a couple of deep breaths, still not looking at him, and gave herself a good 20 seconds to put her thoughts into words.

Confrontation was never her strong point. Charlie, on the other hand, was a salesman with the gift of the gab. He was incredibly quick with his answers and arguments, she always felt like she was on the back foot. He could out-talk her any day and turn any conversation around 180 degrees to prove his point. He often joked that arguing was a sport in his family, and his up-bringing had resulted in his unchallengeable ability to win any verbal war. Sophie was normally as weak as a baby gazelle to a lion.

But not today.

She looked him in the eye, thinking, *This is my moment.*

'I'm sorry,' she said, 'but I kinda meant exactly what I said… I tolerate you.' The words came out perfectly for once. Cool, calm and remarkably detached.

She took another sip from her coffee.

She was on a roll.

'I made a promise to myself at New Year's that I am not going to pretend everything is okay between us any more, because it hasn't been okay for a long time. I just don't love you any more. I haven't for about eight years.' And she returned to her coffee. Cool and calm.

That was it. She had said it. Everything that had been building up in her mind for such a long time. Wow, it felt good! Like a weight had been lifted off her. It was exhilarating and empowering.

'Ummmm.' Charlie was shaking his head, looking stunned. He was momentarily stumped for words. 'What is that supposed to mean?' he asked.

Sophie didn't really know what to say next. She hadn't thought that far ahead.

'I don't really know,' she replied honestly. 'I guess we'll just have to figure it out when I get back from Mexico.'

She had turned an emotional corner. Still cool, calm and collected. And, for once in his life, Charlie had no smart-arse answer or retaliation for her.

What would happen now? She was getting on a plane, heading away for the next three weeks and leaving Hayden behind.

Would he be okay?

Now her confidence began to fade. This always happened. *Dammit,* she thought, as she looked down at her now empty cup.

Just stay strong. A few more minutes. That's all you need, said her inner voice.

And just then, saved by the public address system, her flight was called and it was time to board. The boys were already heading back towards them and Sophie waved to hurry them up.

Oh well, she thought, *I can't undo it now anyway.* It was all said. Too late.

'I have to go boys. Have a safe flight tomorrow, Anton. I love you more than all the stars in the sky. See you in Salt Lake,' and she hugged him in tightly.

'Love you too, Mum,' he said hugging her back, resting his chin on her head. 'See you tomorrow.'

'Bye bud, love you more than the stars. Be good for your dad.' It was Hayden's turn and she hugged him even more tightly than his brother. He had grown so much and was almost the same height as her. But just because he was almost as big as his mum didn't mean he was going to cope for three weeks without her. Especially if his father fell apart.

'I will. Love you too.' Hayden squeezed out his reply under his mother's tight embrace until she let him go. 'And don't forget my sombrero!' he said, grinning. Cheeky boy! Using the last opportunity to remind her that this was the gift he wanted from Mexico.

Sophie looked at Charlie. Was she expected to now hug him too?

He still looked stunned.

'I'll see you in three weeks. We'll talk when I get back,' she said to Charlie with a nod, as if she was farewelling a work colleague. 'Take care.'

And with that, she put on her backpack, picked up her passport wallet and walked backwards to the departures doorway, smiling and blowing flamboyant kisses to both her boys. Then, feeling surprisingly confident and elated, she turned and disappeared out of sight.

Charlie hadn't uttered another word.

Chapter Six

WAITING AN ETERNITY

Thirty-six hours and four flights later, Sophie landed safely in Salt Lake City. The journey had been uneventful, quiet and peaceful – just what every busy mother craves. The connecting flights had gone like clockwork. She didn't really speak to anyone on any of the flights, or in any of the departure lounges.

She had watched four movies and read a third of the novel her friend Katie had insisted she read. It was a love story about two soul-mates who met as teenagers, but were separated when the young man died in a car accident, leaving the girl forever searching for a man who could compare to her lost first love. Sophie couldn't wait to see how the story ended.

In between, and out of necessity, she took half a dozen cat-naps, curled up in her window seat. Cocooned in her own world, she listened to her iPod, with three songs on repeat: 'Sweet Child O' Mine', 'November Rain' and 'Enter Sandman'. She wasn't the most tech-savvy person and somehow, in an iPod syncing incident just prior to the trip, she had managed to erase everything else. As luck would have it, she had been left with three of her all-time favourite tracks.

She wasn't sure how many times she had sighed, still lost in thought, reflecting on the events that had unfolded immediately before her flight had left Auckland. She was proud that she'd found the strength to say what she'd wanted to say for so long. And she was grateful time had run out when it did so she didn't crumble when her resolve began to fade. She felt certain that she could cope with whatever happened next. The ball was in Charlie's court. And he would have three weeks to let everything sink in.

Brett, Anton's team Manager, had a saying that crept into her head now, 'You can't talk yourself out of a situation you have behaved yourself into.' It was true. Charlie had behaved badly towards her for far too long.

Then again, she *had* loved him once, and on their wedding day she hadn't thought for a moment there would come a time she would want to divorce him. When the truth had come out she'd been blunt and matter-of-fact but she hadn't intentionally wanted to hurt him.

Anyway, it was done. She couldn't unsay anything she had said. And actually, she didn't want to take anything back. Plus, you can't unfeel things that you have been made to feel for so long.

Sophie stood alongside the other passengers from her flight at the baggage claim carousel at Salt Lake City Airport, waiting for her suitcases. One was a red, medium-sized case containing her personal belongings. The other was also red, but smaller, and contained her medical supplies. Everyone was becoming restless. Their flight number was clearly displayed above the carousel, but 40 minutes had passed and not one suitcase had come out. The carousel wasn't even moving.

Sophie grew anxious. If her cases were lost, how would she treat the team's injuries?

It was already 10.40 p.m. and she figured the taxi ride to the hotel would take 20 minutes or more. The team would have landed five hours ago. Tiredness had caught up with her. She just wanted a hot shower and a decent bed, and to see her beloved Anton again.

Just then, an announcement came over public address system.

The carousel had broken down, the luggage from the flight was going to be moved manually by staff, and this would take 30 minutes longer. Sophie was relieved the cases were only delayed and not lost, but she would arrive at the hotel even later. She still had to clear customs and then find the taxi stand.

Sophie had absolutely no natural sense of direction and, twice in her life, had become so hopelessly lost in large car park buildings, that she'd had to buzz security to come and rescue her. She was always nervous about finding new places alone. She could read, and she had a tongue in her head (as her mother would say) to ask for directions, so she knew she'd manage.

But it would all take time – maybe another hour. Probably longer. Meaning she wouldn't arrive until well after midnight. The team would be in bed. They were scheduled to be training on the ice early the next morning. Anton would be asleep, for sure.

Damn.

Sophie did her best to wait patiently and, of course, her cases were amongst the last to be brought out. She queued behind the hoards of other passengers now lined up in two queues to clear customs. Her eyes were becoming heavier and heavier.

Eventually she made it through to the other side.

'Welcome to Salt Lake City,' the sign read.

Yeah, great welcome, she thought.

Meandering along, she followed the people ahead of her in the queue, gazing sleepily around at the waiting crowd. All of them there to greet their loved ones.

Now to find the taxi stand. Her vision was becoming blurry and her eyes felt like they were hanging out of her head.

As she looked around for signs that might provide a clue about the direction she should head, she found what she thought must be the exit at the far end. Big glass doors were opening and closing fast, briefly letting in bursts of cold air. She stopped for a moment to take off her backpack and pull her New Zealand ice hockey jacket from her suitcase.

As she struggled to put her backpack on over her jacket, adjacent to the glass doors she noticed a huge mural showing all the surrounding mountains with their ski trails marked out. Sophie stood still, gazing up at it for a few seconds, mesmerised. Wow, it was really gorgeous!

'How was your trip?' Startled from her reverie, she looked around when she heard the familiar Kiwi voice. It was Brett Evans, the New Zealand team manager. He was standing two feet away. Had he come to collect her?

'Hey!' Sophie smiled. 'What are you doing here?' She looked pleasantly stunned.

'Waiting an eternity for you!' Brett laughed, pleased he had surprised her. He turned, pointing up towards the mural. 'I see you found the mountains. Pretty cool, huh.'

'Yes, lovely,' she was looking at Brett now though, not the mural. What an amazingly thoughtful guy. 'Apparently the baggage carousel broke down. I still can't believe you're here! Hey, thanks so much for coming to get me.' Sophie felt blissfully happy.

'Well, what kind of team manager would I be if I made you take a taxi after such a long trip? You've been travelling for a day and a half. You must be exhausted. You look good, considering.'

Sophie blushed and smiled sheepishly. She realised she must look frightful after 36 hours of travel, with no shower, and hadn't even brush her teeth. She hated having 'kitten breath'. But regulations were still pretty tight around things like toothpaste after 9/11.

'Right, c'mon then, let's get you back to the hotel.' Brett took both her cases and turned towards the exit.

Sophie walked beside him. All she had now was her backpack and she felt much lighter. *Wow*, she thought, *he's a gentleman as well!*

In the team van on the way to the hotel, Brett updated her on the latest news. The boys had already enjoyed their first on-ice training that afternoon.

Sophie was highly impressed by Brett's navigational skills. 'How on earth do you know where you're going?' she asked him. First day driving on the wrong side of the van, and on the wrong side of the road, and he handled the vehicle like a pro! He just smiled and carried on telling her about the team.

No wrong turns. No map. No stopping five times to ask directions. *Very impressive.*

In 20 easy minutes they reached the hotel. It was half-past midnight. Sophie found her room, quickly showered, brushed her teeth, and was in bed by 12.45 a.m. Then she slept without moving until her alarm went off just over five hours later.

The first thing she did in the morning after a lengthier, more luxurious shower, and with a towel wrapped around her damp hair, was to find Anton's room and give him a long, tight hug. She was reunited with her son and now her trip was truly beginning.

Chapter Seven

SKATING, EATING, SLEEPING MACHINES

The next three days were a blur of on-ice and off-ice trainings, with breaks for eating and sleeping. Half the team suffered 'skate-bite' – blisters around the ankle bones – and 'lace-bite' – where the laces tend to cut in over the tops of the ankles. Sophie innovated with foot gel-pads. These, taped on with medical paper tape, protected the skin and relieved pain. She gave strict instructions about keeping the skin areas as clean and dry as possible in between training sessions. Infection was the worst enemy. But none of that would stop the boys skating.

Two of the players got 'Charley horses' – deep muscle bruising, usually caused by impact from high speed pucks, or opposition knees or elbows in scrimmage. Sophie always kept ice packs on hand and dished them out plentifully. When the team arrived at the rink, her first job was to find the pit where extra snow was dumped after the Zamboni machine had cleaned the ice – et voila, free ice packs!

Apart from skate-bite, lace-bite, Charleys and a few muscular niggles, the main problems the team encountered were sore throats and colds. At every tournament Sophie had attended, the entire team had caught colds by the end of the training camp. Sophie figured this was due to fatigue, physical exertion and communal living. She had learned long ago to carry two huge bottles of

45

multivitamins and stocked up on three different types of over-the-counter throat lozenges. The boys were triaged to make sure they had nothing more than a cold developing, then asked if their throat was 'a bit sore, a lot sore, or irritated and making them cough,' then given the appropriate lozenge to ease the symptoms.

All in all, the players were holding up pretty well. They had two on-ice sessions and two off-ice sessions every day, a compulsory rest time and repeated feeding and watering stops. At least 100 litres of water, a wheelbarrow of bananas, several cauldron-sized pots of pasta, potatoes, rice and vegetables, plus a handful of multivitamins were devoured daily. These boys burned loads of energy and needed to consume copious calories to keep their engines fully fuelled.

They became skating, eating, sleeping machines.

The players were skating well, communicating well on the ice and gelling together as a team. Everyone was feeling quietly confident about the strength of the unit. The boys were in good spirits, enjoying the camaraderie and loving the rough and tumble of team life.

Each hotel room had two queen-sized beds, and Harry the head coach had allocated two players per room, paired up by their playing positions. The two coaches, Harry and Benny, shared a room, as did the two managers, Brett and Roger. Brett had booked Sophie a room to herself – at her expense but at the group discounted rate. This was her biggest cost for the tour. But the extra shifts she had to pick up to pay for it were totally worth the effort.

Like the other rooms, it consisted of two queen-sized beds, and also had a large modern bathroom, a writing desk with drawers and a fully stocked mini-bar. Luxury! It was the last in a line of rooms occupied by the team on the second floor, which suited her perfectly. A third of the team – all experienced rep players – were on the first floor. The rookie players were on the second floor. They all knew how to find Sophie, and her spot at one end of the hotel meant she could help watch over them, but not get in anyone's way.

The boys were privileged to have Harry and Benny as their coaches. Harry was 36, a Canadian teacher living in Auckland, and the team's head coach. Benny, the assistant coach, was also 36, German-born, and he too lived in Auckland. They were both experienced and had already done several 'tours of duty' with New Zealand rep teams.

In his unmistakable Canadian accent, Harry would say to the boys, 'Sophie's your "away mom". Go see Sophie. She'll sort you out!' Whether it was an injury, home sickness or a laundry problem, they knew they could come to her for anything, and most of them ended up calling her Mum.

Anton had never been a needy kind of a kid. He was quite independent and rarely asked for anything – except the occasional bit of pocket money. Sophie made sure to give him his space and not fuss over him. She didn't want him to feel embarrassed in front of his team mates. He knew he could come to her if he had a problem, but he also knew she wouldn't cramp his style. Ultimately it was his trip and, actually, Sophie felt privileged he wanted her there at all. Most of the boys begged their parents *not* to go! She enjoyed watching her son from a slight distance, and he was having a blast. It was the perfect arrangement.

In Salt Lake City, the team was based at two rinks in opposite directions from the hotel. The first was the home rink of the local AAA rep team – the Regulators. The second rink was the Utah Olympic Oval – an enormous complex that fascinated the Kiwi boys. It had been used for the 2002 Winter Olympics. On the upper level it boasted two ice pads for figure skating, ice hockey, curling or public sessions, and then, around the outside of all this, was a 400-metre speed skating track. Change rooms, a café and bathroom facilities were located on a lower level, along with a four-lane running track, meeting rooms and a banquet room.

Often, while the boys were on the ice, Brett, Sophie and Roger would take one of the two team vans to the nearby shopping mall to stock up on ever-diminishing supplies. An entire training session, including warm-up, kitting up, ice time, unkitting, then cool-down, took three hours. This was Brett, Sophie and Roger's only downtime and they made the most of it, exploring Salt Lake City along the way. The three of them got on famously. They had attended various tournaments together and had known each other for a number of years.

On one excursion, Roger stayed at the rink to sharpen skates while the boys were on cool-down and changing time. Brett had found out about a great little medical supplies store for Sophie to buy more strapping tape. She was as excited as a kid in a candy store, drooling over all the beautiful, modern, state-of-the-art equipment and products. Brett followed her around, patiently waiting for her, and only said something when it was absolutely time to go. It was so refreshing for her. *Such a thoughtful, sweet guy*, she thought.

Later that day, with Brett driving one van and Harry driving the other, they took the entire team to an ice hockey store, and the crowd went wild! The gear on offer was at least a third of the price they would pay in New Zealand, so Sophie bought Anton new ice skates for the following season. Brett's son, Beauden, one of their two goalies, bought a new stick. In fact, almost every player bought something. Many phone calls were made and texts sent home, asking parents for money for this or that.

At home, Roger had had his eye on a pair of new model Bauer skates for refereeing, but he found them here at a quarter of the price. Brett and Sophie were surprised that he had to phone his wife, Wendy, to ask permission, and then had to bargain with her over why he should be allowed them.

Poor Roger, thought Sophie.

Brett and Sophie looked at each other uncomfortably, feeling bad for him because this embarrassing conversation was taking place within earshot of the entire team. Even the boys hadn't had to beg their parents that hard.

On the third evening, after three full days of on-ice and off-ice training, with team-building activities in between, the whole team, including the coaches and managers, gathered around on the second-floor mezzanine of the hotel. It was the sacred daily team talk.

If the New Zealanders were going to uphold their number one tournament ranking and bring home gold, they needed to do everything within their power. On-ice and off.

The only disadvantage of their meeting place was that other guests kept wandering back and forth. Slightly distracting. And some of them seemed quite curious, probably wondering what this group of people were doing in such a small suburban hotel, all speaking with funny accents and dressed in the same black uniform. One young guy in particular, wearing a grey hoodie and faded, ripped blue jeans, walked back and forth several times watching proceedings. Sophie had noticed him and decided he was probably just curious – perhaps a hockey player himself.

Each day, as everyone gathered for these meetings, Sophie sat at the back and had a queue of boys rotating through her care, taking turns to receive massage for muscle knots, heat pack treatments, bandaging and strapping, throat lozenges and other random problems like, 'How am I going to dry my favourite socks for the game tomorrow?' It was the perfect, low-key way to treat the boys while they listened in on what the coaches had to report from their day's work.

On the first day, before Sophie had joined the team, Brett and Roger had made it clear that the boys needed to be in bed by 10 p.m. every night. This meant they needed to see Sophie before that time or wait until the next morning. Roger was a policeman by profession and a stickler for the rules, so he enforced this strictly.

Tomorrow – day four – the boys would play the first of two

preparation games against the under-16 AAA Regulators rep team. The opposition were an average of two years younger, but they were future NHL players. Tough, talented opponents. They would be very fast and very slick, so the New Zealand boys needed to be in top shape.

There were only two more patients in the queue for Sophie's 'Mum-Clinic', and Harry sounded like he was winding down his talk. Soon she would pack up her medical bag, the contents of which were currently strewn out across one end of the mezzanine, then she would race through the shower and hit the sack. Every day was exhausting, especially at altitude.

She rushed through the last couple of consultations. If she didn't hurry, these boys would miss out on whatever they needed because 'PC Plod', as Sophie and Brett had fondly dubbed Roger, would send the boys to bed without treatment.

'What kind of sore throat is it, Steele?' she asked Anton's room-mate. 'A bit sore, a lot sore, or irritated and making you cough?' She would see Brett's son, Beauden, next.

'It's more like an itchy throat, and it's definitely making me cough,' Steele answered. He and Anton had played on the same team since they were 11 and Sophie was pleased they were rooming together. At 190 centimetres, he was the only boy in the team taller than Anton.

'Okay, oh,' said Sophie rummaging through her lozenges, 'it looks like I just gave away my last tickly throat lozenge. I'll quickly run to my room and grab some out of my suitcase. Back soon.'

Without a second thought, she stood up and briskly walked down the hallway towards her room – just going about her business – she had no inkling of what was about to unfold.

Chapter Eight

I'LL BE SEEING YOU

Sophie was swiftly back at her room, humming the Santana song featuring Chad Kroeger to herself along the way, 'She had fire in her soul… And we danced on into the night, ay oh ay oh.' It had been stuck in her head since the first team van trip to the rink that morning.

She was happy. In her element. Looking after the team. But time was of the essence.

She knew exactly where to find the spare lozenge packets in her big suitcase. She took the key card and swiped it through the slot in the door, pulled down on the door handle and stepped inside her room. Then with horror, was instantly frozen to the spot…

Who was this strange man standing in front of her?!

Sophie's right hand was still hovering in mid air, having just let go of the door handle. She should take flight, run. But her feet wouldn't move. She was certain she had read the number on the door correctly – this was definitely her room, and besides it was definitely the last one on the right down the hallway. Plus her key card had worked.

Funny what goes through your mind in a split second.

Was he a burglar? Rapist? Murderer? Drug addict? A hotel employee out of uniform? Or just accidentally in the wrong place? But how had he got in?

Panic set in as she had the sudden realisation that this situation was really, really wrong. It was the young guy she had noticed earlier, watching them during the team talk – the one in the grey hoodie and faded, ripped blue jeans.

In a matter of seconds, as Sophie looked around her, she took in several details. This intruder – who she now realised with horror had been watching *her* intently throughout the team talk – had:

1. Plugged his own cell phone in by the desk, draping the cord around Sophie's suitcase, which was on the desk. Like he was moving in.
2. Laid his phone, wallet, keys and hoodie on the second bed in the room.
3. Had nothing other than what he was wearing and his phone, wallet and keys.
4. Had used the toilet in the en suite (visible to the left from just inside the door), because he had left the toilet seat up.
5. And lastly, and most importantly, had very obviously had a rummage through her suitcase, because things were turned upside down from where Sophie was absolutely sure she had left them.

'Oh, is this your room?' he asked, in what Sophie took to be a broad Texan accent. He wasn't a local then. And he genuinely seemed surprised to see it was her who had come through the door. Was he expecting someone else?

Sophie quickly calculated her options. She was still between him and the door, but he was quite close to her. If she turned around really fast, opened the heavy door and tried to run out, she wouldn't make it out before he grabbed her. Not an option.

'Ah, yes! It is!' she answered him, trying to make her voice sound more bold than she was feeling. She consciously added an angry facial expression to the words. Her heart was racing now, beating through her chest wall.

He was wearing only a t-shirt and jeans. He couldn't possibly be concealing a large weapon, and while his hands were in sight, he wouldn't be able to retrieve a small weapon from his jeans' pockets without Sophie making a run for it.

Then he reached his right hand into his back pocket.

Oh crap, the back pockets, Sophie thought. She was now completely frozen to the spot and inside she was shaking like a leaf.

Remember the wild bear thing. Make yourself seem bigger. It was worth a try.

'So, what's going on?' Sophie said loudly, as if this was some kind of stand-off. She tried to straighten her back to be as tall as possible. He was a lot younger than her – maybe 23 or 24. Perhaps a 'don't mess with me' fierce mother attitude might add credibility to her act.

In that split second, it also occurred to her that he was probably too old to respond to her 'I will count to three!' routine. She could still pull this off with her 13-year-old son. Just.

The man hesitated to answer, seemingly stumped about how to respond. Sophie decided he probably didn't have a clue what to tell her, meaning she had put him on the spot. So his intentions were definitely dishonest. He carried on moving his right hand, reaching into the back pocket of his jeans. He pulled out two key cards.

Whew, no weapon… yet. Keep your cool, but stay on guard. Sophie stood firm.

'Ah,' he hesitated again, 'I told them they put me in the wrong room, but they insisted this was my room, and they even brought me up here an' all.'

This was his answer? Did he really expect her to believe that? Why would the hotel allocate her room to someone else? It was booked under her name! And even if they had somehow made a booking mistake, wouldn't they realise the room was occupied when they brought him up there? Her things were all over the desk and set out in the bathroom. There was no way it could have been mistaken for an unoccupied room!

She decided that now was probably not a good time to argue logic with him. Her first priority was to get him out of the room, to be safe again, and then sort out what to do from there.

'Right, well, best you get downstairs and sort this mess out then!' No longer completely frozen, she was still frowning and scowling as best she could, continuing to act like the angry mother, with her left hand on her hip and her right hand now slightly shakily pointing in the direction of the lobby.

'Yes Ma'am,' he replied as he walked to the bed and collected his phone, wallet, keys and hoodie. 'Ah,' he hesitated again, 'thing is, I came to town to visit my dad for the weekend, but I guess I'll have to go find somewhere else now.'

Was he asking her if he could stay? Did he have no other options? This was a ridiculous story! He was not the 'brightest pencil in the shower' (as Sophie's Aunt Annelise was famous for saying). Why would you come to visit your father and then stay in a hotel? Why would you have no luggage? Not even a toothbrush?

'Well you can't stay here!' she replied bluntly.

'Ah, yeah, so here's your key card, I guess,' he added, as he handed her one of the cards, putting the other one back in his jeans' back pocket. She took the key card and held her stance, planting both hands firmly on her hips.

'I'll be seeing you.' He winked at Sophie as he walked past her to the door.

Don't freak out. Her heart was racing, as she held her breath. He opened the door, walked out and let the door shut by itself behind him.

What did he mean by that? – 'I'll be seeing you.'

For now Sophie was safe. She let out her breath with a huge sigh, nearly collapsing. *Whew. That was a really, really close call.* She sat down on the corner of the first bed, putting her hand on her chest where her heart was galloping at 90 miles an hour.

Thoughts raced through her mind. Too many questions!

And then, *Wait – just one key card. Why would he hold onto the other one? That's not okay!* It was bad enough that he had somehow got into her room in the first place, let alone still possibly having a way to gain access whenever he felt like it. Maybe she had foiled his plan for now but he was obviously already plotting how he might get back in!

Sophie tried to weigh up the situation. He didn't appear to want to harm her. He'd had the opportunity and didn't show any violent tendencies. He didn't seem to have taken anything of value, and he hadn't even touched her backpack…

Perhaps he wanted drugs from her medical bag.

That was it! He must be a drug addict. That was why he had been studying her. He didn't want her and he didn't want money. He was trying to figure out what kind of drugs she had.

Oh, she realised as the penny dropped. She had mentioned within earshot in the hotel mezzanine that she had medications in her room.

The young guy hadn't expected to see Sophie when she opened the door, so perhaps he had been expecting someone else. Maybe an accomplice. A partner in crime. A drug buddy. She knew he probably wouldn't give in so easily. But what would his plan involve next time? No doubt he would be much better prepared, including having a contingency plan for if she interrupted him again.

First and foremost, the question burning in Sophie's head was how he had obtained the key cards?

Sophie was still perched on the very corner of her bed, with her hand on her chest. Her heart was still beating hard, but it had slowed a little. She had buckets of adrenaline on board. It would take an hour or more to settle properly.

Suddenly, she realised she would be safer with the team and out of the room. She figured as long as the man wasn't in the hallway right now, she could get down to reception and have the room re-keyed – that would at least stop the intruder from getting back in with the card he still had. She stepped out into the hallway and shut the door firmly behind her.

Steele and Beauden, who were still waiting for her help, were standing there looking confused. Roger had sent them along to see what the delay was. She must have been gone for 10 minutes or more.

'Who was that guy?' Steele was trying to figure out what was going on.

Sophie was suddenly distracted as she thought she could hear the intruder's voice. Was he talking to someone in the lobby down-stairs? Her heart started pounding through her chest again. Why was he still here? She looked at the boys and motioned her index finger into the universally known gesture for 'shhhh', as she quickly and quietly crept down the hallway towards the mezzanine. She caught sight of him over the balcony railings. He was walking towards the front entrance.

'Sophie, what's happened? You're as white as a ghost,' Steele asked quietly. Harry had stopped addressing the players when he'd seen Sophie creeping down the hallway with Steele and Beauden in tow. Now the whole team was looking at her.

Safety in numbers, she thought. The team would rescue her if she needed it. They would back her up.

Sophie looked down towards the lobby again in time to watch the intruder calmly walk out the front door and then walk away with two other men who had been waiting for him outside.

'Listen to this!' Sophie had regained her normal voice, and with that she marched around the group, down the stairs and straight up to reception. She needed answers!

The seated female receptionist dragged her concerned gaze away from the front entranceway and looked up at Sophie. With a flicker of sudden recognition, her expression immediately changed from concern to horror as she realised who was standing in front of her. She had put two and two together and her face was painted with the sudden realisation that, firstly, she had been taken in by the story the mystery man had told her in order to obtain the key cards and, secondly, something bad had happened as a result.

'So… I'm in room 216.' Sophie gave her this much and waited to see what she would say.

'Oh my goodness. Ms Harding, I am so, so sorry!' she said in a distraught voice as she stood up holding her hands out in front of her as if she was begging for forgiveness.

'Yeah. And that guy…' Sophie pointed out the front doors to where she had last seen the intruder, 'was in my room going through all my stuff. Somehow he had key cards?' she said with a questioning tone. What she would like to have said is, 'How the hell did you get talked into giving him copies of *my* key card to *my* room?' But Sophie could never be that rude, even in this type of situation. Better to give the receptionist a chance to explain.

She still looked horrified. This could easily become a law suit and she would lose her job.

'Ma'am, I am so terribly sorry. He told me he was with you and staying in your room. He said he'd gone for a walk and both the cards must have fallen out of his pocket. I thought he was part of your team. He seemed so trustworthy!' Her explanation seemed genuine. The poor woman had been completely duped.

'But he wasn't in our uniform. Didn't you at least check his details to see if they matched the booking?' Sophie thought she should definitely have checked his name.

'He told me he was staying in your room, 216, and he'd lost both your cards,' she repeated as if pleading her case. 'It didn't cross my mind to check because he was so convincing! And I assumed he was part of your team because I'd seen him around all evening while you guys were all here! Please, what can I do?'

The woman was clearly horrified at her own gullibility, and was begging Sophie's forgiveness. Sophie was feeling sorry for her now. This guy was too smooth!

'Okay,' Sophie sighed. 'What do I do now? Obviously I need my room re-keyed, because he only gave me one of the key cards back, so I'm not happy about that.'

This was at least the first step, then she would talk to Brett and Roger about what would happen next.

Just then, Brett tapped her on the shoulder. Roger was standing right behind him.

'Not good enough,' said Brett, directing his statement to the penitent receptionist. 'We need a new room for her, now. This incident needs to be reported to the police. And they need to get this guy, because he's obviously planning to come back.' Brett was polite, but these were not requests. He had a look of thunder on his face. He was deadly serious.

Then he turned to Sophie and whispered, 'We'll look after you, don't worry,' as he rubbed her shoulder. She was tense and shaky.

'I'm so, so sorry,' the receptionist said again. She looked like she was going to cry.

'It's okay. Look, I'm okay. I don't think he had a chance to take anything,' Sophie replied to both of them.

'No, it's *not* okay.' Brett was not going to allow Sophie to smooth things over just to make the receptionist feel better. 'You've been put in danger. Things could have ended very differently. Sophie, he's probably coming back for whatever it was he wanted.'

Sophie shuddered.

Brett knew Sophie was too nice-natured for her own good. The receptionist had made a serious mistake that had resulted in Sophie's life being put in danger.

'Sir, I will do everything I can. Please let me just see if I can book her into another room.' The receptionist was becoming quite desperate now. She was looking at her computer and tapping on the keyboard, trying to make amends for her blunder. Perhaps she would be able to give Sophie a really fancy upgrade.

Then her facial expression changed to one of utter despair.

'We literally have no other rooms left tonight. Not one,' she said, 'I don't know what to do. What can I do to put this right?' Her hands reached out in supplication again.

Sophie was looking to Brett for an answer too. She couldn't think of anything except re-keying the room. Brett just stood still, slowly shaking his head, thinking.

'Re-key the room,' he said decisively. He had obviously come up with a plan. 'And you'd better alert the night staff to watch that door,' he said as he pointed to the front entrance, 'because I will personally deal to him if he dares to come back!'

With that Brett turned and bolted back up the stairs, taking two at a time, returning to the team. The boys were shocked at what had taken place, and that Sophie had been in such danger, just down the hall from where they had all been sitting.

Brett debriefed the team and, by the time Sophie and Roger had arrived back at the mezzanine after organising the new key cards, the boys had trudged off to bed very, very quietly.

Just the managers, coaches and Anton remained.

'Mum, are you okay?' Anton went up to his mum and hugged her tight. She shed a few quiet tears. She needed this hug.

'Yes bud. I'm okay. He didn't do anything to me, and I don't think he took anything. I think I interrupted him just in time.' She wasn't going to tell Anton that the intruder had kept a key card and was probably already plotting his next attempt. Anton didn't need that kind of worry on his plate.

'Okay. Well as long as you're okay.' He sounded relieved as he let go of his mother. Sophie rubbed his back. Lovely, caring boy.

'I'm fine. Now you hurry up and get to bed. This fiasco has already made you late. Don't want to get in trouble with the coaches!' Sophie winked at Harry, and laughed a little to try and lighten the mood.

'He's alright. He's a good boy, looking after his mom,' Harry offered.

Anton headed off to his room where Sophie was sure Steele would enlighten him further, if he hadn't already been given the full picture. Poor Steele hadn't got his throat lozenge. He would survive until the morning though. And Beauden could ask his dad for help if he was desperate.

'Right, Sophie, I think you've earned a glass of wine! What do you say? You keen? Roger and I have a couple of bottles in our room. C'mon.' Brett's idea certainly appealed. She was still buzzing with adrenaline, although her heart had now settled. A drink might help her sleep. And she really needed to talk to Brett and Roger to get their advice on what she should do if the intruder came back. The thought of going to bed right now wasn't appealing, so she accepted Brett's invitation, packed up her medical kit, and followed the managers to their room.

Chapter Nine

LINE OF SIGHT

Brett and Roger's hotel room was larger than Sophie's, with the exact same layout but in a mirrored floor plan. As well as two queen beds and a large writing desk, they also had a two-seater sofa and a bigger bathroom area with a separated shower and toilet.

As she scanned the room Sophie recognised Brett's things on the first bed. They were folded up and laid out neatly. His big grey suitcase was pushed hard up against the wall in the corner by his bed, lid down. He was organised and tidy. Just how she had guessed he would be.

Roger's side of the room, however, was very different. Clothes were strewn all over his bed and the floor, his suitcase pushed up awkwardly against the far corner, with the lid forced wide open by the extraneous clothing that tumbled up inside and spewed out of it in all directions. It looked like someone had set off a stick of dynamite inside the case, and all his clothes had blown out across his side of the room. As much as she liked the guy, this too was true to the picture she had formed in her mind.

Sophie found it highly amusing and couldn't hide her smile, but managed to hold back the laughter that nearly burst forth. She had the fleeting thought of saying, 'Roger, you should sack your maid!' but decided not to risk offending him.

She felt her mood lift tremendously.

'Australian merlot or Chilean shiraz?' Brett was holding up two bottles and looking directly at her. He had a wee smirk on his face and a twinkle in his eye. He'd caught her body language, her recognition of the difference between the two sides of the room. She smirked back at him.

'Shiraz please. I've never tried a Chilean red. And could I keep the cork?' Sophie had always liked red wine, claiming to be a 'shiraz girl' – unless bubbles were on offer.

She sat down on the sofa, while Brett and Roger perched on the ends of their beds. Roger created space for himself by pushing two pairs of track pants and a sweater off onto the ever-increasing floor pile.

It was a fun few hours. The three of them chatted and laughed about the things that had happened with the boys so far, and how well the team were performing in general. Time ticked along nicely. They finished the Chilean shiraz, then started on the Australian merlot.

Sophie explained she had been collecting wine corks for a number of years so that she could make a noticeboard using corks from all over the world.

They chatted about everything except the evening's incident. Over three hours had passed. Brett had even gotten out his laptop and composed his daily email report to the players' parents. But the evening's incident hadn't been mentioned in that either.

As time went on, Sophie felt herself becoming quieter and more withdrawn as she stared down into her glass of wine, just swilling it about. She didn't know what to do. She would have to bring the topic up soon. It was like they were all purposely avoiding it. The elephant in the room.

At 1.30 a.m., Brett announced he was going to have a quick rinse in the shower. Sophie was now dreading going back to her room. She wouldn't sleep. She was convinced the intruder would come back, but who knew when. She needed a plan. How could she stop him? How could she protect herself?

She could hear Brett's shower running. Roger kept on talking, but she wasn't able to distract herself now. She couldn't think about anything else except the intruder. Before she knew it, Brett's shower had stopped.

'I need to take a leak!' Roger announced as he suddenly leapt up and headed towards the bathroom. Sophie was left sitting by herself. *That was weird,* she thought. She could hear the two of them mumbling quietly to each other between the shower and the bathroom, but she couldn't make out what they were saying. They were probably wishing she would go back to her own room.

She had to say something, very soon.

Just then, Roger came out of the bathroom and stood in front of his bed, arms folded. Then, about 10 seconds later, Brett also entered the room, a towel wrapped around his waist and his hands on his hips. Roger put his hands on his hips now too.

What was this? Sophie looked from one to the other, fully expecting them to order her back to her own room.

Brett and Roger glanced at each other, then Brett locked eyes with Sophie, a serious expression on his face, as he spoke gently but firmly. 'Right, this is the way we see it. You obviously don't feel comfortable about being alone.' This was a statement, not a question.

Was she that readable? She felt so embarrassed. Her eyes started to well up, but she didn't let her facial expression change. She was determined not to cry in front of her colleagues.

As soon as this thought had occurred to her, of course, her eyes started to leak. The adrenaline had long since worn off but only now did she realise how shattered she felt. And the truth was, she was actually terrified of going to back to her room.

Brett continued. 'We all realise this guy is probably coming back. It's just a matter of when. And there is no way Roger and I are prepared to let you sleep in that room without someone to protect you. So, you have a couple of choices, depending on what you feel comfortable with. Realistically it's either myself or Roger… Or Anton as an absolute last resort. But either way, someone else needs to sleep in that second bed while we're still in this hotel. So who would you prefer?'

Brett hadn't moved during this speech. He still stood directly in front of her with his hands on his hips. He meant business.

Sophie looked from Brett to Roger, who took this as his cue to chip in.

'Or we could do alternate shifts. You know, take turns every second night, like bodyguards do,' Roger offered up this fourth choice. It was as though he was trying to fill a police roster.

This was team management pulling rank. They were determined to protect her whether she liked it or not! But actually, Sophie was tremendously relieved. Their show of support was music to her ears. It was such foreign territory to her. So refreshing. Someone truly cared about her safety. And they were deadly serious. Not making fun of her.

Suddenly she was crying properly. Sobbing, in fact. Brett and Roger shifted from foot to foot, looking uncomfortable.

'Oh, now don't cry,' said Roger, passing her a tissue box. 'Just decide!'

She had to pull herself together and think the options through.

Anton was only 16. He was still just a kid, really – he didn't need that kind of responsibility. And, anyway, he could sleep through Sophie vacuuming in his room. It took three alarms in the morning to wake him properly. And he was a peacemaker, not a fighter, except occasionally, when an ice hockey game turned rough! Sophie knew it wasn't right to call upon him to play bodyguard to his mother. Plus, there was no way she would willingly put him in the path of danger. She would die to protect him – it could never be the other way around. Besides this was his trip. He should be allowed to relax and enjoy himself with his teammates, not be stuck having to sleep in his mummy's room every night.

She had taken a tissue from the box that Roger had given her and was blotting her eyes. Her sobbing had stopped, but the tears continued to trickle. She was still thinking.

On the other hand, Brett was a black belt in karate and a karate instructor, and Roger was a frontline policeman. Seriously, what two better bodyguards could a girl want? Roger was about 40, quite tall, but he did look just a little out of shape. Only an hour earlier, he had regaled Brett and Sophie with a hilarious story about how he'd struggled to chase down a thief while on the beat recently.

Whereas, Brett, was a similar age but more disciplined. He certainly had a stronger physique and trained at least six days each week. He wasn't quite as tall as Roger but he had broader shoulders and stronger, sculptured muscles. He would be a strong defender, for sure.

But Sophie didn't want to be a burden or create work for either of them. They both had enough to do on this trip. Plus, she wasn't sure what the team would think if they discovered she had one of them sleeping in her room. What would the boys tell their parents when they got home? And how would it all make Anton feel? Not surprisingly, she didn't dwell so much on what Charlie would think.

So, with her voice cracking a little through the remaining tears, she explained why she thought it was unfair to choose Anton and offered what she suddenly thought was a perfect alternative solution.

'I've got it. It's perfect! I can just sleep on this sofa,' she explained, patting the cushion beside her. 'The guy wouldn't even know I was in here. So when he breaks into my room again and it's empty, he'll think I've left the hotel and then he'll leave!' It really did seem like the perfect solution – so obvious when she thought about it.

Pleased with herself, she stood up, thinking she would just go and pack her other bag.

Brett laughed.

'Sophie, you're forgetting how closely he watched you. If he sees any of the team, he'll know you're here. If he sees you in any of the common areas, he'll be watching to see where you go. What do you want Roger and me to do? Hide you in here for the next week? Besides, as you can see, there's no way we can have another person with two big suitcases living in here full-time. We only have one suitcase each, and that's a struggle!' He was smiling now as he nodded his head towards Roger's side of the room.

'I guess you're right.' Sophie smiled as she wiped away the tears on her cheeks with her finger tips.

She sat down again. She would have to choose which one would be her night shift bodyguard. There was no way around it.

'Hmmm. Then I think it has to be you, Brett. Charlie knows you better, so he would trust you. Not that he wouldn't trust you, Roger. It's just, he doesn't really know you.' Sophie was looking up at them, from one to the other, as she spoke. She felt like she was choosing a partner for the school dance and didn't want to disappoint either of them.

'No, that's fine. I can understand that,' Roger said, nodding his head, hands still on his hips.

Then as she looked down, inspecting her finger tips for smudged mascara, she mumbled, 'Actually, I don't think he'd even care. He'd probably just laugh and say I was being paranoid.'

She suddenly looked up at them both, acutely aware she had accidentally spoken her thoughts out loud. Strangely, they both had slightly sad expressions on their faces. They looked more concerned than shocked.

Brett broke the awkward silence. 'Well, all I can say is you have the whole team to back you up. This was a serious incident. And

I'm more than happy to explain that to Charlie. You *do* need a bodyguard, and it's *not* paranoia.' He was pacing in front of the door and sounded like he was trying to squash down rising anger.

But then something else occurred to Sophie.

'What if Beauden comes to find you? I didn't get to treat him tonight and I don't even know what he needed. And what if the boys see you coming and going from my room? What will they think? And what will they say to their parents?' Sophie was only too aware of how easily rumours started on these tours.

'We don't need to justify anything. The whole team knows what took place tonight. But if we have to explain, we will simply tell them the truth,' Brett stated very simply. And Roger agreed.

'Okay. So we're all in agreement then?' Brett asked. He and Roger were both looking expectantly at Sophie. She nodded.

'Right. Give me two minutes and I'll get a couple of things.' Brett started to gather various bits and pieces. 'Oh, and by the way… While you were downstairs sorting out your new key cards before, I was briefing the team on another part of our plan.' Brett ducked into the bathroom to collect his toothbrush and toothpaste, then continued.

'Roger and I put a 'line of sight' rule in place for you. This means that every second of every day, you need to have one of us in your line of sight. If we can't see you, we can't protect you. If you go to your room, or you're walking around the hotel or the rink, you need to have one of us with you. If we're not available, you take two of the boys with you. If you go to the bathroom, we'll be guarding the door. The boys are all on board with this plan. It may sound a little excessive, but this guy could be lurking around at any time.'

Brett had finished gathering his things into a backpack, and was standing in front of Sophie again. 'Every second of every day. Okay?' He was commanding her full attention and waiting for her final acceptance.

'Okay,' she agreed sheepishly and without argument.
She was going to be protected whether she liked it or not.

Chapter Ten

SAVED BY KIAI

'Shall we?' Brett motioned towards the door. 'It's 2 a.m., which will give us five hours before we have to be up again. And I don't know about you two, but sleep is calling.'

'I'm so sorry about all of this. I feel like such a helpless baby.' Sophie was embarrassed. She was meant to be there to help, not to be a hindrance.

'Sophie,' Brett said softly, 'no sorrys, okay? You don't apologise for something that happened *to* you. Let's go, you must be exhausted.'

'Thank you – both of you.' Sophie was indeed exhausted. And now she would sleep.

She passed Brett one of her new key cards as the two of them walked silently down the hallway to her room. Brett used the bathroom to change into pyjama boxers. No top. Then he brushed his teeth.

Oh my. He did have a great physique. Such a strong chest and shoulders. Sophie couldn't help but notice. She turned away so he wouldn't see her blush.

They didn't speak.

Sophie took her turn in the bathroom, rinsing off quickly in the shower, putting on the long, pink t-shirt she liked to sleep in, and brushing her teeth. When she came back into the room, Brett had

69

already climbed into the second bed and had turned onto his left side, facing the window. Sophie thought he must be asleep already.

Getting under the covers of her bed, Sophie was almost asleep before her head hit the pillow.

'G'night. Sleep well,' Brett said, without moving. He wasn't asleep after all.

''Night Brett. You too.' Sophie drifted off with a wonderfully warm, fuzzy and, most of all, safe feeling.

And she did sleep soundly. For two hours.

At 4.02 a.m., Sophie awoke to a deafening *ka-thud*. It sounded like a truck smashing into a house. She sat bolt upright, thinking, *What on earth was that?* Then there was another resounding *ka-thud, thud*, in quick succession. It was coming from her right, quite close. Time had slowed down to milliseconds. She heard a rustling, like autumn leaves, coming from her left. It was pitch black. She couldn't see anything. And she was terrified of the dark.

Where was she? What was happening? She was momentarily stunned. Completely disorientated.

Two more loud *ka-thud, thuds*, from her right.

Then suddenly everything crystallised in her head. Within a split second she remembered where she was, realised what the thuds were, and then simultaneously realised with absolute terror exactly what was happening.

Someone was trying to break down her door!

She started to hyperventilate. But the terror rendered her silent. She couldn't raise a scream, as she scrambled clumsily out of her bedding and clambered towards the foot of the bed.

It was still pitch black. The *ka-thud, thuds* continued. Time had sped up again to faster than reality, but her movements felt like they were happening in incredibly clumsy, cartoonish slow motion.

Just then, she heard an impressive deep growl, 'Hi-yahhhh!' and one final thundering *ka-thud*.

It came from her right, but sounded like it was inside the room. Sophie had just reached the end of her bed. She leant sideways against the wall where she knew the light switch was. As she flicked the switch on, she saw Brett in a formidable karate stance, facing the door, ready to fight.

It was Brett who made the *kiai* – the karate battle cry. In the seconds since she had heard the rustling of his sheets, he had reached the door.

Once he could see, Brett dropped his karate stance and peered through the glass peephole. Sophie could hear footsteps running from the door, down the hallway.

It seemed Brett's *kiai* had scared them off. And just in time.

The security latch consisted of a round metal bulb attached to the door-frame, with a small bar that pulled across it from the door. The door frame wood was broken up around the lock, and the door had been forced open to the length of the latch. The final thundering *ka-thud* had been Brett's foot kicking the door closed. One more bang from the other side and the latch mounting would have given way completely, causing the door to fully burst open.

'Do you think that was him?' Sophie was trembling now, kneeled on the edge of her bed, hugging the side of the wall.

'No, I think that was him and two mates,' Brett answered matter-of-factly. He was inspecting the door frame to see how he could reinforce it.

'I think they were running at the door with their shoulders. But they won't be coming back any time soon. Pretty sure I scared them off,' he finished, as he rummaged through his backpack. He found his Leatherman tool and then started turning the screws of the latch back in.

'There were three of them?' Sophie's voice was trembling, as her body shook. There was more than one. This wasn't over. What if they came back? Drug addicts had no common sense. They would risk everything for their next fix.

Brett turned around to find her frozen to the wall. He had been too preoccupied to see how terrified she was. He reached across and put his hand on her shoulder. She gave one final shiver, head to toe, then the trembling calmed.

His hand was so warm.

'Soph, I'm not going anywhere. If they come back, I'll be waiting.' He was the epitome of cool, calm and collected. It was the reassurance she needed. She nodded, and he continued, 'I've managed to fix the security latch. So let's try and get a bit more sleep, okay?' He gave her shoulder a little squeeze and she nodded again.

With that, he climbed back into the second bed, turned to face the window again, and quickly fell asleep. It was impressive. Sophie had seen for herself how quickly he could fly into action. Zero to fighting, in a split second. And then back into a state of rest.

She climbed into her own bed, lay completely still, wide awake, listening to every breath Brett took, and hearing every creak and groan in the hotel.

At 6.05 a.m., she was still wide awake, and still analysing every noise. She sat bolt upright again. This time someone was swiping a key card at the door.

'Brett! They're back!' Sophie whispered. She stayed in bed this time and switched on her beside lamp. The swiping continued four or five more times.

Brett had calmly got up and walked to the door. He peered through the peephole. No *kiai* call this time.

The swiping had stopped.

'No one there. Whoever it was, they've given up. Sleep.' Brett sounded exhausted, but totally unfazed.

How did he stay so calm?

Less than an hour later, Sophie's phone alarm went off. It was time to get up.

Chapter Eleven

THE CALM BEFORE THE STORM

While Sophie was showering, groggily trying to wash away the effects of too little sleep, Brett went back to his room to shower and sent Roger down to guard Sophie's door. Roger then escorted her to breakfast and had three boys move to sit at her table. He didn't have to explain why and they responded willingly and quickly.

Brett had briefed Roger, Harry and Benny first thing that morning about the night's disturbances, but no one mentioned it to the boys, at Sophie's request. In fact, no one mentioned the intruder again.

That afternoon at the AAA Regulator's rink, just before their practice game, Sophie went to buy coffee from the rink café. She was barely functioning on two hours' sleep and Brett didn't look much better off. She walked away unannounced, purely because she was so tired she simply forgot to say anything. Ed and Nigel, two boys who were sitting out the game due to minor injuries, immediately ran up beside her and flanked her all the way to the café and back. No one had asked them to. Sophie just smiled at them both. She felt safe, even though the attention did seem a bit excessive.

Later that day, she asked Brett if the bodyguarding was really necessary outside of the hotel.

He looked serious. 'I ran a security check on all the staff and one of them failed that check. Now, I didn't receive any further details than that, but given the incident with the intruder, I'm simply not prepared to take any risks with you. You're far too important to this team.'

And that was the end of that. She remained under permanent protection, 24/7. Like it, or not!

Actually, she hadn't even fluttered an eyelid at the security check thing. Brett's capabilities had far exceeded impressing her. Nothing was now surprising her about this man.

The game against the Regulators came off without any major problems. New Zealand lost as expected, going down 8–1, but the team played reasonably well. It was a good chance for Harry to trial various line combinations and swap players in and out of the lines accordingly. The one goal was a cause for celebration.

That evening, the team had dinner at Applebee's Grill & Bar for the first time. The restaurant immediately established itself as the team's favourite dinner venue and was only a short walking distance from the hotel.

Over the nights they ate at Applebee's, Sophie enjoyed sampling her way through the wine list and collecting all the corks along the way.

Whenever the team returned to the hotel, she would quietly pass by the front desk and ask if the intruder had been seen. The answer was always no. The reception staff became so familiar with this ritual that they would quietly volunteer, 'Haven't seen him,' with a smile as soon as they saw her.

Sophie got used to being bodyguarded. She felt safe and not so jumpy. The whole team were looking out for her, every moment of every day. They made her feel valued, not like she was tagging along, or part of the furniture, or taken for granted. And the added advantage, with her being so directionally challenged, was she didn't have to worry about trying to find places and getting lost all the time.

The rest of the 10-day training camp flew by smoothly. There were some hilarious team moments, which Sophie wrote in her diary so she could amuse her friends when she arrived back home.

On the fifth day they were having lunch in an authentic American all-you-can-eat buffet restaurant. At the end of the meal the boys stacked up their empty food trays and sat them on top of ice cubes. Sophie was puzzled. What on earth were they doing? No one would tell her. They chuckled and whispered amongst themselves. But just as the team was leaving, she understood. The bottom tray was moving very slowly sideways. The brats had worked out that when the ice cubes started to melt, the trays would all come crashing to the floor! They laughed hysterically for the rest of the week about the mess it must have made.

On day six, Kieran spotted three flamboyantly-dressed drag queens on a street corner as the two team vans passed by. It was like a scene out of a movie and certainly not expected in a city like Salt Lake, known for its strong Mormon values. Kieran was one of the youngest boys on the team. He was laughing hard at their over-the-top costumes and exclaimed, 'I love shims and herms, they're the best!' The entire van load of players erupted with laughter, including Brett, Roger and Sophie. Kieran later explained he was trying to say she-hes, and her-hims.

Night five was hazing night. There was a long-standing, ceremonial tradition of initiation amongst New Zealand ice hockey rep teams. The returning players from previous years had the dubious task of designing a wild array of hair styles for the rookies, which were then carved into their hair using an electric razor.

One player had a circular swirl of hair randomly shaved off, while another had only a circular swirl of hair remaining. Another was left with three scattered tufts, and two were given stripes. Bradley sported a 'Krusty the Clown' hair style, which was appropriate, because he was ever the clown. Steele had grown his hair long in anticipation of the ceremony. He had a beautiful mass of shoulder-length, curly black locks. Most of it was shaved off, leaving one long curl behind each ear – like two thick pigtails. Anton's wavy, surfer hair was transformed into a mohawk. And Brett's son, Beauden, who had ash blond hair like his father, was left with a strange and random configuration of short tufts all over his head. This was one topic that was only briefly mentioned in the daily team email. Although most parents respected the tradition and appreciated the before and after photos, some had a tendency to get a little precious about their baby's hair!

It was a great team bonding time. Hilarity engulfed the whole evening and the boys proudly sported their new hair styles for the rest of the training camp. It was a rite of passage. They weren't Junior Ice Blacks until they had been through the initiation ceremony.

In keeping with tradition, the wild hair styles were always left untouched until the team had travelled to their World Championship destination. There, before the first game and the opening ceremony, they would have their hair tidied up with number one or two hair cuts, like army recruits. Until then, they attracted some interesting attention in public.

'My baby's shaggy surfer hair is ruined!' Sophie exclaimed while laughing and pretending to fuss over Anton, stroking the mohawk that remained.

Bradley looked shocked, taking a moment to process what he had just heard. Amazed, he said to Anton, 'Are you serious! Is Sophie your mother?!' Most of the team fell about laughing at this, but there were three other rookies who looked equally as stunned. Sophie could hear them whispering to each other – things like: 'But she's so cool,' and 'Wish my mum was that cool.' These comments were genuinely sweet, but made both her and Anton blush.

Sophie and Brett's night time routine was always the same. After team curfew, Brett showered in his room, while Sophie waited there and chatted with Roger. Brett then gathered a few things and he and Sophie walked together down the hallway to her room. He used her bathroom to get changed and to brush his teeth. Then she quickly showered and brushed her teeth too. When she finished he was always in the second bed, facing the window, but never quite asleep. They exchanged their goodnights, but never spoke much.

Each morning Brett went back to his room and sent Roger to guard Sophie's door while she got ready for the day. Brett was the perfect gentleman and the perfect bodyguard. Sophie trusted him implicitly.

The intruder was never seen again.

Every day was filled with hard work, but also plenty of fun. The weather was crispy cold – around three and four degrees Celsius – with beautiful, clear blue skies. The surrounding mountains were covered in snow and so was most of the township. It was like a picture postcard. Apart from the intruder incident, Sophie hadn't felt so happy and at peace for a very long time.

If she had to pick her favourite day, it would have been their rest day – the only day the team didn't have to be skating, eating, sleeping machines. No trainings, no games, no timetables. Everyone ventured to an enormous shopping complex. There was a monumental Mormon temple nearby. As part of the team's cultural experience, they took a brief look through the beautiful building then most carried on to the shopping complex. Brett had decided to take Beauden and two other boys on a formal temple tour. Meanwhile, Anton and Steele were planning to visit every sports store in the shopping complex. So Roger happily volunteered to tag along and bodyguard Sophie.

Sophie took extra time in a Build-a-Bear store making a gorgeous, pink and white ballet bear, complete with pink tutu and ballet slippers. While she was there, Roger sat on a stool in the window of a bar opposite the store, sipping on a cold beer. To his credit, he didn't take his eyes off her once. He was like a cop under cover.

And if she was honest, Sophie was relieved to have him paying such thorough attention.

Strangely, though, over the course of that day, she realised she was missing Brett and wished it was him standing beside her rather than Roger in the bar across the way. She and Brett had been friends for years, but they had grown closer over the last few days. They now shared an unspoken bond. Purely platonic, of course. She couldn't wait to show him her ballet bear and wanted to hear all about his temple tour.

By the end of the afternoon, while comparing their shopping items, she had shown her ballet bear to Roger, the coaches and half a dozen of the boys, including Anton. They all said, 'Yeah, it's cute.' But she knew no one really appreciated the work she had lovingly put into making her ballerina, and how much she already adored her creation. But Brett would.

Charlie hadn't crossed her mind for days.

The next day, the team were playing their second game against the Regulators. In the change room, prior to on-ice training that morning, the boys had voted for the captain ('C') and two alternate captains ('A's') – positions for the World Champs the following week. The final countdown to the tournament had begun, and it all suddenly became real.

Each player cast one vote on paper. The votes were counted by Brett and Roger as the boys made their way onto the ice. The most popular choice would be the elected captain, and the next two most popular would be were the alternates. The head coach always had the final say, of course, but Harry happened to agree with the team's choices.

Brett smuggled the players' home and away shirts out of their hockey bags in the change room, and gave Sophie the C and A letters to stitch onto them. She managed to get the work done during the training, using the handy sewing kit in her medical bag.

As training drew to a close, Harry made the big announcement to the team: Stephen was the C and Tom and Dave were the A's. Sophie presented the boys with their completed shirts as they stepped off the ice, amidst the cheers and applause of their teammates.

'Thanks Mum!' They said through ear to ear smiles as they received their shirts.

Team spirit was high in the game that evening and they played extremely well. The lines worked better, the passes flowed smoothly, and the score reflected this. They still lost, but it was 5–2 this time. They celebrated with another dinner at Applebee's, and Sophie sampled the last of the Chilean red wines on the wine list.

Another two days of training were all that were left, and soon enough it was Friday. Sophie was once more packed and saying goodbye to the team. And her beloved Anton. It was early in the morning and the team were due at off-ice training. Time stood still for a moment while Anton hugged his mother tightly.

'Love you Mum,' he said, his chin moving up and down on the top of her head as he spoke. She had her eyes closed and was smiling.

'Love you too bud. More than all the stars in the sky. See you in Mexico!' she answered, squeezing him more tightly. 'Fly safe.'

Brett drove her to Salt Lake City Airport to catch the first of her three flights. At least there were no long hauls on this journey, but she still needed to leave much earlier than the team, to arrive in Mexico City only half an hour before they would.

Brett waited with her until she was checked in and her backpack was the last of her luggage she had with her. They sat and enjoyed a coffee by the departures door and watched people come and go. It occurred to Sophie that she was really enjoying herself. It felt easy and pleasant, and not at all awkward. Certainly a contrast to the last time she had sat drinking coffee with a man in an airport.

Finally, Sophie's boarding call was announced. She slid her backpack on as she and Brett made their way closer to the departures doorway. The time had come to say their goodbyes. Brett started by cautioning her.

'Now, you be careful. You're very important to this team, and we're all worried about you travelling alone. Fly safe, and we'll see you in Mexico!'

'Brett, thanks for everything. You've been amazing. From turning up unexpectedly at the airport, to saving me from the druggies!' Sophie was truly grateful. This trip so far would have been very different without him. She threw her arms up around his neck and hugged him tightly. He hesitated momentarily. Then he reciprocated, carefully placing his arms around her waist under her backpack. He held her tight for a few moments.

'See you in Mexico!' Sophie grinned as she gently pulled away from the hug then turned and disappeared through the doorway towards her gate.

She had felt sad saying goodbye to Anton earlier, and now to Brett. But she would see them both again very soon.

Chapter Twelve

A LONG WAY FROM HOME

Sophie enjoyed her three flights and two short stopovers. Her bags were checked right through, so all she had to carry was her backpack. She didn't feel rushed and all the connections went smoothly. Everything was well signposted so she didn't need to talk to anyone during the journey. Best of all, she had the whole day to herself. It felt like freedom. Peace and quiet.

There were no movies on these shorter flights, so she seized the opportunity to delve back into the novel Katie had insisted she read. She hadn't picked it up since she had landed in Salt Lake City 10 days ago.

The girl in the story was now 30 and was still endlessly searching for the elusive man who might measure up to her first, lost love. At 28, she had settled and married a 'good man', but divorced him a short time later. Sophie had reached the third to last chapter. The young woman had accepted that her life was going to be one of solitude and was visiting the tourist spots alone in Paris, the City of Love. She was sitting at an outside table in front of a back-street Parisian café, planning her day at La Louvre, when she was approached by a familiar-looking man who had recognised her. It was a one in a billion chance meeting. He was the older brother of her lost love! The young woman had only met him briefly in the past. He sat down with her and they started to reminisce. He, too, still mourned the loss of his brother. Sophie thought he seemed like such a gentle, caring and attentive man.

Just then, the plane wheels hit the tarmac and Sophie had to quickly pack her book into her backpack, which she had stowed under the seat in front. She had been completely distracted and her flight had already landed in Mexico City. She couldn't wait to read the last two chapters to see how it ended. But that would have to wait.

As the plane taxied up to the arrival gate at Terminal 2, Sophie switched on her cell phone. An automated 'Welcome to Mexico' text message came through immediately. As the passengers disembarked, she was surprised to see she was one of only six Caucasian people on the plane. Looking around further, she was even more surprised to realise she was the only blonde woman in sight. She was attracting curious stares and whispers. Maybe they hadn't seen many blonde women in real life.

The signs were all in Spanish, so she simply followed the other passengers and quickly reached the immigration desk. Her immigration officer took her passport and custom's declaration card without saying a word, looked at the photo for one second, and studied her face for about 10 seconds. Sophie just smiled. He looked at the passport and declaration card again for a few more seconds, then handed her passport back, waving her on towards the carousel.

She decided maybe he didn't speak English or just couldn't be bothered. Either way, she had nothing to declare, and he obviously wasn't going to make small talk.

The further she walked, the bigger the crowds became, and the more she was being stared at.

Sophie hauled her two red suitcases off the carousel, cleared the last customs desk under the curious gaze of two officers, and then followed the crowds to what appeared to be the exit area. Only then did she stop, briefly standing up her right-hand suitcase next to her, to check the time on her cell phone. 5.30 p.m. already. She one-handedly sent a text message to Brett and Roger. 'Arrived safely, making my way to Terminal 1.' She estimated that the team should have just landed, so Brett and Roger would get her text as soon as they switched on their phones.

When she looked up again, she could see cars and taxis parked in a covered loading bay outside large automatic glass doors. The sun was low. Another hour and it would be dark outside. There were so many people coming and going in the wide concourse that the doors barely had a chance to close. She could feel a wave of beautiful, dry warmth blowing in. She had researched the climate and knew that, at this time of the year, it should be about 28 degrees Celsius during the day and about 12 at night. Although the sun was going down, the temperature was still quite balmy. *Mmmm. Nice contrast to Salt Lake.* She took off her black team sweater and stuffed it into her backpack.

When she looked left and right, she could see the airport building continued for a long way in each direction. *Wow.* And this was only one of two terminals. It appeared that Benito Juarez International Airport was rather large!

There were oceans of people everywhere. But still no signs in English.

Damn. Not helpful for the directionally challenged!

All she needed to do was find an information desk and get directions. Terminal 1 would surely be within easy walking distance. Most airports were like that. She just had to find out which direction to go. Sophie had been in this kind of situation often enough that she was confident she could figure it out. It would be a piece of cake... Hopefully.

Here goes.

Backpack secured on back. *Check.*

One suitcase handle in each hand. *Check.*

Passport wallet in inside pocket of backpack (for security). *Check.* Smile. *Check.*

Time to take on the crowd!

Sophie headed left along the inside of Terminal 2 and made her way through the ocean of people. The crowd stretched as far as she could see. It was like a mosh-pit at a concert – complete with the pushy, sweaty people. It seemed like every second oncoming person was staring at her. As she got closer to them, they seemed to either smile wildly like she was their long-lost friend or look really perplexed. Sophie thought these were strange reactions, but didn't have time to analyse.

Several taxi drivers, sporting various uniforms and attempting to drum up business inside the terminal, politely asked, 'Taxi?'

'No thanks,' she replied, smiling politely to all of them.

After fighting the crowds for about 10 minutes she finally came across an information kiosk.

Whew.

See! That wasn't so hard!

'Excuse me. How do I get to Terminal 1?' she asked, smiling. The woman behind the desk looked stunned, then abruptly stood up and spoke loudly at her, a million miles an hour, in Spanish. She pointed and motioned further in the same direction Sophie was already headed.

'Oh, okay, thank you,' Sophie replied, still smiling. She thought it was a strange reaction to her simple question, but took the woman's gesture to mean she needed to carry on in the same direction. Maybe she was trying to tell her that someone at the next kiosk spoke English.

Just then, Sophie's phone whistled, so she stood her right hand case up to check the text. Brett had answered: 'Team landed, collecting last of bags now, still have to clear thru customs, meet at main door Term. 1.' Clearing customs was a lengthy process with

24 of them altogether. They would still be a while. No need to answer him yet.

Sophie carried on fighting her way through the crowd of people staring at her, past several more polite taxi drivers, and saw nothing but Spanish signs, for what seemed like another 10 minutes. The numbers of people started to thin out, but then, one minute later, she realised why. The long length of Terminal 2 had come to an end.

Obviously *not* the right direction to get to the other terminal!

As she looked around her, the only two doors remaining seemed like small, private, locked entry ways. She could see a few scattered signs, but again, all in Spanish. To the left, set up in a corner was a desk with two very relaxed, uniformed women, lounging back on their chairs, with arms folded, legs crossed, staring at her, but talking to each other. All this staring was starting to feel even more strange. However, she hoped one of women might speak English. Sophie turned and made her way towards them. As she approached, their expressions changed to one of bewilderment, as if they were looking at an unexplained apparition.

'Excuse me. How do I get to Terminal 1?' she asked again, smiling. The two women didn't move but continued to stare at her, seemingly at a loss for words, for about 20 seconds. Then they looked back to each other and simply carried on their conversation for about half a minute, completely ignoring her. *How rude!*

'Excuse me. I'm lost and I need to get to Terminal 1.' Sophie interrupted them, feeling a little cross and speaking a little louder this time. Both women looked up at her, obviously surprised to see her still standing there. One of them said something dismissive and gestured to her right. Then they resumed their conversation once more. Apart from the arm movement, they hadn't moved at all.

'Well, thanks for your help!' Sophie muttered sarcastically to herself, as she turned to retrace her steps, back through the building. This was getting tedious. The team would nearly be through customs by now and she really wanted to be there at the other terminal to greet her darling Anton.

Thinking the situation through logically, Sophie came to the conclusion that Terminal 1 must obviously be past the place where she had first exited the customs area, in the opposite direction. So she carried on, battling her way back through the thickening, staring crowds, and several more polite taxi drivers. She felt at least a bit more confident that she was now on the right track.

After about six minutes of walking, she spotted a funny-looking staircase and checkpoint to the left, on the outer edge of the building. She hadn't noticed this when she had first passed it. She couldn't see where it went, but there was a sign in English that read 'Sky Train'. Was this the way to Terminal 1? There were no other clues. She would go and find out.

While she queued at the checkpoint for a few minutes, she took the time to reply to Brett. 'I'm a bit lost but will be there soon.' Then, she was at the front of the queue.

'Excuse me. Is this the way to Terminal 1?' she asked, smiling to the male guard. He was a giant, with an enormous 'Magnum P.I.' moustache and wore what looked like a policeman's cap.

'Pasaporte,' he declared, as he held out his hand. He looked serious – not a person to be messed with.

'Oh, no. I don't want to buy a ticket. I just need to know how to get to the other terminal,' she replied, hoping he would understand something.

'Sky Train. Pasaporte,' and he held out his hand again.

'No, I'm *not* giving you my passport. Does anyone speak English?' Sophie was starting to lose her cool now. These people were wasting her time. Looking around, she was very aware she was holding up the queue of people, now choking up behind her. It had been a long shot that this Sky Train would take her to Terminal 1 anyway, but she most certainly was not going to hand over her passport! She had cleared customs. Done!

The people behind her now started to yell at her in Spanish, and the checkpoint guard also spoke to her angrily, pointing back in the direction she had come, and then toward the Sky Train, wherever it may go.

Time to get out of the way. Sophie turned and fought her way through the choked up queue, dragging her cases, and feeling the animosity of those who had been yelling at her. She had no clue where to go next, except that there was still the far end of this terminal to explore. So she carried on.

And on.

Her phone whistled again, but she didn't stop. Then, after another few minutes, she recognised her surroundings. She was back to the original spot where she had first emerged from the building after clearing customs. On her left were the wide automatic glass doors.

This was the landmark she had been looking for. Terminal 1 must surely now be only a few minutes away. Forty minutes had passed since Sophie had cleared customs. It was rapidly getting dark outside. The team must be through customs at the other terminal and almost on the bus waiting for her by now.

Then she remembered her phone had whistled. She stood her right case up again so she could check the text. It was Brett. 'Cleared customs, on the bus, where are you??'

Sophie thought it was best for her to answer him in a way that wouldn't make him worry. 'Bit frustrated! Cant find Term. 1, nobody speaks Eng! Be there asap :)' She put the smiley face on so he knew she was safe and in good spirits.

Firmly gripping the handles of her suitcases again, Sophie headed towards the unexplored end of the building. Her backpack was starting to feel like it was full of bricks. But at least the crowds appeared to be thinning out again. People still stared at her, smiling or bewildered. Sophie now completely ignored the taxi drivers. She knew she was now wearing a slightly worried look on her face.

She had walked for about five minutes when she came across another information kiosk. Without holding high hopes of finding someone who spoke English, she approached the desk where two uniformed women were seated.

'Excuse me. How do I get to Terminal 1? Ter-min-al 1?' She repeated the second Terminal 1 very slowly, in case the Spanish word was similar.

To her surprise, one of the women smiled sweetly at her and answered her in English!

''Ello, goot ebening,' she started, 'Wow-come to Me-Hico. Caan I helb you?' Okay, it was broken English, but it felt so good to hear it! Sophie couldn't help smiling, she was so relieved.

'Yes please! I'm trying to find Terminal 1. My son and his sports team are there and they are all on the bus waiting for me, because I've ended up so hopelessly lost. Which way do I go?' Sophie asked, still smiling.

'Solly. I no speako Engliss,' the woman replied.

All Sophie's hopes were once again dashed. The woman continued to smile sweetly, then she began talking a million miles an hour in Spanish, while the other woman started chuckling and shaking her head in amusement. It must all have been a great joke to them. They probably did this to tourists all the time.

'Oh, great. Thank you very much for your help!' Sophie said sarcastically, this time out loud. She knew they couldn't understand her and she was annoyed beyond belief at this well-rehearsed prank. *Where on earth is Terminal 1?*

Sophie was growing increasingly worried.

With no other option, she turned and carried on through the

building. Now she stopped each person who looked like an official to ask, 'Do you speak English?' Of course, none of them did. She was still being stared at and the taxi drivers were still asking 'Taxi?' but she was now walking very quickly, frowning heavily leaving the taxi drivers in her wake.

After five more minutes, she reached the other end of the building and only slowed a little as she turned a loop at the end to ask three officials, 'Speak English?' One shook his head. The other two didn't even bother responding. They all stared at her as she walked away, back towards her starting point. Again.

Sophie estimated she'd be back at the automatic glass doors in less than 10 minutes, especially now that she had sped up her pace and there were fewer people around. She continued to ask anyone who looked like an official, 'English?' as she passed by them. Most didn't answer. Some shook their heads.

Sophie felt a long way from home.

Chapter Thirteen

HOW TO DISAPPEAR IN MEXICO

Back at the glass doors, it was time to take stock. Put an action plan into place. Sophie stood still in the middle of the large concourse, firmly gripping the handles of her suitcases. Backpack now dragging down on her shoulders. Full frown on her face, looking at her feet.

Think logically, Sophie, she told herself. *This is not rocket science. You can work this out.* She needed to explore all avenues of common sense.

In New Zealand when she got lost, she would simply ask for directions. No English. So that had failed.

Or she would read the signposts or find a map. Unhelpful people. No English signposts. No airport map. So that had failed.

What else could she possibly do? Maybe she had to go outside the building, but then it was very nearly night-time now. She was in a strange city and terrified of the dark at the best of times. So, *nope*!

Sophie's only option was to carry on looking for Terminal 1. Maybe look into the Sky Train again?

She turned and started walking.

Just then, out of nowhere, two huge men in taxi driver uniforms came running towards her and flanked her on either side.

'No thanks,' she automatically and firmly replied. But they

weren't looking at her face. They were focussed intently on her hands and suitcases. The men were blocking her way and not allowing her to continue walking.

Then she figured out why.

In a split second, the men had each wrapped a huge hand around Sophie's tiny wrists. Then they also grabbed her suitcase handles, fully encompassing her little hands where she maintained her own grip. She was trapped.

Boy, these taxi drivers won't take no for an answer! Sophie thought. She began pulling and wriggling against the vice-like hold the men had on her, but there was no breaking free. Her hands and wrists were hurting. A lot! She would have to tell them once and for all.

She shook her head vigorously and shouted, 'No! I don't want a taxi! Let me go!' She repeated herself several times, raising her voice louder and louder, still trying to wriggle free. The giants only tightened their grip even further. Surely, even if they didn't speak English, her body language should convey the message clearly! She did *not* want a taxi!

At that moment, time slowed down to slow motion. Sophie suddenly understood with absolute clarity their ill intentions, as the freeze-frame pictures playing out in front of her clicked into place, like a thousand little pieces of a jigsaw puzzle…

They weren't offering her a taxi.

They weren't after her suitcases.

They wouldn't know she was carrying drugs.

And they certainly didn't want her clothes or toiletries.

As the last elusive piece of the puzzle fell into place, Sophie realised with absolute terror… They wanted *her!*

In the same moment, to her horror, the men proceeded to pull her, drag her, and lurch her, as she kicked and screamed, towards the automatic glass doors.

As her surroundings and situation became more surreal, Sophie thought about the weird and illogical things that had begun flashing through her mind when she realised her life was in danger. She could see Anton and Hayden's distraught faces when the news was broken to them that their mother had been kidnapped by two huge Mexican taxi drivers, never to be seen again. Anton wouldn't be in any fit state to play at the world championships. She would never hug her darling sons again. And who would be on the benches to look after the injured players? They would have no medical supplies. How would the boys get their favourite socks dry? Who would do the coffee run for the coaches?

Wait!

How ridiculous!

This is not okay!

This cannot happen.

She could *not* allow these men to take her.

And just like that, Sophie knew she was quite literally fighting for her life.

She thrashed, and fought, and screamed, and kicked, harder and louder than she ever thought possible. She found the epic adrenaline rush she had read about in books.

But despite her adrenaline-fuelled efforts, with each slow-motion millisecond, she was being manoeuvred closer and closer to those perpetually opening automatic glass doors.

As she struggled, she was peculiarly distracted by a line of approximately 25 armed policemen to her left, only about 20 feet away. They were queued in front of a small bank kiosk, with one person serving them. *They have guns! Why won't they help?*

She continued to fight. She even tried to scream in the direction of the policemen, hoping to attract their attention.

Only 20 feet away! Surely they could all hear her!

Screaming was universal language, wasn't it? Didn't they understand she was fighting for her life? But only three of the policemen were turned towards her. Their arms were folded, like they were casually waiting in a supermarket queue. They stood there, watching. Not one of them moved towards her, instead the three began pointing, chuckling and joking amongst themselves.

Sophie was on her own.

But she would thrash and fight and scream and kick until the end.

She had been pulled and dragged perilously close to doors and would soon disappear into the night.

Her wrists and hands were burning.

Then, just as suddenly as the giant men had run up and grabbed her, they dropped her hands and suitcase handles, threw their arms in the air as if they were surrendering, then ran out the doors, laughing raucously all the way. They looked back several times as they ran, but not at Sophie.

Despite the balmy evening, Sophie was shaking from head to toe, frozen to the spot, suddenly incredibly dizzy and ready to faint, rubbing her burning, red wrists and hands. She was exhausted.

But it didn't make sense that they would suddenly give her up.

Nothing made sense. She had been a helplessly weak opponent, even with a bucket-load of adrenaline on board. Her screams had done nothing. The policemen hadn't posed even the slightest threat to the monsters. So why had they suddenly let her go?

Oh no! Were they planning to come back with more men? First the experience at the hotel in Salt Lake City, now this. Why was it happening to her again?

She had to move, and quickly. But where to?

Sophie hastily grabbed her suitcase handles and turned to get away from the doors, only to realise immediately why the huge taxi drivers had surrendered her...

There stood an even larger man, an armed security guard, less than three feet away. He looked relaxed, even bored, with his arms lazily folded over his very large belly. He stared at Sophie with an air of mild irritation, no doubt unhappy that the drama she had been part of had disturbed an otherwise quiet shift.

Sophie nodded to the guard in thanks. He had just saved her life, even if he seemed disinterested in the whole situation. In response to Sophie's gesture of thanks, he simply blinked, showing absolutely no other facial expression, then turned and sauntered, very casually and slowly, his arms still folded, back to his original spot against the corridor wall. He must have been standing there that whole time. He almost blended into his surroundings. He was so still. The perfect camouflage. No wonder Sophie hadn't seen him during her struggle.

She weighed up her next move, and for now it seemed like a good option to go and stand near the guard. He may be camouflaged like a chameleon, and he may move like a tortoise, but at least he had a gun, and at least he would act as a deterrent if her assailants returned. And if she fainted, perhaps he would look out for her.

Chapter Fourteen

RESCUING SOPHIE

Sophie stood a respectful three or four feet away from her temporarily appointed, apathetic bodyguard, and tried to act casually as she took out her phone. Her wrists and hands were red hot and burning, and she was still quivering as she sent a much more succinct text to Brett. 'Can't find Term. 1, not feeling very safe. Pls come find me ASAP. I'm at main doors. PS. I'm ok.'

No smiley face this time.

She didn't want to panic Brett, but where the hell was her chief protector when she needed him more than ever?!

If he could see her face. She was trying unsuccessfully to hide the panic stricken state she was in. That warm, fuzzy, cocooned, safe and blissfully peaceful feeling that she had grown to absolutely adore in his presence over these past few days had evaporated in the blink of an eye. In its place instead, was an absolute terror, a burning nausea in the pit of her stomach, and a tremor from head to toe.

Sophie could stand near the security guard for a while, but eventually he would probably walk away to take a meal or bathroom break. Her eyes darted back and forth as she scrutinised every person that came within a 10 foot radius of her.

She checked her phone. It was eight minutes since she had texted Brett. Where the hell was he? Had he even received her message? What if the team bus had been moved along and they had no choice but to leave? What if he didn't come to find her? What would she do?

She knew by now that she couldn't rely on the police for help. The security guard wasn't overly perturbed about her predicament. Did he even know she was standing beside him? He hadn't looked at her again. He had done the bare minimum he could to help her, albeit at the critical moment. Thankfully, it was enough. But he wasn't going to stand there all night. What if the huge taxi men were watching her? What if they saw him walk away?

The tremors took hold with a power surge shudder that travelled down her body from head to toe.

C'mon Sophie, think!

She could call the New Zealand embassy! Maybe they would send someone to help. But she had no roaming data on her phone, so how would she even find the phone number? Plenty of tourists must come through this airport every day. Surely they couldn't all speak Spanish. How did they all find their way?

'Oh, this is hopeless,' Sophie whispered, checking her phone again and rubbing her aching wrists and hands. Still no text. 'C'mon Brett,' she muttered to herself. It was 17 minutes since she had text him to come and rescue her.

Then, way off in the distance to her left she spotted a muscular young Mexican man towering above the thinned out crowd, with a focused and serious look on his face. He was charging through the seemingly tiny people in front of him, almost mowing them down. His eyes were fixed on Sophie and he was pointing directly at her.

She wanted to scream but could only hold her breath, eyes wide with terror.

She quickly checked that her makeshift bodyguard was still standing near her. He was oblivious, looking in the opposite direction.

Maybe her assailants had sent another man to secure their prize once and for all? When would this end? What else could she do? She was already exhausted, and her wrists and hands would surely break this time. Should she say something to the guard? Would he even understand her? And even if he did, would he just ignore the situation this time, like the policemen had? What was the point of him carrying a gun when he could hardly be bothered unfolding his arms? And what would it take to make him jump into action? She had to try – she had no other option.

Sophie was still holding her breath, as she watched with terror as this newest threat closed in, his eyes still fixed on her. She briefly turned her head and waved her right arm in the direction of the security guard, trying to get his attention.

The security guard did *not* look in her direction. He did *not* move. The threat was only moments away. Sophie finally managed to let go of her breath so she could scream for help… but instead she quietly exclaimed 'Oh!'

The young man wasn't alone. Next to the Mexican and striding beside him was a normal-sized blond man. His eyes too were fixed upon her. He was focused and serious, with a worried, pained expression on his face.

It was Brett…

Brett had come to rescue her!

Sophie had no words. She threw her arms around Brett's shoulders and burst into tears. She had never felt so relieved in all her life.

'I am so happy I found you!' Brett said gently into her ear. 'Are you okay?'

'Hi,' was all she could squeak back as she nodded and sobbed out loud. Brett was holding her tightly. Squeezing her in. She needed this. These strong arms to hold her tight. To reassure her she was safe again. No harm would come to her now.

The muscular young Mexican man stood nearby, watching them both, intrigued.

Sophie suddenly felt self-conscious at her bizarre, needy display of emotion. She was usually so composed, even under stress. She pulled away from the bear hug and quickly regathered herself with a few deep breaths.

'Sorry,' she whispered, as she carefully wiped the mascara raccoons from her eyes.

Brett introduced Carlos, one of two World Championship hosts assigned to the New Zealand team. The young Mexican spoke perfect English in an American accent, and had been on a hockey scholarship at the University of California, Los Angeles. He would have been on the Mexican ice hockey team, but he couldn't play because he had busted a knee three months previously and was waiting for surgery.

Sophie shook his hand and profusely thanked them both for coming to rescue her. Brett and Carlos each took one of Sophie's suitcases, and the three of them headed out through the automatic glass doors.

It was completely dark outside now. After walking briskly for two minutes they arrived at the taxi van that was waiting for them, then drove for eight minutes through airport traffic to the team bus at Terminal 1, three kilometres away.

Sophie gave Brett the one minute abridged version of her near miss. She could embellish the story with all the terrifying details later. Brett silently shook his head. His demeanour had changed.

He had shifted into high alert, ready to fight anybody with any kind of weapon at the merest sign of malice.

He filled her in with his side of the story. After he had received her uneasy text while sitting on the team bus, he'd tried to phone her. But because the networks worked so differently in Mexico City, he had dialled a local number by mistake. He was temporarily puzzled when a gruff-sounding man answered the phone in Spanish, but was then mortified to hear a woman crying and screaming in the background. He immediately hung up, leapt out of his seat, grabbed Carlos by the collar, and said, 'Come with me, *now!*' He didn't want to alarm the team, and specifically not Anton. So he simply announced, 'We're going to get Sophie. She's, ah, lost.'

Sophie smiled to hear this. It was a very believable alibi. No one would be surprised to hear she was lost.

Carlos had hailed a passing taxi van and Brett didn't hesitate even though the corrupt driver demanded the equivalent of NZ$200 up front. They sped towards Terminal 2 and screeched to a halt outside a set of glass doors that the driver swore to Carlos was the main entrance. They were in a different location to Sophie but, as luck would have it, because Carlos was so tall, he had almost immediately spotted the only blonde woman in the terminal.

Brett and Sophie spent the last two minutes of the ride back to the bus in total silence and stillness, staring out the window, each painfully aware that things could have turned out much worse. Brett was relieved to have found Sophie in one piece, despite her evident emotional trauma and the wrist and hand bruising that was already visible. He pictured how it would have been, having to break the grim news to her husband that she'd been kidnapped, raped, and murdered. And on his watch!

Sophie had more explicitly graphic images tumbling through her mind, but of the exact same circumstances. Only, her version included Brett breaking the news to Anton and Hayden.

She didn't think about Charlie.

Brett and Sophie shuddered at the same time. He reached across to her hand, gave it a reassuring squeeze and held it until the van pulled up alongside the idling team bus.

Without talking, Brett and Carlos moved Sophie's cases to the bus's luggage compartment. Once onboard, Brett sat down beside Roger, and Carlos returned to his seat beside another large Mexican, the team's other host, Julio. The amusing, weird hairstyles of the rookies were a welcome sight as Sophie looked around for an empty seat. She prepared to settle herself at the front of the bus.

As she slid her backpack off in one smooth movement, she spotted Anton's mohawk half way towards the back. He looked up, waved and said, 'Hi Mum,' then continued chatting with Steele. It was clear he had no idea of the nightmare his mother had just been through. Sophie smiled, relieved and answered, 'Hey bud,' as she placed her backpack on the aisle seat, then sat down beside the window.

Chapter Fifteen

CONADE CASTLE?

It was 6.50 p.m. and pitch black outside. Sophie was grateful that the light in the bus was dimmed down as they drove, and the front seat was perfect for her. She felt sure her eyes would be swollen, with mascara raccoons, and she needed to collect her thoughts before the team arrived at the Conade Sports Village, where they were staying.

It was cooler outside now, and cooler again on the bus, and Sophie welcomed the comfort and warmth of her black New Zealand team sweater. It would also hide the evidential bruising on her wrists and hands.

She had already decided not to worry Anton with any details about what had happened to her and if he didn't have reasons to ask, she wouldn't have to lie to protect him. He had some serious games of ice hockey coming up that needed his full attention. None of the team, including Harry, Benny or Roger, had noticed her smudged eyes or her bruises. And she didn't feel like divulging her story.

Thoughts suddenly popped into her head of what Charlie's response would be, if she told him. He would probably laugh at her. Then tell her she was being completely paranoid, that she was imagining it, and that the men were just offering her a taxi. Either that, or he'd make out it was her own stupid fault that she had nearly gotten herself kidnapped.

She decided she would never tell him.

Her mind went numb.

From then on, the bus ride from the airport to the sports village was a 30-minute blank for Sophie as she stared out the window into dark oblivion.

Further back in the bus, Brett also remained quiet, deep in his own thoughts.

Everyone else on the bus was a little tired after their early morning off-ice training and two flights. They were all looking forward to some dinner, finding their rooms and getting a good night's sleep. But they were animated with excitement and anticipation about being in a new country.

Time to focus on hockey again!

Thank goodness, thought Sophie.

On-ice training tomorrow, 10 a.m. Back to some sense of normality.

Mexico City had two ice rinks. The one in the northern districts had hosted New Zealand teams at world tournaments on several previous occasions. But this was the first World Champs to be hosted at the southern district's San Jeronimo Rink. None of the New Zealand team members had been there before.

Sophie had done her homework and was fascinated by the Conade Sports Village. Conade stood for 'Comisión Nacional de Cultura Física y Deporte' – Mexico's National Commission for Physical Culture and Sport.

The complex was set on a hill. It had quite a history, having provided accommodation for the Olympic Games in 1968 and hundreds of international sports training camps and tournaments since. It slept approximately 500 people and covered a large acreage. The gymnasium was said to be world class and the surrounding grounds included a swimming pool, football fields and basketball courts. It sounded amazing!

It was 7.20 p.m. by the time the team entered the village compound. To their surprise, they passed through three armed, gated, security checkpoints before reaching the top of the hill and the reception area.

'Wow, they take security seriously round here,' she heard the player behind her remark. Sophie wasn't unhappy about that.

The team piled out of the bus in a disorderly fashion, collected their bags from under the bus, and headed towards the reception lobby on the ground floor. Everyone waited, happily chatting, while Brett, Roger, Harry and Benny waded through the boys and bags to the front desk. Sophie had silently followed them before planting herself in the middle of the chatty group. As truly exhausted as she was, it was now second nature to surround herself with the safety of this sea of comforting, familiar black uniforms.

Then a commotion broke out. 'Nope! That's *not* okay! *Not* good for the team! *Not* gonna work!' Harry exclaimed loudly, banging his fist on the reception desk to emphasise every *not*. Sophie jumped slightly each time. Harry was leaning with the fisted hand on the counter top, the other hand on his hip, shaking his head, and looking at Brett, like he would have all the answers.

The boys' happy chatter quietened somewhat, as some of them were distracted by what was going on.

'That's not right.' Brett was echoing Harry's sentiment, but quietly, calmly and slowly to the man behind the desk. 'Our team cannot fit into six rooms. For a start, the five management members are supposed to get a room each. It's in the rule book.' This he said tapping his finger on the folder he had with him. 'Please find us some more rooms.'

'One moment please,' replied the man behind the desk. He picked up the phone and proceeded to speak in Spanish for what felt like 15 or 20 minutes.

Roger, Brett, Harry and Benny muttered to each other, and

Sophie just wanted to lie down. She started feeling dizzy and faint again, so she sat on some nearby stairs. Half the boys were now dozing off, sitting against their hockey bags, and the other half were fidgeting and talking even more animatedly in the background. Her ears were ringing. Eventually she got up and squeezed into the huddle that Roger, Brett, Harry and Benny had formed.

'What's going on?' she asked quietly.

Brett was the one to answer her.

'They've put four boys in each room, the four of us blokes in a single room, they have no room allocated for Carlos and Julio. And... ah,' he hesitated as he looked directly at her now, 'he's looking for another room... Now don't freak out, but he's saying you have to stay in the women's quarters. They don't allow women in the men's quarters.'

No sooner had Brett said that than the man abruptly hung up the phone.

'No. Sorry,' he said with a fake smile, and folded his arms onto the desk.

'*No!*' Sophie physically recoiled at the news. She turned and looked at Brett and Roger to her right, obvious panic on her face. She had just been able to regather a small sense of safety and equilibrium on the bus and there was no way she was going to stay in a completely separate part of this vast sports village. This man was going to throw her into a four-bedded room with three other women she wouldn't even know?! This was not a good idea. What about her lack of directional sense? Plus she needed to be accessible to the team.

The survival instinct screamed out within her. She needed her bodyguards like she needed to breathe!

No one was going to tell her no. Not today! Not after all she had been through!

Then out of nowhere...

'*No!*' she growled out loudly into the seated man's face. Sophie found herself leaning over the counter, and realised she was now the one banging her fist on the counter.

'I – am the *team medic* – and I – *need* to be with *them*,' she said forcefully, angrily, slowly, pointing around at the team. The boys' chatter had ceased instantly, as the whole team looked on at the unfolding spectacle.

Oblivious, Sophie continued. 'I – am *not* staying anywhere else. So – *you*,' now pointing at the man, *'find us more rooms!'* She hammered her fist on the counter, staring him down.

Even Anton was shocked. He had never heard his mother sound so menacing.

'Okay. One moment please,' said the man behind the desk, still wearing his fake smile. He picked up the phone and again proceeded to speak in Spanish, for what felt like another 15 or 20 minutes. Sophie leaned on the counter top, mostly so she wouldn't fall over, and stared at him with a look of thunder for the duration of his conversation. Now, more than ever, Sophie wished she spoke more than just English and fragmented French from her childhood.

Eventually the man hung up.

'Sorry madam. Cannot help. We no rooms left. We full,' he said, holding his hands up in a gesture of surrender, looking smug.

This can't be happening, Sophie thought in despair, still leaning on the counter top and staring at him, feeling dizzier than ever.

At the same time, Brett had been ferreting in his backpack for something and just then found it.

'Aha!' he said, withdrawing a computer disc and placing it on the counter top, with his other hand on Sophie's shoulder to reassure her that all would be well. 'This is the rules of the International Ice Hockey Federation regarding Olympic-sanctioned World Championships. And I think you will find that Mexico, as the host of these World Championships, is obliged under these IIHF rules, to provide separate rooms for each member of the management team.

Sophie is part of our team and we need her with us. So…,' Brett was ever the diplomat, 'what can you do to help this situation?'

How did he stay so calm? Sophie was now highly embarrassed by her out-of-character outburst, which hadn't made a difference anyway.

The man's smug look slid off millimetre by millimetre. The smarmy bastard! He'd known the rules all along. He just didn't *want* to help! He sheepishly stared at Brett for all of 20 seconds while Brett stared silently back. Then the man caved. He picked up the phone and, with a different tone, began speaking animatedly, like he was reprimanding the person on the other end. This went on for at least another 10 minutes.

When he abruptly hung up this time, he clasped his hands together and looked up at them all with a wide smile on his face as if he was the hero of the day.

'I get two more rooms. But manager, coach, share. Two in room.' Then waving his hands at Carlos and Julio he said, 'Incluido.'

That sounded like a musical finale. A concluding statement. No room for any further negotiation. Rule book or not!

He handed the teams' ID security lanyards to Harry and said, 'You put on. Wear all time.'

The happy chatter resumed once more, with Harry sorting the boys into groups of four, doubling up on the room arrangements they'd had in Salt Lake City. Each group of four boys received one room key to share, and their personal security lanyards. Their rooms were spread over the first and second floors. There was no elevator in the building, so all the suitcases and hockey bags were dragged by the bedraggled team, banging and bouncing up one or two flights of stairs.

Sophie was absorbed in thinking about how the room configurations were going to work for the managers, coaches and hosts. The boys rooms she understood: four beds multiplied by five rooms, equalled 20 players – done. But, two managers, two coaches, two hosts and her…? Seven was an uneven number to fit into three rooms. As bright as she was, she was a little dyslexic with maths and, for the life of her, she couldn't come up with a solution in her head that was going to work.

She had been given her ID lanyard, which she put around her neck straight away. But she hadn't been the lucky recipient of a key. She hadn't paid proper attention once Harry had started sorting people into rooms. So it was all guess work, at best.

Uh-oh. Maybe Harry had forgotten about her…

Now her brain hurt.

One thing was for sure – there was no way she was going to the women's quarters.

'Well, I'll just sleep on the floor.' Sophie resigned herself, not realising she'd spoken her thoughts out loud.

Brett just smiled in response.

Sophie followed Brett and Roger, clumsily banging her suitcases up the first part of the stairs to the landing. Thank goodness the cases had wheels! She then turned around, swapping her aching wrists and hands to hold the suitcase handles backwards, and reversed up the second set of stairs to the first floor. Brett and Roger had stopped at the top to wait for her. Then they turned left, with Sophie trundling along behind.

'So, meet back here in five then?' Roger asked Brett.

'Yeah, then we'll round up the boys for dinner,' he answered.

Roger banged on the door in front of him, and Stephen, the team captain, opened it to let him in. Brett carried on walking to the end of the hallway and used his key to open the last door on the right-hand side. Sophie wasn't sure whether to follow him, so she hesitated. She was the last one left standing in the corridor.

'By the way, we have a bedroom each,' he said with a wide grin to Sophie.

'C'mon.' And he stepped through the door. Sophie smiled a vague, confused smile back at him. How on earth did he work that one out? The guy downstairs said two to a room.

Then it all became apparent.

Sophie had stepped into a small entry hall. To the right was an enclosed toilet and shower, and a bathroom basin on the left. Ahead were two closed doors. Sophie opened the door on the left, and discovered a modest double bedroom. This would be her home for the next nine days, and Brett would be staying in the room through the other door.

Sophie's room contained two single metal-framed beds, with copious rust patches breaking through their old white paint. There was an old-fashioned set of wooden drawers that didn't close properly, complete with broken handles, and with one drawer missing altogether. The beds were each covered with a thin hospital-style cotton blanket. She would need to use both blankets and hope she would be warm enough if the temperature dropped to 12 degrees overnight.

Over the drawers were wide wooden-framed windows, which didn't close properly and were fitted with external security bars. Sophie shuddered at the thought that security bars might be needed. The ceramic tiles on the floor were chipped, and there was a line of water meandering through the grouting, all the way from the bathroom sink in the entry hall to the outside wall. There were two thin towels, but no facecloths, no bath mat, no kettle, no hairdryer, no TV, no telephone, no internet, no fridge, no radio, no clock, no soap, no shampoo and no conditioner.

Talk about basic!

'Well, it's clean,' said Sophie, trying to make the best of it, 'and we know the running water works!' She was smiling at her glass-half-full irony.

'Hmmm. Doesn't look like they've done any maintenance since

they hosted the 1968 Olympic Games, let alone any renovations.' Brett sounded quite disgusted at the state of the accommodation. 'And this definitely does *not* meet the minimum three star requirements of the rule book.'

'Well, at least it's clean!' Sophie repeated, laughing this time. 'But I was looking for a moat, 'cos it's a lot like a castle, what with the security bars over the windows and the security checkpoints. It does seem a bit extreme, but at least it feels like we'll be safe here.' She sounded more serious now – and by 'we' she really meant herself.

'Conade Castle!' said Brett smiling. 'Ha! That's funny.'

'I think it might be as cold as a castle too. And someone stole the drawer with all the warm blankets!' Sophie giggled as she pointed to the space where the missing drawer should have been.

Brett watched as Sophie removed the thin blanket from one of the beds and overlaid it on the other. He disappeared momentarily, reappearing with the spare blanket from his room.

'Here, have this. I won't need it. I'm pretty hot,' he said with a completely straight face, the double entendre escaping him.

'Thanks!' Sophie smiled. Secretly, she had always thought he was 'pretty hot'. She added the new blanket to her bed and was glad to have her back to him until the heat went out of her face.

She lifted her suitcases and backpack onto the spare bed, causing its wonky metal legs to clatter and groan on the floor tiles. She soon discovered that her own bed made the same sound when she sat on it. It would wake the whole building every time she rolled over! She was laughing now at the very basic level of amenities. Compared to Salt Lake City, Conade Castle was like a prison camp.

'I can fix that too,' Brett smiled, as he once again disappeared into the other room. This time he reappeared with two pairs of socks.

'I packed emergency furniture levelling equipment,' he said with a laugh. Sophie got up and stepped aside. He placed a folded sock under each bed leg, then sat down to test his work. All quiet. He wriggled. The bed didn't rattle at all.

'Problemo solved!' Brett said bouncing up and down a couple of times.

'Wow! A gentleman *and* a handyman!' Sophie was laughing hard now. 'That's genius. Thank you.'

While they finished unpacking, Brett playfully teased Sophie from the other room. He said she'd looked like a puffer train with steam coming out her ears at the front desk. She felt embarrassed and humbly apologised for her outburst.

'Don't worry about it,' Brett chuckled, 'it was like playing 'good cop, bad cop'.'

Sophie giggled. She had certainly excelled at playing the bad cop, but it was Brett who had saved the day – again. And she told him so.

Chapter Sixteen

CASTLE HOSPITALITY

Soon after Sophie and Brett had finished unpacking, there was a knock at the door. Roger was standing in the main hallway, waiting for them.

'Bring your backpack with you, Sophie. I don't trust these people at all,' Brett said.

Sophie fetched her bag from her bedroom, without questioning his judgement or rationale. She never went anywhere without it anyway.

The three of them made their way along the corridor, Roger and Brett knocking on doors, summoning the troops for dinner. As the boys emerged from their rooms, Brett collected their passports. He put a giant rubber band around the booklets and placed them at the bottom of Sophie's backpack.

Sophie was nervous about the responsibility. But because of the 'line of sight' rule that was still in effect she would be guarded for the remainder of the trip, thereby keeping the passports safe too. Plus, as Brett had pointed out, who would ever suspect that the little lady of the group was carrying such a precious cargo?

Once all the team members had been gathered, they made their way downstairs for dinner. At the front desk, they encountered the same smarmy man, who informed them that the restaurant had closed at 8 p.m. and, as it was now 9.30 p.m., there was no food for them.

The whole debacle about their rooms had cost them the better part of two hours, and their dinner!

'Okay, thank you so very much. You've been so very helpful,' Brett said ever so slightly sarcastically, but with a huge smile.

Carlos and Julio suggested a grocery store 20 minutes' walk away, which was open until 11 p.m. So the entire team, led by their young Mexican hosts, with Sophie cocooned in the centre of the mob, set out, down the small hill, through the three security checkpoints, then along a flat road.

Having arrived at the store, the boys bought their own supplies, including drinks and snacks. Other late night shoppers looked at them with amusement, taking in their array of interesting hair styles. Sophie got 'the Mexican stare,' as she had now dubbed it, from several people, then the team made their way back to Conade Castle.

As they walked along, they happily chatted about the various things that had happened, gone wrong, the state of their rooms, and how much nicer Salt Lake City had been. The boys were experiencing some culture shock, but the walk was a good opportunity to let off steam. The whole group were wilting and quite subdued by the time they arrived back at the gates of the sports village.

They had no problems getting past the three security checkpoints on their way back up the hill. However, upon re-entering the accommodation quarters, their old friend at the front desk took great delight in informing them that they would now need to go through the entire check-in process again, because they had broken the 10 p.m. Conade curfew.

Another time wasting exercise! There was a curfew? Who knew? This man was infuriating!

In one corner of the lobby, some of the boys were laughing and chatting amongst themselves about the absurdity of the over-the-top rules and security, and a rude new nickname for the sports village – Conade Concentration Camp – was born.

The following morning, Sophie jumped out of her skin as she awoke to a loud knock on her bedroom door. She had gone to bed exhausted but now felt worse than the night before – completely rung out, physically and emotionally. She had suffered continuous night terrors, over and over, about the previous day's near kidnapping incident. She couldn't remember details of the dreams, but the sensation of panic stayed with her, and the sound of the screams she had made in the nightmares was still ringing in her ears.

The knock was Brett. 'Sorry to wake you,' he said through the closed door, 'but breakfast finishes in 45 minutes.'

Because she had only snacked the night before, Sophie was famished. Brett had apparently been up for a while. He had already been through the shower, and had knocked on the players' doors to wake them, making sure the whole team was accounted for. Then, as he waited patiently for Sophie to get ready, he sat on his bed fine-tuning the schedule for the day.

Sophie showered and dressed, and attempted to style her fly-away hair, which looked like it had also suffered from night terrors. She threw on some mascara and lip gloss, then tossed her backpack over one shoulder.

Sophie and Brett met the waiting team in the corridor, and the sea of black uniforms proceeded down the stairs to the front desk, complete with ID lanyards. Luckily. Because, at the front desk they each had to show their ID, sign their name, and have their fingerprints taken, before being handed a ticket for their food! Apparently, this was standard procedure, and they would be required to scan their fingerprints for every single meal. With that level of security, Sophie imagined the food must be a buffet fit for a king, served on 18 carat gold platters.

After a short walk outside on a narrow footpath, around some trees and a few corners, they arrived at the restaurant.

'Restaurant' was too glamorous a term. The place looked more like an army canteen or mess hall, complete with plastic chairs. And, in typical Mexican style, the entrance was manned by two armed guards, who were sitting either side of the open double doors. Were they expecting a robbery?

The New Zealand team piled inside and found tables, eyeing the South African and Chinese Taipei teams as they sat down. Mexico and Mongolia had apparently already been and gone.

The buffet was spread out at one end of the hall. The boys haphazardly found plates and picked out their food, grumbling as they trudged along.

Sophie needed coffee, first and foremost. Strong and black. To help her get over her 'night-terror-hangover'. She slid her backpack off, set it under her table, and sipped from her cup. *Mmmm. Oh yeah, that is good.* Now she felt famished again. Brett and Roger kept an eye on the backpack as she went to the buffet to find something to eat. The offerings were slim pickings indeed, and in no way fit for a king. No wonder the boys were grumbling.

She surveyed the thin strips of overcooked chicken, cornflakes, dried out refried beans, bananas, and yoghurt tubs that were sitting in a big tray of warm water. There were three different fruit flavoured drinks in large glass tanks, and small sealed bottles of water. Sophie took another coffee, a banana and a large bowl of dry cornflakes. *Cornflakes can't brew much bacteria*, she thought.

That's when alarm bells went off in her head. Looking around at what the boys had taken, most had overcooked chicken, cornflakes, bananas, or a combination, and some had refried beans. All had the sealed bottles of water. Only one had warm yoghurt, but he hadn't begun eating it. Whew! She made a beeline to his table.

'*Don't* eat the warm yoghurt, and *don't* drink the juice!' she whispered to each player, as she completed a circuit around each table. The boys nodded, understanding why she had issued the warning. She didn't need to explain. She didn't want to sound like a nagging mother, but she needed to let them know. Sitting down at her own table, she gave Harry, Benny, Roger and Brett the same advice.

The chicken was so overcooked it would render it safe to eat, but if the yoghurt tubs sat in warm water for long enough, they could cause food poisoning. And in any tournament, any unsealed drinks – especially those provided in a communal living environment – could easily be spiked with an illegal substance, causing players to fail drug testing.

The cornflakes were a bit dry, and tasted like cardboard. Not a surprise. But they were taking the edge off Sophie's hunger, so she went back for a second bowl. She usually she went home from these trips having lost weight. And by the look of this buffet, she wouldn't be the only one this time. She would save her banana for later in the day. No doubt she would get peckish, or one of the boys would.

While the managers and coaches made do with the food on offer and sipped their tea and coffee, Brett briefed them on the three concurrent one-hour tournament meetings scheduled for 8 p.m. that evening.

Brett and Roger needed to attend a management meeting at the hotel where the games officials were staying. Tournament rules stated that the hosting country were required to use two places of accommodation to provide separation for the referees, linesmen, supervisors, IIHF delegates, and especially for the tournament's biggest VIP – the IIHF tournament supervisor and chairman. Harry needed to attend a Team Rule Information Meeting (also known as a TRIM meeting), which was run by the IIHF referee supervisor for the head coaches. This would be held at the rink, and Sophie was also due there for a medical meeting. Two team buses would take them to the two venues, leaving Conade at 7.30 p.m. Lucky Benny, who wasn't required for any of the meetings, would get to stay behind and chill out with the players until the 10 p.m. Conade Castle curfew.

As the team exited the mess hall, some of the boys carried out bananas and half-drunk bottles of water for later. Without warning, the two guards at the door jumped out of their seats and started yelling at the boys in Spanish, trying to confiscate their backpacks. Roger and Brett stepped forward to find out what the problem was, but the guards just yelled more loudly and gesticulated more wildly.

'They say you can't take food and water out of the restaurant,' Carlos interpreted. Sophie hadn't even noticed he and Julio were present.

'Tell them we are supposed to have food and water supplied to us each day,' Brett replied. Carlos relayed this information but the guards became even more incensed. One was positively spitting in anger. Sophie held her banana behind her back.

'They say you have to eat and drink in the restaurant and then leave. If you want water and bananas you have to finish them here, now,' Carlos said simply. 'And they want to search your bags.'

'No, they are *not* searching our bags! And what's the difference whether we have the food and water here or take it with us?' Brett was getting a little heated now too. 'We are supposed to have three meals, three snacks and six litres of water a day, each. Ask them where these snacks and water bottles are. *And*, leave our bags alone!'

'Do they think we hid their refried beans and warm yoghurt tubs in our backpacks?' Sophie chuckled quietly to Harry, who was standing next to her. He laughed out loud.

Carlos and Julio both spent the next two to three minutes arguing with the guards, all of them yelling and waving their arms around, but to no avail.

'They said they are just the guards and they have been instructed that no one takes food or water out of the restaurant. All the meals must be eaten in the restaurant. 'They know nothing about snacks. And they just want to look in your bags,' Carlos concluded, making it clear that this was the end of negotiations.

'Oh, for crying out loud!' Brett muttered under his breath. Then out loud to Carlos, 'Well, they have guns, so they win. It looks like we'll need another trip to the grocery store!' Brett turned to face the boys, now gathered around him. 'Right, team. Hand the food and water back so they can't accuse us of stealing anything. Open the zips of your bags so they can look inside. Then back to your rooms. We'll meet in the lobby in 10 minutes. Full uniform, and remember your ID tags.'

Chapter Seventeen

YOU'RE FAMOUS!

As the team filed out of the mess hall everyone surrendered their bananas and water, and had their bags checked. They felt like criminals. Sophie was careful to show just enough of the inside of her backpack to satisfy the guards without them being able to see the passports at the bottom. Luckily, her Spanish phrase book and team sweater camouflaged the stack of booklets nicely.

Brett and Roger stopped at the reception desk and prepared for battle. Where were the team's water supplies? Snacks? How would lunches and dinners be provided when the restaurant had such limited meal times? How could the team get breakfast at 5 a.m. or dinner at 11 p.m. when games ran at absurdly early and late times throughout tournament week?

The rules clearly stated that the competing teams were to be provided with: six litres of water per player per day in the form of tamper-proof, sealed water bottles; three high quality meals; and three sets of substantial snacks. With the rising daytime heat in Mexico City, the players would burn through even more water than they had in Salt Lake City and continue to chomp their way through loads of food at all times of the day. Team funds would quickly dry up if they had to buy their own supplies for the remainder of the tour.

Best leave the managers to sort it out! thought Sophie as she was escorted by half the team to the first floor. She discovered that Anton and Steele's room was right next to hers. It felt nice to have Anton close by. They talked for a little while about the sports village. Anton wasn't worried about how basic the rooms were, even though he'd been too cold to get to sleep, and had needed to put on his whole tracksuit to stay warm.

'Just like being in a tent at the beach!' he laughed. He and Steele had been exploring and had found the gymnasium, which was apparently huge and well equipped.

As they finished chatting, Sophie hugged Anton tight and told him she loved him more than the stars, because she knew he wouldn't mind with just Steele watching. She gave him some more spending money, then they made their way downstairs to meet the rest of the team in the lobby. Once again, the whole group set off down the hill, via the three security checkpoints, and along the road to the grocery store.

The walk was much more interesting in the daylight, as they trekked past an eclectic mix of grey and colourful tin shacks and posh mansions. Sometimes a crazy, up and down roofline would extend the length of an entire block, with various building designs underneath. Sophie took photographs and tried to make sense of everything she was seeing.

The road was three lanes wide on each side and the bumper-to-bumper traffic moved exceedingly fast, as vehicles sped by unpredictably, erratically, accompanied by tooting and hooting like some cacophonous orchestra.

Halfway to the grocery store, the team passed under an overhead pedestrian crossing. There were about 15 men working on the bridge with hammers and power tools and, as the team approached, the men put down their equipment and stared at Sophie. Then they turned to the other side of the bridge in order to continue staring as the team passed underneath and walked away. A couple of the boys noticed, pointing up at the workmen. The situation didn't escape Brett's keen bodyguarding eye. He stared right back at the men.

'You're famous!' Julio exclaimed to Sophie, in his American accent.

'Yeah, I'm famous because I'm the only blonde in Mexico!' Sophie laughed, feeling slightly embarrassed and uncomfortable. But she was surrounded by 26 blokes so at least she felt safe.

Coming up on the left corner just before the grocery store was a large, turquoise-coloured building.

'That's the mall,' Julio said to Sophie, pointing up at it. 'It has some great fashion stores.' It looked rather run down from the outside. Paint was falling off the walls and graffiti had replaced it. 'We could go there if you like.'

'Maybe another day if we have time,' Sophie answered with a smile. *Hmmm, looks missable!* she thought.

At the grocery store, Brett told the team they had 10 minutes, as they all filed inside. Once again the boy's hairstyles attracted strange looks from other shoppers and Sophie was stared at ad nauseam as they bought their junk food snacks and drinks. The junk food wasn't ideal but it was predictable and unpreventable, and hopefully healthy foods would be available to them in abundance soon. Sophie bought fresh fruit and dark chocolate, and a bottle of Chilean red wine. She sampled a small piece of freshly made, warm corn tortilla and instantly fell in love with it, buying two more to snack on later.

Her phrase book came in handy when she had to ask, 'Dos agua por favour,' for two bottles of water. Extra stocks of water had to be brought in from the storeroom out the back, due to demand from the team. Almost every player carried a five-litre bottle in each arm, along with a four-pack of one-litre bottles in his backpack. Of course, it took 20 minutes to get everyone through the checkout. It wasn't a large store, but rounding up the boys was still like herding cats.

On the way back, past the wonky houses, the overcrowded roadway and the staring workmen on the overbridge, the team were junk food satisfied and loaded up with water bottles as they walked along, chatting happily.

Chapter Eighteen

STINK RINK!

It was the team's first full day in Mexico City. Having stocked up at the grocery store, the schedule for the rest of the day included a drive to the San Jeronimo Rink to check out the venue and to drop off and secure their gear. Then they would head back to the sports village for lunch, where Brett was hoping to discover that the meal/snack/water situation had been resolved. The boys would have a couple of one-hour off-ice training sessions in the afternoon, with a few periods of downtime throughout the day to break things up. They needed to adjust to the slightly higher altitude and much warmer climate. At 11 a.m. it was already 27 degrees Celsius. The team would meet at the mess hall for dinner at 6.30 p.m., then Benny and the boys would get to chill out while the tournament meetings took place.

The team bus, labelled with 'NZ' and a small silver fern flag, which Sophie hadn't noticed amongst the trauma of her previous day, waited for them outside the main building at Conade.

The driver spoke no English. And his skills behind the wheel were not unlike those Sophie had seen on the road earlier that day. Thankfully it was only a 30-minute drive, or half the team might have been vomiting by the time they reached the rink.

Sophie's home city of Auckland boasted one major motorway

interchange, where traffic from the four corners of the city converged, winding around itself in all directions. This meeting of roads was fondly called 'Spaghetti Junction'. The 30-minute drive to the rink in Mexico City travelled through two junctions that were twice as large and twice as complex, making Spaghetti Junction look like something out of a quaint little hick town. Thank goodness Sophie would never have to drive there!

The team offloaded safely at the other end, looking slightly green around the gills, and dragged their hockey bags and sticks out from the storage lockers under the bus. The IIHF rules stated that the host rink was to provide secure storage for the players' gear although, given their experience in Mexico so far, Brett and Sophie had grave doubts about how good that security might be.

The crowd of black New Zealand uniforms came to a halt outside the double glass door entrance way to the San Jeronimo Rink, while Brett and Roger spoke to the young woman at the front desk with Carlos interpreting. She handed Brett a key to their allocated change room and told Carlos how to find it. Brett set off in that direction with the team following along behind.

Upon entering the main arena, the smell was overwhelming. It stung everyone's nostrils and left a sensation, on exhale, of having burnt its way deep into the lungs.

'Poo! What's that smell?' asked Stephen, the captain, shaking his head in disgust. The boys were all pulling faces.

'I think someone jizzed all over the rink then peed on everything in sight, like three weeks ago, and now everything's rotting!' Everyone laughed raucously at Kieran's response.

Typical teenage boys, thought Sophie, smiling to herself. Sometimes they just plain forgot she was there. Stephen was right though. It was a disgusting smell. She screwed up her nose as her sinus cavities burned and she suddenly felt rather headachey.

Just when they thought the smell would be the worst feature of the rink, the team now stood in disbelief in the centre of their allocated change room, taking in the disgusting sight. Lockable metal caging surrounded three sides of the room, with decrepit hockey gear stored up to the roof behind it. The gear stunk and was literally black with mould. The locking system for the cages consisted of two cheap padlocks. The rubber on the floors was slimy. The showers had black mould along every edge, and slime collected in each tray.

It was like the bad smell in the rink was concentrated into this one changing room. Brett grabbed Carlos and disappeared, while everyone else wondered whether the place was safe and whether it had ever been cleaned.

No one put down their bag or stick. No one sat down.

When Brett and Carlos reappeared, Brett simply said, 'Follow me. Bring everything.'

Everyone followed him to the opposite side of the rink where he opened another changing room. This one was directly behind the players' benches, much bigger, with seating throughout. It was cleaner and fresher, and didn't have rotting gear stored behind cages, or mould, or slime. It had a huge padlock, half the size of a fist, on the door.

'Okay, listen up,' Brett said, commanding attention from all. 'We have been upgraded to the Mexicans' change room from here on. We need to respect that. There aren't any showers, but compared to the shit fight in that other room,' he said, pointing across the ice, 'I think that's the least of our problems!'

Brett's choice of words was so unlike him that everyone sniggered at his show of disgust.

'We need to be humble, because they are *not* going to like the fact that we have been given their change room!'

With his usual diplomacy, Brett had approached the rink manager and explained that the first change room would never allow the team's gear to dry. Refreshingly, the man spoke excellent English. After some feigned reluctance and a US$50 bribe, he had agreed to allow the New Zealand team to use one of the main change rooms.

Once the change room situation had been sorted and Brett was reasonably happy that he had the only key to the padlock, the team went on a quick exploration of the rink.

Sophie was horrified. It wasn't just bad, it was actually incredibly unsafe.

The ice itself was horribly groomed, and so wet that it was more like a lake. Deep, thick, figure-skate grooves were chiselled into the surface. Players could easily trap their blades in these deep cuts and trip over or break an ankle. Nowhere on the entire ice pad did the edge of the ice meet the panels of the low walls (boards) that surround the ice, as it should. In two areas, the gap was at least 10 centimetres from the boards. Forget getting their skate blades trapped, the boys could lose an entire skate down there!

Inside the confines of the two players' seating areas (players' benches)… Well, first of all, where were the actual benches? Were the players expected to stand while they awaited their turn on the ice? And then what should they stand on? There was scant rubber matting in other parts of the arena, but not in the benches. The bare concrete floor would ruin the players' skate blades by the end of the first game. Only one of the four benches' gates opened properly. The others appeared jammed closed. This wasn't ideal but it was only cosmetic in terms of what the team needed. The boys could easily climb over. They often did anyway. Just so long as the gates didn't open under force if the players crashed into them at speed. The one gate that did open had a broken lock, was wobbly, and wouldn't stay closed. The hinges were rusted and the handle was broken.

The boards that surrounded the ice were half a foot shorter than the international standard, only coming up to waist height.

This meant the boys could sustain more rib injuries than usual. Looking down the length of the rink, Sophie could clearly see that the boards crookedly zigzagged their way to the end. Screws jutted out in several places. Given how perilously close to the boards the players would skate, and how fast, frequently taking or dishing out 'hits', someone was going to get quite severely cut up on one of those screws. Lastly, the high, protective glass that extended up from the boards was completely missing in several places. Not very protective for the crowd.

The entire rink was a disaster zone. The team was understandably scathing as they walked around the outside of the ice pad.

In three places, they passed cleaners with big buckets and mops, lazily mopping the old rubber flooring that was obviously breaking down with age. They were simply slop-mopping cleaning product all over the rubber, then letting it dry.

'This rink stinks! And it's a stink rink!' said Sophie, summing up the situation.

Brett had out his digital camera and was taking photographs all around the arena.

'Yep. I've seen enough,' he said, disgusted. 'Let's go get some lunch.'

Once again, the team followed on behind, back to the parking lot and onto the bus, grumbling loudly all the way.

En route to the sports village, the adults sat together in the front of the bus and discussed the poor condition of the ice, the rink facilities and Conade Castle.

They vowed to each raise the same issues at their respective meetings that evening, so that their concerns would be reiterated at every level throughout the tournament's organisational hierarchy. The list of problems was long and they knew things could get ugly.

The team gathered for lunch at the mess hall at 1 p.m. after passing through another security rigmarole, and were no more impressed with the food on offer than they had been at breakfast time. The spread consisted of oranges, cornflakes, plain white bread (with no spreads), warm yoghurt tubs (probably the same ones) and some sort of unrecognisable, dried out, rubbery, brown meat. 'I wouldn't feed that to my dog,' said Brett, prodding at the meat with a pair of tongs.

Throughout the afternoon, the team got on with their off-ice training stints and enjoyed their downtime, napping, chatting, reading, wandering the Castle corridors and exploring the grounds. Some used the rest time to see Sophie about headaches, sprains and strains. Most found the gymnasium and sung its praises. Anton and three others shot some hoops, playing two-on-two on the outdoor basketball court adjacent to the gym.

When she wasn't distracted by players needing Mum and ongoing conversations between Harry, Benny, Brett and Roger about how they should approach the evening's meetings, Sophie found herself having vivid flashbacks of the horrid events of her near-kidnapping the day before. She only hoped she would be so tired by bedtime that she didn't have night terrors again.

Dinner soon came and went, in the form of another unappetising meal, with the same indistinguishable meat as at lunchtime, but this time presented in roasting dishes with small slices of plastic-looking cheese, slightly melted on top. Also on offer were the same cornflakes, refried beans and warm tubs of yoghurt. There was also the exciting addition of dry, lumpy, mashed potato that tasted like it had been made from dehydrated ingredients. No other vegetables. No fruit. It wasn't like the team had been expecting a seven-course dégustation, but at least they could have been served something fresh and edible!

Brett discretely took photographs of the food. More evidence for the meetings.

Juan introduced himself to Brett. He was the Mexican coach

and the president of the Mexican Ice Hockey Federation. At about six and a half feet tall, he towered over Brett. They chatted for 15 minutes.

Early in the evening, the management and coaches of various teams gathered then set off by bus for their respective meetings. Harry and Sophie joined a group of head coaches and medics, and waved goodbye to Brett and Roger who were left waiting for their transport along with the managers from the other teams.

Sophie had been in this situation before, but in that moment she once again realised that, across all the teams' officials, she was the only woman.

The 30-minute bus ride to the rink passed quickly as the coaches and medical staff from New Zealand, South Africa, Mongolia and Chinese Taipei introduced themselves. It quickly became evident that New Zealand's concerns about the facilities and food were widely shared and it seemed everyone was on the same page. It was reassuring to know that all four visiting teams would support each other in the meetings.

Turning her head away from the animated discussions on the bus, Sophie looked out the window. Not for the first time in the last 10 days, she took a deep breath to maintain her equilibrium. There had already been more drama than anyone would care to experience – she just hoped that the seemingly inevitable showdown with the tournament officials would lead to a positive outcome. She could do with that right now.

Chapter Nineteen

AMIGOS AND PROMISES

The pungent, burning, chemical smell punched Sophie and Harry in the face as they arrived back inside the San Jeronimo Rink, reminding Sophie to add that to her list of issues to bring up. It seemed stronger than when they had visited earlier in the day. In unison, they both screwed up their noses then laughed at each other. They arranged to meet outside the front entrance later in the evening, then made their way to their respective meetings.

Along with the medical representatives from the other three visiting teams, Sophie entered a meeting room containing a long, head table, with three other shorter tables set up to form a square. Behind the main table sat three Mexican officials. Sophie smiled to herself as a wild vision suddenly popped into her head of three men on top of donkeys, with huge sombreros and crazy moustaches. She silently dubbed the officials 'The Three Amigos'. The men seemed pleasant enough but didn't stand up or offer to shake hands as she and her colleagues entered the room. Sophie gave them the benefit of the doubt – perhaps they weren't rude – perhaps it was just a cultural difference.

The medic from Chinese Taipei took a seat at the first smaller table, followed by the representatives from Mongolia and South Africa who also positioned themselves around the square. Sophie took the last remaining seat directly to the left of the officials.

The middle amigo stood to address them. At about five-foot-nothing tall, he was of the shorter Aztec stature and it appeared that he was the only one of the three who spoke English. With shoulders back and chest puffed out, he introduced himself as 'the officially appointed Tournament Medical Supervising Doctor'. The other two men were introduced as volunteers. He finished his little speech with, 'I am at your service!' Then he took a small theatrical bow and smiled directly at Sophie.

Sophie gave a slight nod and smiled politely.

Creepy, she thought. *Note to self, don't get stuck alone in a room with him.*

The young Chinese Taipei representative was in his mid-twenties. He stayed seated and, in his smooth American accent, introduced himself as Frank. He said he had been selected as his team's medical liaison because he spoke good English. He was actually the assistant coach, and had no medical qualifications, apart from a first aid certificate, and said that he would welcome all help from the other representatives.

The Mongolian gentleman looked to be aged somewhere between 60 and 70. He stood abruptly, stated, 'I. Am. Medical… Mongolia,' then bowed and sat down again just as quickly. This declaration appeared to be a rehearsed phrase and the only English he knew. Sophie wasn't exactly sure what he had meant by 'medical', but from past experience she knew it could be anything from a basic first aider to an orthopaedic surgeon. Hopefully the latter.

Next up was Felix van Houten. He was in his early fifties and, without standing, he introduced himself as the doctor for the South African team.

Sophie followed his lead and also remained seated as she introduced herself, 'Hi, I'm Sophie and I'm medical for New Zealand.' No one asked her to clarify her qualifications, so she didn't offer anything further.

Before airing any of their own concerns, all four representatives allowed the tournament medical supervising doctor the courtesy and time to speak about medical preparation and involvement for the forthcoming tournament. He didn't say much of any importance, except how wonderful his staff were, that there would be two ambulances in attendance with two paramedics, and that there would be two large oxygen cylinders available if required. Oh, and had he mentioned how wonderful all his staff were?

And then, the moment they had all been waiting for…

'Any questions?'

Concerns and queries flooded over the Mexican head table from the three English-speaking medicals. Mr Mongolia remained silent but, despite his limited ability with English, Sophie was pretty sure he got the gist of things.

Frank, Felix and Sophie were careful not to come across as offensive or accusatory. Instead they were respectful and polite in addressing the head amigo, whose smile had quickly turned to a scowl. Felix and Sophie both quoted the rule book with regard to international games standards.

Finally, the Mexican doctor reapplied his smile as he made reassurances and promises that he could, and would, fix everything, immediately. The multiple complaints, comments and recommendations of the teams had been heard loud and clear!

Over the course of the meeting however, the atmosphere had turned from being official and formal, to tense and chilly – like a frost over a frozen lake. By the end of it, Sophie diagnosed herself as having developed a pretty bad tension headache.

The head amigo wrapped up the meeting 10 minutes earlier than scheduled, looking rather dishevelled. He must have quietly briefed the other two gentlemen as they gathered their papers, because the three suddenly seemed to be in a hurry to usher the four medicals out of the room and get the door closed behind them.

Sophie and the others respectfully said their goodbyes and thank-yous while shaking the Three Amigos' hands, then silently made their way out of the building through the front doors. They stood quietly in the entrance way for about 20 seconds until they knew they were completely out of earshot.

Then Felix turned to Sophie and Frank and broke the silence.

'Well, that went well!' he said laughing. He'd summed it up, both beautifully and sarcastically, in his broad, South African accent.

Sophie and Frank laughed with him. Even Mr Mongolia was chuckling. They had all felt the same tension.

'I think they bloody rude not standing when a lady enters their room though,' Felix continued. 'And how was that greasy little pervert, taking his little bow, 'I'm at your service'!' he exclaimed, performing an even more exaggerated bow, mocking the chief amigo. The other three laughed at his imitation. It was very good!

'All I can say is, I hope he keeps his word.' Frank's comment had a sobering effect. 'This whole thing has given me a headache!'

'Yes, me too! Tense atmosphere, I guess,' Sophie replied. 'But I don't trust that Mexican doctor. And not just because he's a creep.' Felix and Frank looked at her quizzically.

'Don't even ask!' she added shaking her head, as she pushed the image of her would-be kidnappers to the back of her mind. 'Anyway, I was very pleased to hear you're a doctor, Felix.'

'Oh, actually,' Felix hesitated, 'I've been an oncologist for 30 years. Put it this way – I haven't worked in emergency since my house surgeon days. So, about 35 years ago! But what did you say your field was?' Felix enquired of Sophie, knowing full well she hadn't yet stated her expertise.

'I'm an emergency nurse,' Sophie said matter-of-factly.

'Oh, that's perfect! You'll be so much more useful to my team than me!' Felix laughed.

This made Sophie laugh too. She was chuffed by his compliment, and she had so much more respect for an honest and humble doctor who didn't think he was a god.

'Thanks! I'll be sure to boss you around if we get a full-on resus then!' she joked back in good nature. 'Anyway, I'm sure you'll be light years more helpful than our creepy Mexican friend. He's probably only a podiatrist anyway!'

They all laughed.

Just then, the head coaches joined them. They reported a similar outcome in their meeting – loads of promises.

It was 9.30 p.m. when Harry and Sophie arrived back to Conade. Both were weary and were suffering from headaches but they were feeling quite positive. Brett and Roger arrived back shortly afterwards. They too had received promises, but luckily, no headaches to match. Of particular interest was a comment made at their meeting by the IIHF chairman and tournament supervisor, a Slovakian, Mr Friderik Babic. He had admitted that the committee and officials were less than happy with the quality of the rink or the ice and, two days previously, the committee had provided the host staff with a list of items that urgently needed to be addressed before the first game puck was dropped.

That was music to Harry and Sophie's ears!

On the down side, Brett and Roger were spitting tacks about the palatial accommodation with which the officials had been provided. Given how the committee members were living it up in their five-star digs, the Hotel Pedregal Palace, perhaps calling the teams' quarters 'Conade Concentration Camp' wasn't so rude after all.

By the time the 10 p.m. curfew arrived, the boys had been ushered into their own bedrooms for the night. The adults retired to Harry and Benny's unit on the second level, to find Benny lying on his bed reading a book.

While they were all at their meetings, Benny had got bored and taken half the team back to the grocery store for another junk food fix. Brett had said he wanted an even bigger and sturdier padlock for their change room at the rink, just in case someone else had a key to the existing lock. Benny had found one twice the size. He'd also bought a small bag of ice, a large plastic bucket and a 12 pack of Corona beer, which he'd set up in readiness for when the others arrived.

Sophie had discreetly carried her bottle of Chilean wine up to Benny's room in her backpack, also to share, but then realised they didn't have any cups. So, she and Roger made a short trip back downstairs and collected a supply of paper drinking cones from beside the water cooler in the entry foyer.

They'd all had enough talk of Conade and the stinky rink by then, so they boycotted those topics. Tonight they could socialise, because tomorrow would be their last day of serious training before the tournament commenced and Brett had scheduled a sleep-in for the team.

They chatted about their families, jobs and hobbies until around midnight. As much as they were all quite good friends, there was still a lot they didn't know about each other. And they enjoyed each other's company.

Benny was from the south part of Auckland and married with a young daughter who had just started peewee hockey.

Harry lived on the North Shore of Auckland. He was single and told them that he hadn't yet met 'the one'. Brett asked him what his ideal woman would be like, and they all laughed raucously when he divulged far more saucy details than anyone could have imagined or expected!

After they finished laughing, Sophie made a quiet, solemn, throwaway comment, 'Well, Harry, you take your time, because you're a long time married to the wrong person.'

The five sat silently for a minute contemplating this. Brett and Roger looked at Sophie pensively. She felt a little embarrassed because her flippant remark had just kind of popped out and broken the flow of their lovely conversation.

Roger broke the silence as he told the group a bit more about himself. He was from Christchurch in New Zealand's South Island, a hockey referee and player, and they pieced together that his wife was rather a difficult and demanding woman.

Then it was Brett's turn.

Brett was seven years older than Sophie and lived in the east part of Auckland. He was a qualified engineer and general manager of a steel engineering company. He had Beauden, who they all knew of course, and a lovely daughter named Nicole who was 14. Nicole was very sporty, had been a gymnast, but now played netball and inline hockey.

Sophie's mind drifted back to the previous year. Nicole had been dead-keen on switching codes to ice hockey and could skate quite proficiently, but couldn't stop. Sophie had offered to teach her during a public skating session, and Brett had also gotten on the ice to try skating for the first time ever. Sophie was happy to help them both and it had been a fun afternoon.

Brett spoke proudly about Nicole and all her school and sports achievements. Sophie could tell he was really missing her. They must be close.

Everyone knew Sophie's boys so when it was her turn, she talked about their hobbies outside of ice hockey. She talked about Anton being on the school surfing team and about his talent as an acoustic guitarist. And she talked about Hayden being a talented drummer and told them about the school music competition he and his band had recently won.

Then Harry asked about her job at the accident and emergency centre. They wanted to hear stories about the weird and wonderful injuries she had come across. Sophie indulged them with a few examples, with no names of course, but loads of gory detail. She loved this topic. The more blood and goop the better! Harry, Benny and Roger all cringed and pulled revolted faces as she got more and more graphic, while Brett was genuinely fascinated and asked multiple questions.

Midnight soon arrived and it was time for sleep, so everyone headed off to their beds.

As Sophie happily drifted off to sleep that night, reflecting on all that had been said, two strange facts occurred to her about the evening's discussions. Firstly, she hadn't mentioned Charlie and nobody had asked about him, and secondly, Brett hadn't mentioned his wife, Kristine. In fact, Sophie realised for the first time that she had only ever clapped eyes on Kristine twice in all the years she had known him. And he never talked about her… very strange.

She slept fitfully once again, tossing and turning. The night terrors were clearer this time, with evil, cartoonish taxi drivers pulling her towards a black tunnel, laughing hauntingly at her, stuffing her into the boot of a car in absolute darkness and tossing her two suitcases in on top of her. Then she dreamed of a blond knight in full shining armour coming to rescue her on his galloping white stallion, wielding Excalibur in his hand.

Despite the dream rescue, she awoke again with an overwhelming sense of panic and her own screams echoing in her ears.

It was so unlike her. She usually excelled at sleeping. She would joke that it was one of her hidden talents and said that if it was an Olympic sport she would win gold every time. Shift work never bothered her. Jet-lag never bothered her. She could sleep anywhere, anytime.

All too soon, it was morning once again. A precious sleep-in. Wasted by night terrors.

For breakfast, they had to go through the same security rigmarole again: scan fingerprints to get meal ticket, guards check tickets at mess hall door – all this, to eat slop!

It should have been the breakfast of champions but the food was equally as poor as the day before. In fact, it could well have been the exact same food. The chicken looked familiar but even drier. Apparently the messages relayed at the previous evening's meetings hadn't yet reached the chef. At least that's what Brett and the others told the boys. He had his doubts that anything would change, and Sophie had to admit she agreed with him. Still, they would keep trying.

South Africa, Taipei, Mongolia and Mexico were all at breakfast too, and the grumblings about the food were certainly not confined to the New Zealand tables.

Sophie was the only one to bother taking her backpack down to the mess hall. It was now a security requirement that all bags should be left with the armed guards at the door. So the five adults sat at the closest available table and took shifts going up to discreetly check that all was well with the precious backpack.

Off-ice training came and went, then another unremarkable lunch of the same slop, before the team loaded onto their bus for their final on-ice training session. The pungent stink hit them again as they entered the rink. However, it did seem to dissipate over the two hours they spent there.

Like the food, the state of the rink had not yet improved – except that the staff had laid water to fill the ice gaps around the edges and were now waiting for it to freeze. Brett was relieved to see the padlock on their acquired change room was still intact, but decided to replace it with the giant one Benny had bought the night before anyway. He wasn't taking any chances.

The boys trained hard and fast knowing this was their last opportunity to practise the drills they had been working on so hard. With pride, Sophie noticed that Anton had never looked so accomplished and smooth in his skating, passing and shooting. The whole team was shining.

Tomorrow was Sunday – game day.

Crunch time.

Time for the New Zealand team to prove why they had been chosen to represent their country and why they were ranked number one for the tournament.

Time to play for gold!

The boys hung their gear to dry in the change room and boarded the bus back to Conade. Most of the team were experiencing headaches, so Sophie dished out a few paracetamol tablets and took one herself.

It was no surprise to discover that the food/snack/water situation had still not been remedied. So, for some much needed fresh air and supplies, the team took their customary walk in a balmy 26 degrees through the three security checkpoints to the shops.

The workmen on the bridge downed tools and stared at Sophie, just like the day before.

That afternoon, there was another hour of off-ice training and a compulsory rest time, before dinner was served – a rubbery pasta dish with what appeared to be watery tomato ketchup. Not to forget the inevitable cornflakes, lumpy mashed potato, warm yoghurt tubs and overcooked, dried out chicken.

The first activity after dinner was tidying up the rookies' hair styles. This was a much quicker and far more serious procedure than the hair sculpting frivolity in Salt Lake City. Over and done within 30 minutes. Respectable hair styles once more – albeit very short.

The haircutting ritual was followed by one final classroom session in the gym, run by Benny. By the 10 p.m. curfew, the entire team were tucked up in their beds with a book, music or already fast asleep, readying themselves for their big debut the next day.

Chapter Twenty

SUNDAY, GAME ON!

Sunday.

Game one.

Followed by the opening ceremony.

Today was going to be *big!*

It was also the seventeenth birthday of one of the players, Nigel, and Sophie planned to buy a cake during the day and gather the team for a surprise celebration after the game.

Sophie had slept poorly for the third night in a row, once again haunted by evil taxi drivers. Only this time she awoke before the knight could rescue her.

These troubled sleeps were taking their toll.

She had to be awake and responsive today, not half comatose. The boys needed her fully functional. No distractions. Thankfully she had a little time to pull herself together. The first half of the day was to be one of quiet reflection and focusing prior to the game.

The whole team arose at a respectable time and met for breakfast at 9 a.m. as planned. This was followed by a rest, then back to the mess hall for lunch at 12 noon. The food was shocking, as usual, but the boys made the best of each meal, trying to pack in enough crucial calories.

After lunch, they took a brisk walk to the grocery store, past their old 'friends', the gawping workmen. The boys loaded up on healthy snacks this time, and more water. Sophie sneakily bought a Black Forest Gateaux for Nigel's surprise birthday celebration. She kept it hidden in a grey plastic bag then squirrelled it away in her room.

The boys had more downtime for the remainder of the afternoon. Sophie went from room to room, checking on the players, and everyone was feeling good. She provided strapping for injury niggles, done in private so that no one from the other teams could identify potential weaknesses.

New Zealand's first game was against Mongolia and was scheduled for 4 p.m. The bus would need to leave Conade at 2 p.m. to be there by 2.30 so the team could have a decent off-ice warm up. They would then gear up and be ready for their pre-game pep talk at 3.30, then the on-ice warm up at 3.40 p.m.

Brett had raised the food/snack/water problem yet again and the team were finally provided with dinner boxes to take with them on the bus. These provisions would be vital as the boys wouldn't be returning to the sports village until about 10 p.m., and by then, the mess hall would be closed for the evening.

Sadly, true to form, the kitchen lived up to the team's diminishing expectations. Brett and Roger were heartily disappointed when they opened two of the dinner boxes. Each box contained two pieces of plain, dry white bread. Slapped in between was a piece of luncheon meat, so dried out that it looked like it was three days old, and a slice of plastic-looking, pale cheese. Half the boxes also included a warm yoghurt tub, and the others had an apple. There was a plastic bag of a dozen small 300ml water bottles. There were 20 players. Were they meant to share?

These sleeping, eating, skating machines should have been powering through three times that many calories, five or six times a day, and that was supposed to be dinner? After a tournament game, no less.

'They said that's all there is,' Carlos and Julio translated after many attempts to bargain and plead for a larger quantity and better quality of food. 'They are trying to make American food for you because they don't think you will like our Mexican food.' Even they looked mortified at what was on offer.

It was too late to change anything, so each player begrudgingly took a dinner box and boarded the bus. The front desk assured Brett there were more water bottles at the rink. But it was obvious the team would need to buy some serious food after the game. Carlos and Julio promised they would help find a restaurant.

The bus trip went as planned, haphazardly weaving through traffic, and thankfully, there were no problems on the roads. The team disembarked in the rink's parking lot and made their way through the front doors into the pungent stink.

Despite a few comments such as, 'Oh geez!' 'Pooh!' 'Whoa!' and 'Man that's bad!' plus the obligatory screwing up of noses and fake gagging, every member of the team stayed focused on the game ahead.

A public skating session was on, with disco lights, loud music and a crowd of people. Some were already leaving the ice to take off their hire skates. Sophie figured the session was nearly finished. Three staff members were at three different corners of the rink, slop-mopping cleaning product onto the rubber floor around the ice. The team navigated their way, single file, past the casual skaters and the cleaning staff to their change room.

Off-ice warm-up went like clockwork and the players changed into their gear while the public session was wrapping up. They were feeling invigorated, lost in their own thoughts, psyching themselves up for the battle ahead. Brett managed to commandeer two large crates of water, which he hid in the change room, behind the empty stick bag and with a gear bag on top. Matthew and Kieran had already developed headaches and asked Sophie for paracetamol.

She ordered the whole team to guzzle half a bottle of water on the spot. They should know by now that dehydration was the biggest cause of headaches! She drank some too, as her headache was also amping up.

Brett disappeared again and returned with a bag full of towels. Sophie wasn't sure what they would use them for – there weren't any shower facilities in their change room.

While the coaches had the team's full attention for the pre-game pep talk, Brett, Roger and Sophie made their way to the players' bench beside the ice. At this point in proceedings, it was best that the three of them stayed out of the coaches' way!

New Zealand had been lucky enough to be allocated the benches with the one gate that opened. Sophie then understood why Brett had wanted towels. The rink staff had put skinny pieces of rubber matting down in front of the two short benches that had also been placed there, but this wouldn't be sufficient to protect the players' skate blades from the concrete. So Brett and Roger began laying out the towels, double thickness, over the remainder of the exposed floor. The boys would be able to stand safely, even if there wasn't room for them all to sit down between shifts.

Brett and Roger then spread the water bottles throughout the benches for the players. Sophie arranged her medical bag on a towel just inside the door to their bench area, but out of harm's way. It needed to be accessible, but not so that anyone could pilfer her supplies. The kit had cost Sophie $2000 of her own money to set up, and none of it would be easily replaceable if it got raided.

Sophie looked around the rink. She nodded and smiled at Mr Mongolia in the opposition players' benches next to theirs. He and the other managers had followed Brett and Roger's lead and were also laying down towels. She spotted the tournament doctor and nodded politely to him, but without a smile this time.

Creep, she thought.

Looking around, she was delighted to see that the grandstand was already half full with spectators. A small pocket of around a dozen New Zealand black jackets were visible in one area. Sophie recognised most of the people wearing them. A beautiful Mexican girl stood and waved flamboyantly. Then Sophie realised who it was.

'Oh look, it's Gabi!' Sophie smiled and waved back, as did Brett.

One of New Zealand's Senior Ice Blacks, Marcus, had met a lovely Mexican girl named Brigid when the New Zealand team had last played at a World Championship in Mexico four years previously. The couple had become quite serious and Brigid now lived in New Zealand with Marcus. Her sister Gabi had visited the year before.

Brett and Sophie waved to the other New Zealand supporters as well. It was nice to see some familiar faces. Continuing her visual scan around the arena, Sophie saw there were two television camera crews set up on opposite diagonal ends of the rink.

Wow, TV coverage! Ice hockey rarely received any media attention in New Zealand. Several official volunteers were also now dotted around.

Roger guarded the team bench and Sophie's medical bag while she and Brett set off to collect snow for the ice packs, then hand over their game sheet to the score bench officials. When they returned, they discovered two ambulances had parked outside the back doors, between the two closest change rooms, and the paramedics had just finished placing two large oxygen cylinders outside each of the players' benches.

'Gracias,' Sophie thanked them as they disappeared out the back doors. The tournament doctor had delivered on one of his promises at least.

The scoreboard clock seemed to tick down to game time very quickly, as the boys came out of their change room, completed a solemn half-ice warm up adjacent to the Mongolian team, then retreated hastily to their change room for a last-minute pep talk from Harry and Benny. There, they had their traditional hands-in cheer, and waited for the two referees and two linesmen to complete their on-ice warm up and ice inspection.

Amazingly, but predictably, the ice passed the inspection. It was still in the same shocking state as it had been two days earlier, and Sophie wondered why the referees even bothered going through the charade of checking it.

The referee sounded his whistle. Brett gave the signal into the change room, and the New Zealand team poured into the arena, accompanied by loud cheers and clapping from the grandstand, as Brett locked the change room door behind them.

The two teams lined up in the centre of the ice, facing each other, and the game announcer stationed in the music booth performed the player introductions. He spoke in Spanish, and then in very fast English, with a heavy Hispanic accent. The sound system was poor and his voice, along with various microphone feedback squeals, ricocheted off every wall.

As he called out each of the players' names, ripples of subdued laughter could be heard through the line-up of players on the ice, and their friends and family in the crowds.

Sophie even laughed out loud when the man theatrically announced her son as, 'Antonio Harading-o.'

The national anthems of New Zealand and Mongolia were played, then the team captains swapped souvenir pennants and badges. New Zealand performed their haka, the traditional Maori war challenge, and finished with an almighty 'Heee!' as they jumped into the air at the end. They looked formidable on the ice. A force to be reckoned with. The haka always sent shivers down Sophie's spine. The spectators stood, clapped and whistled, and the New Zealand supporters went wild. Wherever the haka was performed around the world, it was always a crowd-pleaser.

The starting line of six players, with Nigel in goal, took their positions, while the others returned to their benches, sitting or standing wherever they could.

Everything was in readiness. The referee blew the whistle and dropped the puck.

The game burst into a flurry of action.

Sophie's heart leapt in excitement. Butterflies soared in her stomach. Nerves went on high alert. She quickly cracked open a stick of gum. She knew if she didn't chew something, she would end up chewing her lip or holding her breath.

The first period flashed by. The game was proving to be fast and easy for New Zealand, with the lines changing up quickly. Everything was going to plan. Anton was playing right winger on the second line and looked pretty sharp. He had assisted two goals already.

As the buzzer sounded to mark the period break, and the Zamboni came out to clean the ice, New Zealand were up 7–0 on the scoreboard. Sophie followed the team to the change room, medical bag in tow. The boys were electric with excitement.

Sophie was kept busy in the period break treating several more players who had developed headaches. She plied them with paracetamol and more water. Four boys were a bit dizzy and light-headed, and two felt breathless. She wasn't really concerned, assuming it was probably nerves and the intensity of the game, mixed with the slightly higher altitude. She asked Brett to wheel one of the big oxygen tanks into their change room. A quick dose of oxygen would fix any altitude issues.

Harry and Benny talked all through the period break:

Strategy. Technique. Passing. Shooting. Formations. Speed. Intensity. Focus.

Soon enough, the buzzer sounded, and the boys made their way in single file back to their players' bench. Brett once again locked the change room door behind them. The starting line up entered the ice, and with a whistle, the puck dropped again.

New Zealand were determined to continue their dominance. Beauden subbed out Nigel in goal halfway through the second period. Nigel had kept a clean sheet. The boys played out their practised formations with purposeful and accurate stick head to stick head passes.

So far, so good!

The game became more physical. Anton dished out two seriously great hits, and assisted another goal. And, like Nigel, Beauden was an impenetrable wall.

The second end-of-period buzzer sounded. New Zealand had put a further 10 goals on the scoreboard, and the teams once again retreated to their respective change rooms while the Zamboni cleaned the ice. Harry and Benny kept up their patter, while Sophie continued to treat the players for headaches, dizziness and breathlessness.

'Geez, I didn't think this altitude would affect us the way it is, given all the training we've done,' Sophie confessed to Brett. But she didn't let the boys know she was now a little concerned. She reassured them, 'It's fine. It's just the altitude, boys. Lucky we've got that oxygen tank. I think that Mexican doctor knew we would need it!'

The buzzer sounded and the boys made their way to the players' bench. This time, Sophie asked Brett to wheel the oxygen tank into the benches. The starting line entered the ice, the whistle shrilled, and the puck dropped again.

The third period was a little slower than the first and second. Both teams had visibly slowed their skating pace and made silly mistakes. Not surprisingly, Mongolia looked like they had succumbed to inevitable defeat. And the New Zealand team had lost some of their hunger. They were playing a different game now, with less intensity.

Sophie encouraged the boys to take a small hit of oxygen if they were feeling breathless between shifts on the ice. Four of the boys took up the offer and said it helped.

Despite all this, the New Zealand team scored 12 more unanswered goals. And Beauden once again let no goals through.

The final buzzer sounded and the score stood at 29–0. The refereeing had been fair and consistent. The first and second lines had had the most ice time, but every player had been on for at least a couple of shifts. And Anton had played one of his best games ever, with four goal assists.

Both teams, including coaches and managers, entered the ice for the handshake, then waited for the 'Most Valuable Player' to be named. Sophie waited in the benches.

Several players were slumped forward, hands resting on knees. *Poor kids*, Sophie thought. They had skated hard and played hard.

Then three of those players sat down on the ice. Sophic had never seen a player sit on the ice after a game. They were obviously feeling exhausted. The presentation would only take 10 minutes, then they could all relax, enjoy the opening ceremony and watch the next game.

A couple of minutes into the presentation, one of the players sitting on the ice stood up, moved away from the line-up, and skated and stumbled his way towards the benches. Sophie thought he might not make it. It was Matthew. As he approached her, he was shaking his head. Something was wrong.

'I feel really sick,' he said.

'Okay, come with me,' Sophie said, just as he collapsed, unconscious, through the one gate that opened properly, into the benches. She managed to grab hold of the trunk of his body to break his fall. Thankfully, he wasn't much bigger than her. As she crouched down at his side, he became conscious again so she helped him back up, flung one of his arms over her shoulder, and helped him towards the change room. As they reached the doorway, his legs started to buckle and she realised he was collapsing again.

Oh darn. Brett had the key. The change room was locked! She twisted the unconscious Matthew, making his legs cross, and was lowering him to the floor, butt first, just as Brett came up behind her carrying her medical bag.

'What happened? I saw him collapse when he got off the ice.' Brett was visibly worried.

'I don't know,' Sophie replied truthfully, 'but he just collapsed again. Can you please open the door, then run and get that oxygen tank for me?'

In 10 swift seconds, Brett had unlocked and opened the door and dumped the medical bag in the centre of the change room. Sophie dragged Matthew onto the central bench, unclipped his helmet chin strap, removed the helmet, grabbed a nearby team shirt, crumpled it up like a pillow to support his neck and tilted his head back to open his airway. No sooner was this done than Brett returned with the oxygen tank.

Sophie quickly placed the oxygen mask on Matthew's face and cranked the flow up to 10 litres.

His airway was open and he was breathing spontaneously. *Whew!*

Sophie was seated beside him now, checking his pulse – it was racing. She grabbed her portable blood pressure kit. Blood pressure was very low. He was hot, clammy and a rosy, flushed colour. At least he wasn't pale. One good sign.

Suddenly he opened his eyes, looking dazed and confused.

'Welcome back. How are you feeling now?' she asked.

'Terrible. Headache. Dizzy. Like I wanna throw up,' Matthew replied through the oxygen mask. He sounded like he was on the verge of tears.

'Just stay lying down with the oxygen on and you'll feel better, okay? I've got you.' Sophie's voice was soothing and reassuring.

'Thanks Mum,' he squeaked out, closing his eyes as she stroked his forehead. He was scared and worried. The boys knew Sophie didn't fuss over them. But sometimes they just really needed a mother.

What she didn't say was that she had a whacking great headache of her own and felt quite dizzy and nauseous herself. Dizziness was not unusual for her in the heat, but she had never felt like this in the cool, dry air of the rink.

The MVP presentation finished, with the crowd bursting into applause once again. The remainder of the team entered the change room moments later.

'I feel better now,' Matthew suddenly exclaimed, pulling off the oxygen mask and promptly jumping up as the first of the boys walked in. Sophie smiled as she reached to turn off the oxygen. She realised his bravado was kicking in.

He stood up smiling, hand outstretched to shake Beauden's hand, congratulating him for his 'shut out,' allowing in no opposition goals. He managed to say, 'Good game Beaud…' just as he passed out again, toppling straight backwards this time. Luckily Sophie was still sitting in the same spot and stood just in time to catch him. She lowered him back onto the central bench and placed the oxygen mask back on him.

The boys gathered around, firing questions at Sophie. Kieran exclaimed he also felt 'quite yuck,' and Stephen answered, 'Yeah, me too.' Much to Sophie's surprise, many of the team joined in, loudly offering up how horrible they were feeling.

'Okay, everyone calm down!' Sophie raised her voice to the team. 'We only have one oxygen mask. Have some water and rehydrate, then start getting changed. See how you feel when you're finished.'

How strange, she thought to herself. She hoped they weren't all coming down with some horrible virus. She had to keep them calm. It was probably the altitude affecting them, but she had developed a deep-seated feeling of intuitive discomfort.

Something was wrong. And she couldn't put her finger on it.

Matthew came round again, so Sophie offered the oxygen to Kieran and then Stephen. Any thoughts about infection control went out the window. They would have to share the one mask.

After Stephen had taken a few deep breaths he gave the mask back to Matthew. A few rounds later and they all felt a little better. Even Matthew sat up, and slowly, under Sophie's watchful eye, started to change out of his hockey gear.

The coaches and managers were milling around, helping some of the boys hang their gear and collecting up the hockey sticks.

'Speed it up boys. Five minutes until the opening ceremony. Zamboni's nearly done. Remember to put your hockey shirt and skates back on.' Brett was the voice of the time keeper again.

'I'm not going on the ice,' Matthew spoke quietly, slurring his words a little as he leaned in towards Sophie.

'That's for sure!' she said back reassuringly and quick as lightning. It was her way of politely laying down the law, and she had intended to be bossy if needed. He grinned. 'You're waiting in the benches with me where I can keep an eye on you,' she stated matter-of-factly. He nodded, still grinning.

As the minutes floated by precariously and the boys seemed to settle down a bit, Sophie felt a little more comfortable. But the ill-at-ease sensation in the pit of her gut didn't leave her.

Something didn't add up. And she still couldn't put her finger on it.

The Zamboni had finished. The announcer made some unintelligible, echoey statement, which the team interpreted as 'It's time.' So they made their way out of the change room. The Mongolian team were already lined up behind the second benches. South Africa and Chinese Taipei were lined up behind Mongolia, and moments later Mexico were lined up behind the New Zealand side.

And so the ceremony began.

Chapter Twenty-One

THE TRAIN SMASH

The official music for the opening ceremony of the world hockey tournament blared through the tinny sound system at the San Jeronimo Rink. They all knew the drill. Each team had a Mexican ice hockey player, around eight years old, as their mascot and flag bearer. On the ice, each mascot, wearing their assigned team's shirt, led the players as they glided around in their lines like a well-choreographed, synchronised ice dance, until the music finished.

At the end, the five teams had formed a near perfect semi-circle, almost the length of the rink, facing the score bench. The announcer in the music booth made another garbled announcement, then slowly and clearly, introduced the guest speaker: 'The International Ice Hockey Federation Tournament Supervisor, and Chairman of these World Division III Championship games, all the way from Slovakia, Mr Friderik Babic!' The crowd applauded and cheered loudly.

Was he a celebrity or something? Other than a passing mention by Brett, Sophie had never heard of him. He was at least 70 years old and as round as he was short. Sophie couldn't help but giggle as he waddled out onto the red carpet that was laid on the ice. He looked like a Womble!

Mr Babic addressed the crowd and the players for about five

minutes. Most of what he said was obscured by the terrible sound distortion and feedback, but everyone understood when he exclaimed slowly and clearly at the very end…

'I now, officially, announce, this, International, Ice Hockey, World Division III games… *open!*

The crowd, players and officials applauded, cheered and whistled, even more loudly this time. Cameras flashed around the rink. Sophie watched Anton's face, relishing his excitement and happiness. The atmosphere was amazing!

It was a proud mummy moment. A moment to cherish forever. A moment of true elation.

The sense of excitement and happiness stayed with them all as they made their way back to the change room, and the players continued their enthusiastic chatter once again. Skates and hockey shirts came back off and shoes and jackets went on. Then they made their way back out into the arena and up the nearest stairs to their small posse of supporters to watch the next game from the grandstand.

Mexico was dominant over South Africa but it was definitely tighter than the New Zealand versus Mongolia game had been. The score at the end of the first period was 6–0 to Mexico. South Africa appeared to be experimenting with lines, swapping players in and out. Some players used at the beginning of the game didn't get any further shifts. Three players even left the benches during the period and went back to their change rooms. By the end of the first period South Africa was operating with only two lines.

'Bit late to be sorting their lines out now, isn't it?' Sophie overheard Benny commenting to Harry during the period break.

Sophie had sat towards the back of the group and was keeping a watchful eye on Matthew, Kieran and Stephen. Matthew was quite subdued, sitting quietly, chin resting on hands, elbows resting on knees, not really talking to anyone. Kieran and Stephen were chatting to other teammates. She was aware that her own headache was worsening.

'Anyone need anything? I'm going to get some ibuprofen,' she said to the boys around her. Several boys stood. At first, Sophie thought they were volunteering to bodyguard her. Matthew was amongst them. As she turned to make her way towards the change room she heard gasps and several exclamations of 'Sophie!' from behind her. When she looked back she saw Edward, one of the biggest boys, holding on to Matthew, who had passed out yet again. Nigel jumped up to give him a hand and Brett raced over as well.

'Back to the oxygen?' he asked.

'Yes, I think so! Hurry boys,' Sophie said to Ed and Nigel. It suddenly occurred to her that they were in possession of one of only two oxygen tanks, and it was locked in their change room. South Africa was now playing from the same benches they had, which meant they didn't have a tank. So she sent Roger to give the South African team manager their apologies, and suggest they commandeer the tank from the Mexican side because the Mexican boys would be acclimatised to the altitude and wouldn't need oxygen.

Brett led the way as Ed and Nigel hauled the unconscious Matthew back to their change room. Around half the team were now following them. Ed and Nigel laid Matthew down on the central bench again. Sophie placed the oxygen mask on him, and cranked it up. He was breathing spontaneously. His pulse was racing, blood pressure was very low, but he was still a good rosy colour.

The boys all stood around and watched with concern. After about 15 seconds of oxygen, Matthew came round again.

'Matthew, don't move, okay. You need to keep the oxygen on.' Sophie had flipped into work mode. 'Right, who else needs something?' she asked the boys who had followed her.

Several of them wanted ibuprofen even though many had taken paracetamol prior to the game. Sophie consulted her notebook where she had made a record of who had taken what, before she handed out more medication.

Headaches, dizziness, shortness of breath, some were a little confused and disorientated, and two were complained of burning nostrils. *Hmmm. Strange set of symptoms,* she thought.

Kieran was lying down on another bench groaning, 'I don't feel so good.'

'Kieran, move closer so you can take some oxygen too. Boys, swap benches so Kieran can take this one.' Sophie handed out directions, moving traffic with her hand gestures, so she could treat Kieran as well.

Outside in the rink, the Zamboni had finished grooming the ice, the whistle had blown and the second period had started.

'The game's starting again,' one of the boys commented, but nobody moved towards the door to go and watch it.

Dave, one of New Zealand's leading goal scorers, then gave the five second warning, 'I think I'm gonna faint,' before doing exactly that, toppling into the catching arms of Ed.

'You're getting good at that!' Sophie laughed, trying to the keep the mood light. The nagging sense of unease in her gut was growing by the second. 'Bring him over here please, Edward, and lay him down on this bench on my other side.' She took the oxygen off Matthew and put it onto Dave. He came round a few seconds later.

Roger entered the change room at that moment, looking visibly disconcerted.

'Sophie, it's not just us. The South African kids are all feeling like crap too. They're down to two lines. Felix says even with the oxygen now, they're dropping like flies.'

'It's got to be the altitude. How's Mexico feeling?' she asked, trying to gather more pieces of the puzzle.

'They seem to be mostly okay. Only two or three of their players are sitting it out. I think they're the boys that were living in LA,' Roger answered.

'Okay. Well, that fits with the altitude theory. If those boys haven't been back long, they won't have reacclimatised yet.' Sophie was thinking out loud. But what she was saying seemed to make sense.

'Sophie! Look! Beauden!' Bradley shouted from one corner of the change room.

Everyone looked around to see Beauden crumpled into an unconscious heap. Sophie and several of the boys jumped up and dragged him out into a clear space on the floor.

'Brett, get the oxygen!' she barked at him, as he stood, momentarily frozen to the spot in shock at the sight of his own son in this state. Horror was written all over his face.

Brett jumped into action, wheeling the oxygen to Beauden, while another player, Theo, grabbed the mask off Dave and raced it over to Sophie. Like Matthew, Beauden was breathing spontaneously, pulse racing, blood pressure very low, but with very rosy cheeks and lips. It took a whole minute for him to come round, and even then, he consistently dropped in and out of consciousness.

Sophie decided they needed to be in a place where they could access ambulance equipment more readily.

'Guys, we need to move to the first aid room. A-sap. Ed and Nigel, you take Matthew. Stephen and Hugh, you take Kieran. Theo and Brad, take Dave. Brett and Roger, you take Beauden. Keep the mask on him and I'll follow with the oxygen tank. Craig, can you take my medical bag? Okay everyone? Let's go.' Sophie was in resus leader mode. Clear and direct. Everyone nodded.

'He'll be okay,' she gently said to Brett, as she put her hand on his chest. Brett nodded, still with a look of shock on his face.

'Nigel, get the key from Brett and lock the change room door behind us please,' Sophie said as an afterthought. Last thing they needed was to lose all their gear to theft in this time of crisis.

Swiftly, the sick players were moved towards the first aid room. As they passed the South African benches, Sophie could see several of their boys hunched over, with Felix hovering over them. He looked worried. He glanced up just in time to catch Sophie's eye as she pushed past with the oxygen tank. She noticed that the second tank, which had been parked outside the Mexican benches, was now missing, but it didn't look to be at the South African benches either.

The first aid room wasn't much bigger than the change room. But without the clutter of hockey gear, there was much more available space. Sophie had Beauden and Matthew lying on two plinth beds, with Dave and Kieran on the floor, their heads all in close proximity so the one oxygen mask could be shared around more easily. The boys were dropping in and out of consciousness. Extra oxygen was the only thing that would keep them awake.

Then Sophie had a startling thought. Where was Anton? Was he okay? He was bigger than most of the boys who had become sick. And actually, that was a point… Those who were suffering most were the smaller players in the team, and all on the first and second lines. The big players seemed okay. Apart from Beauden who had only been on the ice for the second half of the game. *Hmmm. Interesting. Relevant?* she wondered.

In the meantime, Stephen had joined the fainting few, partially collapsing while helping Kieran through the door into the first aid room, before fully collapsing from a seated position on the floor. Then it was Hugh and Bradley's turn.

'I can't believe the altitude has affected us so much. I mean, we've trained so hard for this. We acclimatised so much more quickly in Salt Lake City. And it's only the smaller players from the first and second lines, plus Beauden. It doesn't make any sense.' Sophie was thinking out loud again, but Brett answered her.

'It's almost like there's something else going on. Not just the altitude,' he said.

That's when the eureka moment hit Sophie like a bullet from the blue.

'Of course! That's it! The smell! That smell in the rink each time we came in – it's some kind of poison, like a gas or something!' Taking action, Sophie barked instructions. 'Ed, Nigel, go find the rest of the team and get them out of the building! *Now!* The boys bolted into action.

'Roger,' she added, 'can you get a team list to Harry so he and Benny can account for everyone. And get one of the paramedics for me on your way back please.' Roger obeyed immediately.

Before Sophie could come up with a plan for evacuating her intermittently conscious boys, members of the South African team poured into the first aid room. Several semi-collapsing players were amongst them, propped by their teammates and accompanied by Felix and the South African coaches. One player was wheeling the second oxygen tank.

'Sophie, I don't know what's happening!' Felix exclaimed to her. 'We stopped the game halfway through the second period. Forfeited. We had only five players left standing. My boys are dropping like flies!' Sophie counted eight South African players being lowered to the ground in various states of consciousness and confusion. Felix was crouched over their goalie, who was completely unconscious.

'Some of the team were collapsing on the ice. And these boys went to the change room then passed out cold. Sophie, what must I do for these boys? Please, tell me what to do!' Felix pleaded.

Felix, the highly trained medical doctor, was looking for direction. From Sophie!

'I'm flying blind here,' she replied honestly. 'I don't know what this is either. Maybe some sort of gas poisoning. But we just need to go back to our basics. Get oxygen into them. Swap it between them as they become conscious.'

Felix agreed with her theory about toxic gas. They had noticed the same pattern in their team as the New Zealanders had seen – the smaller players from the first and second lines were the worst affected. The only part that didn't fit the puzzle was Beauden, and he was suffering worse than anyone. He had been mostly unconscious for the better part of 15 minutes, even with the oxygen.

Everybody in the first aid room was busy helping somebody else. Slightly panicky chatter rippled across the group.

Sophie then noticed one of the Mexican paramedics. Roger had brought him in. He was in a navy-coloured uniform with 'Paramedico' on his epaulettes, arms folded.

'Do you speak English?' she asked him.

'Yes,' he answered succinctly.

'Oh, thank goodness. Can you get me some IV stuff: tourniquet, cannulae, tubing, saline, tape. I want to put up a line for this boy,' she nodded towards Beauden and mimicked putting a needle into a vein with her finger, in case he had trouble understanding her instructions.

The paramedic looked completely disinterested and walked away, with no urgency and no acknowledgement. Arms still folded.

Bugger, thought Sophie, *I bet he didn't even understand.* His reaction was all too familiar – reminiscent of the security guard at Mexico City airport. *What is wrong with these people?!*

As she was thinking this, two of the Taipei boys and the three suffering Mexican players also arrived in the makeshift resuscitation room. The group had now expanded into the adjacent referees' room. Both areas were full to overflowing. Felix was stepping over players, swapping the second oxygen mask between those who needed it, reporting vital signs to Sophie. The symptoms were the same across the entire group. Pulses were racing, blood pressures were very low, but all the boys had good colour.

Sophie was relieved when the paramedic returned a couple of minutes later with a tourniquet, some intravenous needles, tubing and two 500ml bags of saline.

'Oh, that's great, thank you!' she smiled up at him. He did understand, even if he didn't care.

Two young Mexican girls from the grandstand had followed him in.

'They sick,' he stated very simply to Sophie, then stepped back out of the way, folding his arms again. Felix offered them oxygen, which they both accepted. They took a few breaths each then left the room.

Sophie quickly had the IV bag and tubing set up, then skilfully slipped the needle into Beauden's arm, taped it down, opened up the tap and let the saline pour into him at full speed. Brett was given the task of holding the saline bag above his son's head.

At that moment, the tournament doctor appeared at the door.

Thank goodness! The doctor has come to help, thought Sophie.

At first she was relieved, but that feeling soon turned to disgust. In the middle of this life-threatening, crisis situation, and of all the bizarre things to suddenly be aware of, Sophie realised the creepy little pervert was looking down her top. She had been bending forward and her blouse had gaped slightly. *The despicable little weasel!*

Too bad, she thought. *Now's not the time to worry. More important things to worry about!* At least he was there to help.

But then, the biggest shock of all.

Like some slow motion scene from a comedy farce, Sophie watched the doctor skulk over to an unconscious Matthew, who was currently wearing one of the two oxygen masks. He pulled the mask off Matthew, sucked four or five big deep breaths of oxygen himself – so much that he collapsed the reservoir bag each time – dropped the mask back down on Matthew's chest, then skulked back out the door!

The room had turned to stone cold silence. Everyone was suddenly motionless, like heat-stunned flies, staring at the empty doorway in utter disbelief. Felix snapped to, quickly placing the mask back on Matthew's face.

'Unbelievable!' Brett exclaimed, mortified.

The panicky chatter quickly resumed. Within a few minutes, Matthew had come round and the mask was transferred back to Beauden.

After two more minutes of oxygen, Beauden came round at last, tried to sit up, then promptly vomited three times into the oxygen mask. He then faded out once more, as a result of Sophie taking the vomit-filled mask off him.

The paramedic continued to watch on, not offering help to anyone, not moving at all.

'*Hey!*' Sophie shouted, waking him from his trance. 'Can you get me another oxygen mask?' She was going to lose her rag with this guy shortly.

He looked at Sophie and the vomit-filled mask in her hand, then walked away with the same lack of urgency as before.

'Not the brightest pencil in the shower!' Sophie commented to Brett, using her Aunt Annelise's famous misquote. They seemed to be the right words for the situation and summed the paramedic up beautifully.

He returned with an infant-sized resuscitation mask.

'*No!* This is for a baby!' Sophie cried in exasperation. 'These boys will suck that reservoir dry in about a quarter of a breath. I need a big one, an adult one. Bigger!' She motioned bigger with her hands.

Really? Did he really speak English? Or was he just that thick?

Finally, he came back with another adult mask.

'Thank you!' Sophie barked sarcastically at the paramedic. *Rookie!* she thought to herself. Here they were struggling with a bunch of really sick kids, and this paramedico was proving to be nothing more useful than a fetch dog.

He stepped to the back of the room again, out of the way. This time Sophie thought he would be better to stay there, out of the way, or she was likely to give him a piece of her mind.

As Sophie placed the fresh mask on the unconscious Beauden, she took a couple of seconds to look around her and take in the scene. She counted 20 teenage boys in varying states of conscious-ness: seven New Zealanders, eight South Africans, three Mexicans and two Taipei players. Most of them were on this trip without their parents. And they were literally struggling for their lives. By her estimation, probably half of them were critical, and the other half were deteriorating rapidly. It was like a scene from a small train crash. And it was happening on her watch!

Just then, Ed and Nigel burst into the room.

'Sophie, the rest of the team are all outside the building. All accounted for,' said Ed excitedly.

'Good job boys. How are they all feeling?' she enquired.

'Actually, everyone's feeling much better in the fresh air,' answered Nigel.

Good. That meant Anton must be out there too. And he must be okay. Her heart sang with relief! But to confirm…

'Anton?'

Nigel stepped up, and put his hand on her shoulder. 'He's fine.' The words she longed to hear.

Whew. She bowed her head momentarily in relief.

'Right! That's it then.' Sophie stood up. Now she was speaking to the whole room. 'Whatever this is, it's reversible. We need to get these boys up and out of here as quickly as possible. Felix, your boys too. And you lot.' She waved in the general direction of the Taipei and Mexican players.

'We'll aim for a high concentration of oxygen, one person at a time, and as they become conscious, get them outside the building, as far away from the main entrance as possible. Okay?'

Everyone nodded, and the procession began. One by one, the boys had a decent hit of oxygen until they came round, then, flanked by an able-bodied player on either side, the exit strategy was implemented. Roger led the way. Beauden was last. Sophie managed to get half the second bag of saline into him, then took the drip out, stopped the vein bleeding and, at the last second, removed the oxygen mask yelling, '*Go!*' Brett and Nigel helped him up and out, partially dragging him all the way.

Sophie grabbed her medical bag and followed them. As she made her way to the front entrance, she saw that the large doors at the back of the rink were open and that the two ambulances were driving out of the rear driveway, with lights and sirens on. She recognised her hopeless paramedic driving the front ambulance. Maybe they were taking sick people from the crowd to hospital.

Wait, that can't be! She had seen him leave the first aid room just 30 seconds ahead of her. Both oxygen tanks had been left behind. Neither ambulance had their cabin lights on. So they couldn't possibly have patients on board. They were simply running away!

Sophie noticed the rink was now almost empty. No sign of the tournament doctor either. He had obviously scarpered as well.

'Glad the good doctor saved himself!' she said out loud sarcastically. There were no officials. No volunteers. The TV crews had packed up and disappeared. Only two staff members were visible, milling about, picking up rubbish.

The parking lot outside the front entrance was mostly empty except for the sick players. The last big bus in the parking lot was full of people and was just leaving. Some of them were hanging out of the windows, yelling in her direction. Sophie recognised they were New Zealand players and waved, until she had a sudden realisation.

'Wait! That's our bus!' Sophie was horrified. Someone had made the call to take the well players back to Conade. Anton must be on that bus. How would they get the sick players back?

Roger came running over.

'It's alright Sophie. The players that feel okay are going back with Harry and Benny. We told them to keep all the windows open in the bus. The officials have all buggered off – so we're gonna take their bus – so,' Roger puffed, as he updated Sophie and Brett, pointing to the slightly smaller, but beautifully modern bus parked on the far edge of the parking lot, 'so we can go straight to the hospital.'

'*Hell* no!' Sophie could not express herself any more plainly. There was no way on earth she would take her boys to a Mexican hospital unless the situation deteriorated beyond what she could handle herself. The poisoning appeared to be reversible. The players were reviving, beginning to think more clearly, and nobody had passed out since leaving the rink.

'You saw how hopeless and unhelpful the paramedic and tournament doctor were,' she said to those standing around her, with fire in her eyes.

She reinforced her point by reminding them of a tale they had heard from the last New Zealand ice hockey trip to Mexico City. One of the New Zealand players had been taken to a local hospital.

'They waited nine hours to be seen,' she said, adamantly punctuating each word with hand gestures, 'and the emergency department was full of gunshot victims and locals carrying guns! Not only that, it is proving very difficult to find anyone who can actually speak English or with any actual medical training! No thank you!' she declared.

Sophie's plan was to phone the toxicology consultant at the New Zealand National Poisons Centre when she got back to Conade, and gain some input and direction from him. As she relayed all this to Roger, Brett and Felix, while every player in front of her listened in, everyone instantly and unanimously agreed.

One by one, the casualties – a mixture of New Zealand, South African, Mexican and Taipei boys – were helped onto the bus. Sophie organised a buddy system in which each recently critical player was seated beside an open window, with a not so critical player next to him in the aisle seat. The sickies and supporters filled the smaller bus to capacity.

Chapter Twenty-Two

CONADE GRAVEYARD SHIFT

Despite her own high level of nausea, Sophie sat at the front of the bus facing backwards the whole way back to Conade, keeping watch over the players.

Some dozed off and, when this happened, Sophie had their neighbour poke them to see if they were asleep or unconscious. They were just sleepy. Some played on their phones. Only one vomited – right out his open window.

Thankfully there wasn't much traffic at that time of night so the trip was straightforward and quiet.

Roger passed round a few bags of potato chips and some 300ml water bottles, and Sophie encouraged the boys to eat and drink. Snatches of conversation floated down the aisle towards her. The comments she overhead were mostly derived from fear. 'They'll have to cancel the games.' … 'That was scary.' … 'I just wanna go home.' … 'I'm *not* playing again.' … 'I thought we were gonna die.' … 'They can't make us play.' … 'We would have died without Sophie, eh.' … 'I do wanna play, but only if it's safe.' … 'They can't cancel the games, cos our parents spent too much money getting us here.' And then the inevitable, 'I'm starving.' … 'My head hurts.' … 'I wanna throw up.'

And lastly, 'I can't believe I almost died on my seventeenth birthday. This is one birthday I'll never forget!'

Poor Nigel – in all the commotion, everyone had completely forgotten about his special day.

'You've been one of my heroes today, Nigel,' Sophie told him. 'Helping the players out of the rink the way you did.' Then she told him about the birthday cake, promising that they would celebrate tomorrow instead.

Surprisingly, Beauden was quite chirpy. Despite previously being the most critical, he looked and sounded more together than most of the sickies, and said he was feeling much better. Brett sat next to his son and they talked all the way back to Conade.

At 10.40 p.m., the bus turned into the driveway of the sports village – well past curfew. It occurred to Sophie that they may have a problem getting through the three security checkpoints without Carlos and Julio.

Speaking of whom, thought Sophie, *where* are *Carlos and Julio?* Sophie hadn't seen them since before the New Zealand versus Mongolia game. She also realised she hadn't seen any of the Mongolian team since the opening ceremony. *What happened to them?*

The bus slowed for each of the three gates to open, but continued driving each time. The armed guards gave a simple wave to the bus driver from inside their booths. Sophie figured out what was happening – they were in the officials' bus, getting the royal treatment! *Hmmm.*

Outside the main lobby, Sophie was first off the bus with her medical bag, and Felix was right behind her. She made a beeline for the reception area where the remainder of the New Zealand and South African players were waiting. She wanted to check on each one but, most of all, she wanted to clap eyes on Anton.

Someone had arranged five rows of chairs, so both teams could sit down. Anton was in the middle of the waiting group, chatting to a South African defenceman. Sophie was instantly relieved. Her baby was okay!

The two teams were getting along famously. As soon as Anton saw his mother, he came over to hug her. He was equally relieved to see that she was okay. Then Sophie and Felix were engulfed in a flood of animated questions.

'Wait! Everyone find a seat and we'll tell you what's going to happen,' Sophie said loudly. The boys quietened, and made their way to the chairs.

'Felix, will you check each of your boys, and I'll check ours. One at a time, okay? Nobody goes anywhere,' she announced to the group, 'not even to your room, until we say you're good to go. Got it?' Now was the time to lay down the law. They all nodded.

Sophie systematically worked her way through the playing lines, starting with the first then the second line. She recorded pulses, blood pressures and lists of symptoms, including a grading, out of 10, for their headaches. Most were between eight and 10.

She and Felix briefly discussed the safety of adding specific med-ications into the unknown mix of chemicals the boys had already absorbed. He decided it would be reasonably safe and shouldn't create further toxicity. So she topped up doses of paracetamol, ibuprofen and anti-nausea tablets. The more critical patients were pointed to a designated 'sick corner' and told not to leave.

Sophie talked non-stop to Anton as she checked him over from top to toe. She told him she loved him more than all the stars in the sky, and that she had been incredibly worried. She figured this was one occasion when she would be forgiven for fussing over him.

'I'm fine, Mum. Just a really bad headache and my brain feels kinda fuzzy, but I'm fine,' he tried to convince her. However, Steele told Sophie the full story.

When the two boys had first left the rink on Harry and Benny's say so, they had sat down just outside the front doors and had both passed out for a few minutes, until a player from the South African team found them and helped them move further away from the entrance.

Sophie shook her head in concern, but now that they were safely back at Conade, the boys' vital signs were stable, so Sophie pointed them to the 'okay corner'.

Most of the players had slightly fast heart rates and lowish blood pressures, which could be expected at altitude, let alone after some kind of gas poisoning. In addition to general symptoms of headache, dizziness and nausea, some were still slow to process their thoughts and some felt a little breathless.

Theo, Nigel and Benny also complained of burning nostrils and watery eyes, and all their blood pressure readings were high. Sophie recognised these symptoms were slightly outside the pattern.

The players in the 'okay corner' were buddied up, and sleeping arrangements were reconfigured so that those boys could keep an eye out for each other. They were told to drink lots of water, to have a snack from their personal supplies – even if it was cookies and potato chips – and to sleep with their windows wide open. They were warned against taking any medication without first checking with Sophie.

Sophie made them promise not to be heroes, but to find her if someone needed help. This instruction went double for Anton's buddy, Verne. Sophie knew Anton was so stoic that he would have to be really, really sick before he bothered anyone.

Finally, by 1 a.m., all the 'okay' boys had gone to bed, and so had Roger, Harry and Benny. Felix, and one of his coaches, were still in the lobby with three sick South African players. Sophie was keeping a close eye on six of the seven particularly sick New Zealand boys. Theo had pleaded to be able to return upstairs, and Sophie had made the arrangement conditional on him bunking with Craig, just across the hallway from Sophie's room. Brett was also still in the lobby because Beauden was one of the most critical. Sophie was grateful. She was glad of his help and company.

The four adults discussed how they would monitor the sickest boys, and tried to figure out the best way for Sophie to phone the poisons centre toxicology consultant in New Zealand.

As they were talking, two Mexican men came into the lobby. Sophie recognised one as Juan, the Mexican team coach and president of the Mexican Ice Hockey Federation. The other man was holding a wet towel, and immediately approached Sophie and Felix, introducing himself in surprisingly fluent English.

'I am doctor, and I come to update you on what happened at ice rink tonight. It was just only carbon monoxide gas,' he stated without concern, like the casualties had just got a little bit wet in the rain.

'The Zamboni has malfunctioning,' he continued, 'and was put out carbon monoxide from exhaust. So everyone will be fine. No problema.'

'Okay thanks,' said Felix, trying to take the news at face value. 'So what must we do for these boys now?'

'You all just only need breathe through wet towel, like this!' He put the wet towel across his face and gave an over-acted demonstration of breathing, in case they had forgotten what breathing looked like.

'Also you can take antihistamine to make feel better. Thank you, that is all,' he concluded.

It was clear the doctor wasn't interested in any line of questioning or debate. But Sophie was feeling too cynical and wasn't going to have a bar of it. She stood to face him head on.

'How do you know it was 'just only' carbon monoxide poisoning? Where is your proof? You could just tell us anything. And I can't possibly see how breathing through a wet towel is meant to help?

And the antihistamines? This is *not* an allergic, histamine-type reaction. The antihistamines could just add another chemical to an already near-lethal cocktail!' She glanced at Felix to see if he could make any medical sense of the Mexican doctor's advice. Felix shrugged his shoulders, indicating he didn't know how antihistamines could possibly help.

So Sophie continued. 'I'm not sure it's only one gas or one chemical either. We found differing symptoms so while there is a definite pattern, some of the symptoms didn't fit that pattern. How are you going to prove this carbon monoxide theory?' she demanded.

He looked dumbfounded. No response. So she dismissed him. 'Thank you, but you can go. *We* will take care of our boys.'

And with that, she turned her back to him and sat back down, crossed her legs away from him, and returned to discussions about the logistics of phoning the toxicology consultant.

Juan and the doctor slunk away with their tails between their legs. As the lobby door closed, Sophie could no longer contain herself: 'I bet *he's* a podiatrist too!' Everyone laughed. But Sophie was being serious.

Felix and his coach took their players to their rooms on the third floor, while Brett and Sophie sorted out a plan for the New Zealand boys. Sophie would take the sickest of the three – Matthew, Kieran and Stephen. Brett would take Beauden, Hugh and Dave. Matthew would sleep on Sophie's spare bed and Beauden would sleep on Brett's spare bed. The other four would collect the mattresses off their own beds and sleep on the floor. They would keep both doors between the adjoining rooms open, and have the windows open wide, despite the cold night air. Sophie could continue monitoring the six casualties until she was satisfied they were stable enough for her to get some sleep herself. Their welfare was paramount. Her sleep could be caught up.

Eventually.

When the night terrors stopped.

Brett needed his rest because it would be his job to deal with the tournament organisers in the morning. How they could go on with the competition, Sophie didn't know. She wasn't prepared to put any of the boys in danger again until their safety could be guaranteed.

Sophie quickly moved all her bags off the spare bed in her room, then made sure Kieran and Stephen didn't put their mattresses near the trickle of water that was still snaking across the floor from the leaky bathroom sink.

Once everyone was settled, she changed in the bathroom into her long, pink t-shirt with a sweater over the top and turned out all the lights except the one in the shower. This would give enough light to work with, just like a graveyard shift at the accident and emergency clinic.

Sophie sat cross-legged on the floor in the foyer of the rooms and pulled out her cellphone. She scrolled through her contacts until she found Bella, her charge nurse back home, and began composing a text message. It was 1.30 a.m. in Mexico City and 8.30 p.m. in New Zealand. Bella would have her kids in bed by now and Sophie knew she would happily drop everything to help when she heard about the medical emergency.

So began what turned out to be a nearly two-hour text conversation marathon between Sophie and Bella. Sophie had sent a text to Nate Thompson, the New Zealand Ice Hockey doctor. But he hadn't responded. She wasn't sure he would know enough about this very specialist area anyway. Bella phoned the toxicology consultant, passing on the questions that Sophie sent through, and replied with the consultant's answers. He proved to be very knowledgeable about carbon monoxide poisoning and advised Sophie that she had responded to the situation correctly. Removing the source was the first step, then administering oxygen at high concentration, pushing fluids and treating the symptoms.

Sophie asked if she should take the boys to hospital for blood tests, but the consultant advised that there would be no advantage in that course of action. He explained that carbon monoxide is an odourless gas that binds with haemoglobin in the blood, forming carboxyhaemoglobin, which leaves the body within four to five hours of poisoning, meaning that the boys' blood work would already have returned to normal. He told her that after unconsciousness and vomiting, the next symptom for carbon monoxide poisoning is seizures … then death.

They had got out of the rink just in time.

But one anomaly remained. Why did Theo, Nigel and Benny have burning nostrils, watery eyes and high blood pressure? Was there something else? The consultant advised that these symptoms were not consistent with carbon monoxide poisoning.

Sophie asked Bella to tell the consultant about the rancid, putrid smell in the rink, which had grown steadily worse each day. Bella wrote back with his reply. He agreed that there may have been some other factor in addition to the carbon monoxide, but didn't know what.

Sophie typed her sincere thanks to Bella and the consultant. It had been a relief to touch base with home and communicate with knowledgeable and caring people.

In between texts, every 15 minutes she checked on her six patients, recording heart rates and blood pressures, and tickling eyelashes to check levels of consciousness.

She also sent texts to her family, letting them know that she and Anton were okay, in case news of the emergency had somehow filtered through to New Zealand. Her Aunt Annelise, who held a senior position within the New Zealand Corrections Department, text her back offering to contact a friend in Foreign Affairs who could pull some strings should they need any further assistance.

Sophie was grateful for the offer and held it in reserve in case the situation worsened.

Sophie felt like she was cutting herself off from the civilized world as she signed off all contact with New Zealand and put away her cellphone.

She checked on the boys again.

'All quiet on the Western Front?' Brett whispered as she left his room. He had gone to bed long ago, but she wasn't surprised he was still awake.

'Yeah, all stable. And the tox consultant was happy. I think we can safely get some sleep now,' she whispered with a smile. 'I'll get up and check them every half hour for a couple more hours. Thanks for all your help tonight, Brett. I couldn't have done it on my own.'

Brett had climbed quietly out of bed and before she knew it, he had wrapped his arms right around her waist and was resting his forehead down on her shoulder, quietly sobbing, with his knees partially buckling under him. He had held it together all night, until now. In response, she wrapped her arms tightly around his shoulders.

'He nearly died,' Brett sobbed quietly, releasing his emotion about what had happened to Beauden. Then several deep sobs later, 'He *would* have died,' sob, 'Thank you,' sob, 'from the bottom of my heart.'

'Hey, it's okay,' Sophie whispered to him, as she rubbed his shoulders. 'I was honestly just doing my job.' She had never seen Brett this vulnerable. 'But I'm very glad I was there.' She was crying now too. They were holding on to each other for dear life, as the enormity of just how tragically the evening might have ended hit them both.

A full minute passed, but it might as well have been an hour. Neither wanted to let go of the other.

Sophie broke the silence.

'When I've had the worst, most stressful day at work, sometimes it's all I can do to say, 'Well, at least no one died.' But, you know what? It's true. No one died today. We all lived to tell the tale. And maybe one day I will!' She was trying to lighten the mood.

'Yeah!' Brett exclaimed as he finally pulled away from her. 'You could write a book! But would anyone believe the story?'

'Probably not. We skated on thin ice, for sure.' Sophie smiled an exhausted smile. 'Anyway. Bedtime. Little bit shattered now. Gonna have a huge day tomorrow. Lots to sort out!' Sophie patted Brett's shoulder one last time as she turned and navigated her way through the obstacle course of leaking water, Kieran, Stephen, her backpack, and two cases. Utterly exhausted, she crawled into bed at last. It was 3.30 a.m.

Chapter Twenty-Three

MONDAY, MUTINY!

'Sophie, wakey wakey. It's nearly 9.30 a.m. They want a medical and managers' meeting at 1 p.m. at the officials' hotel and we need to meet with the other teams before we go to that.' It was Brett. He was fully showered and dressed, the boys and all the mattresses were gone from her room. She hadn't heard a thing!

How does he do that? she thought as she groaned and stretched, then clambered out of bed. Then out loud, but quietly to herself, 'It's like he's in stealth mode, like the SAS…'

Brett smiled to himself as he retreated to his room.

Sophie's head hurt and she felt nauseous and dizzy. She had slept like a brick since her last half hourly check at 5.30 a.m., and had been mercifully free of night terrors.

She rushed through the shower, tied her hair in a bun, threw on some blue Capri jeans and a pale pink t-shirt, then grabbed her backpack and Nigel's Black Forest Gateaux, still camouflaged in the grey plastic bag.

They had to celebrate poor Nigel's birthday somehow! Her original plan had gone completely out the window in the commotion of the night before. She had decided to smuggle the cake into the mess hall, although she had no idea how they were going to eat the contraband without being discovered by the guards.

She stepped out of the foyer of her room to find the entire team sitting on the floor, lined up on either side of the corridor, awaiting their morning check-up.

'Oh good!' Sophie suddenly came up with a Plan B for Nigel's celebration. 'Seeing as you're all here, I've arranged a pre-breakfast snack!' And with that she pulled the cake out of its grey plastic bag, while singing the first few bars of the happy birthday song.

The team joined in and sang along quietly. The hip-hoorays at the end were categorically the most pathetic she had ever heard, and there were no candles to blow out. Nevertheless, Nigel grinned with pleasure all the way through – he hadn't been forgotten.

'Thanks everyone. This is one birthday I will *never* forget!' he exclaimed enthusiastically.

'Let them eat cake!' Sophie laughed. It was a questionable nutritional choice – the cake would either be a welcome relief from the mess hall slop, or it would make the boys feel even more nauseous. Using their fingers, most of the players picked out a little chunk of the gateaux. After all, it might be the only decent food they got all day.

It wasn't long before the whole cake had been polished off, so Sophie decided the boys must be stable enough to wait until after breakfast for their check-ups. The team headed down towards the mess hall, had their fingerprints scanned, and received their meal tickets, just in time to catch the last of the same old slop. Thank goodness for the cake!

Brett and Roger quietly talked to the coaches and managers from the South African, Taipei and Mongolian teams. Mexico was present for breakfast too, but they sat at a distance from the other teams, and didn't join in discussions.

The four sets of adults arranged to meet in Felix's room on the third floor at 11.30 a.m. They intended to compose a formal joint letter of complaint, listing a range of issues that needed to be addressed. Mexico were not invited to the meeting.

Straight after breakfast, Brett called a meeting of the New Zealand team. They had a scheduled on-ice training session at 11 a.m. and then a game against South Africa at 4 p.m.

'No way in hell these are going ahead. Obviously!' Brett declared.

The boys gathered on the basketball court for their meeting and, while Brett provided an update on what would be happening that day, Sophie checked everyone over, paying most attention to the six patients from the previous night. Then she fussed over Anton for a few minutes. Everyone still had thumping headaches and felt a little dizzy and quite nauseous, but they had definitely improved. Considering he had been the most critical, Beauden continued to make a remarkable recovery. He had only a mild headache and no dizziness or nausea. Sophie concluded that the IV fluid replacement he had received at the rink must have made the difference.

The players that spoke up during the meeting were adamant they would not set foot inside the rink again, let alone play hockey there. They just wanted to go home. The whole group discussed various scenarios. They had come here to play hockey after all… Could they change to Mexico City's second skating facility?… What if changing rink could resolve the problem?… After all, it had taken a mighty effort and a huge cost to get to Mexico in the first place… Shame not to play… Some boys voiced that they wanted to play again, but only if it was safe.

A small group of four boys led by Stephen, the captain, became angry and dissident, throwing wild comments at the coaches and managers. 'You just want us to play at any cost.' 'We could have died.' 'You can't *make* us play.' 'You don't even care about us.'

Sophie recognised they were simply scared, but…

'*Hey!*' she finally yelled, commanding their attention. She had been quietly stewing in the background, and now she was really mad.

'Let's stop right there with the negative! I know you're scared. Yes, we had a brush with death last night, but we survived to tell the tale! Not one of you has asked how I'm feeling. I have a whopper of a headache too! And I feel sick too! Just remember,' she said gesturing to the other adults in the room, '*we* were there too!'

Some of the boys were embarrassed and looked down at their feet. Even Anton looked a bit shocked. Sophie had had multiple occasions on this trip when she'd needed to stand up and say her piece, despite her usual calm and quiet demeanour, and now was no exception.

'What you don't know is that I spent nearly two hours last night talking to one of the top toxicology specialists in New Zealand, while *you* were all asleep. And Brett and I were up most of the night monitoring the sickest of you. We've only had four very broken hours of sleep! Because *we* were looking after *you!*' She had their full attention now.

'You're also forgetting that my son is on this team. Do you think that I would *ever* put my own son in danger? I would *never! ever!* put *any!* of you in danger!' Her voice had risen to top volume as she pointed around the team. What were they thinking? That she wouldn't protect them with her own life?

'I. Am. An. Emergency nurse!... and *this*... is what I do! I have been in seven full-on resuscitations in my career!... I have *never* lost a patient on my watch!... And I am *not* about to start now!... Also, no one is going to *make* you play! I am promising you, right now, these games will *only* resume, firstly, when and if I know you're medically safe to play... and I'm gonna talk with Dr Nate, the New Zealand Ice Hockey doctor, or my tox guy, tonight. And, secondly, when we know the rink has resolved whatever the problem was. So, if and when we can *guarantee* your safety, *we* will make a decision whether the games go ahead, and then *you* can decide if you want to play.'

Wow. Stroppy, shouty Mum! She was really cross with them. It looked like her speech was over, but she had one last parting shot...

'And, you know what? You lot are *much* bigger than me. What in the world makes you think I could *make* you play, anyway?!' she growled. Now she was staring and pointing directly at Stephen.

Then, for maximum impact, she turned on her heel and marched away.

Brett and Roger followed her through the exit. That would give the players something to think about. Stephen still looked defiant but the rest of his dissident posse looked rather sheepish. Meanwhile, the boys who wanted to play were starting to look more hopeful.

Sophie and the two managers had planned to leave the boys with Harry and Benny to talk, play basketball and hang out in the gym until the emergency tournament meetings were over. All going well, they would be able to return from the meetings with a plan of how things might proceed.

The first thing Sophie wanted to do was to get on a computer to research carbon monoxide poisoning. She wanted to be armed with all the facts for the meeting. Brett thought that an email should be sent to all the parents advising what had happened and what actions had been taken. The grapevine was no way for a parent to hear that their kid had nearly died.

So Brett, Roger and Sophie went to the front desk to ask about using the internet. The sports village 'boasted' one computer room equipped with one very old computer attached to a very slow dial-up modem, but now they needed to make use of it.

The same smarmy official who they had dealt with on arrival was at the front desk. *Oh great*, thought Sophie. In his usual unhelpful manner he advised them with a fake smile that bookings for the computer had to be made well in advance. 'So how about 5 p.m. tomorrow?'

'No. We need to use the computer *now!*' growled Brett, thumping his fist down on the desk.

The official then pulled out the Conade rules which clearly

stated that the computer had to be booked in advance and was only available from 5 to 9 p.m. His fake smile only grew bigger.

'Look, I'm sorry. We nearly died last night,' Brett was perfectly calm again, trying to appeal to the man's human side, 'and we need to do some research. Our boys are still really sick. So will you *please* let us use the computer?' he pleaded. 'Or… will I phone the tournament supervisor and tell him just how very *helpful* you have been?'

The official's fake smile had fallen off his face. He passed Brett the key without further hesitation. It had the room number on it.

'One hour,' he said.

Felix came downstairs just at that moment. Perfect timing. The four of them quickly found the computer room. Sophie scrolled through the documents she found on the internet and Felix read over her shoulder, while Brett and Roger drafted an email to the parents on paper.

Sophie found several interesting articles by reputable medical websites, listing the affects of carbon monoxide poisoning. The severity depended on the amount and duration of CO gas exposure. She printed off two key pages that listed potential delayed symptoms and ongoing complications:

- Brain related symptoms: memory loss, confusion, seizures, hallucinations, irritability, loss of balance and speech, depression, Parkinson-like syndromes, a type of blindness and hearing loss, and urinary and bowel incontinence.
- Heart related symptoms: potential damage to the heart, particularly older people and anyone with existing heart disease, decreased heart muscle blood supply, chest pains, enlargement of the heart, heart attack and death.
- The incidence and severity of brain and heart complications increases with the age of the patient.

- And complications for unborn babies: brain damage, heart problems, low birth weight, early foetal death, stillbirth, and behavioural problems for some babies who survive it.

Judging by what Sophie had found in the documents, the severity of their exposure and the length of their exposure had indeed been very serious. Everything confirmed what the toxicology consultant had said – they had gotten out just in time. She also discovered the reason why none of the boys were pale. Carboxyhaemoglobin shows as a characteristic cherry red colour. That was why their skin had looked so rosy.

It stood to reason that the smaller players on the first and second lines, who had been on the ice the longest, became the sickest. They would have been sucking in the largest quantities of carbon monoxide and, with their smaller body masses, they were overcome more quickly. Beauden had become the most critical of all the boys and now she understood why this was too. For the last period, when the carbon monoxide levels would have been at their highest, Beauden was in goal right in front of where the Zamboni was parked.

However, there was still mystery around the atypical symptoms some of the players had experienced.

Sophie, Felix, Roger and Brett all briefly checked their emails and were surprised to find a number of very panicky messages from parents. Unbeknown to them, some of the boys had been texting home and two had been able to receive phone calls. The parents had heard differing stories from various sources about what had happened and were extremely worried.

Gabi, who had been in the grandstand with her parents and little brother, had contacted her sister, Brigid, in New Zealand, who had emailed a number of parents with some parts of the story. Apparently there had been nothing on the news in Mexico City.

Oddly, however, one email from New Zealand said that a New Zealand television station had reported that the team had received lead poisoning and had been sent to hospital!

The rumours that were circulating needed to be dealt with, and swiftly.

Sophie typed up Brett and Roger's drafted email, as she was the fastest typist. The men decided that the email should come from her, as she was the medical professional. Henry, the president of New Zealand Ice Hockey, Jolana, the chef de mission, and Dr Nate, the New Zealand Ice Hockey doctor, were also copied in.

There was no point beating around the bush. The message needed to be honest and up front. Yes, the players' lives had been in danger. And yes, some had been critically ill. But they had all survived, and would get better each day. Sophie felt it was imperative that the parents and New Zealand officials knew she had been in contact with one of New Zealand's top toxicology specialists, and that he had assured her that her actions had been exemplary. The boys had been, and would be, safe in her hands.

Brett and Roger read through the email one last time. Both were happy with how it was worded, so Sophie hit send. Brett noticed she hadn't taken the opportunity to send any personal emails, whereas both he and Roger had.

'Don't you want to email Charlie?' he asked politely.

'Oh… no… that's okay. He'll get the group email,' she said quietly.

She had thought of Hayden, but not of Charlie. She simply felt detached. And anyway, the less Hayden knew about it all, the less he would worry about his mum and brother.

Armed with the documents she had printed from the internet, Sophie and the others made their way to the scheduled meeting.

There were 10 of them huddled in Felix's room, some seated

across the two beds and some standing. Sophie inquired about the wellbeing of their players.

As usual, Mr Mongolia hardly spoke. He wasn't able to elaborate much due to his lack of English, but did manage, 'We no stay, we sick, mmmm, okay now.' Apparently this meant that the Mongolian team had left the rink immediately after the opening ceremony because their boys were feeling sick, but were doing okay now.

Frank and the Taipei team were very grateful for the help their two very sick players had received. They had only come to watch the last period of the New Zealand versus Mongolia game, take part in the opening ceremony, then watch the first period of the South Africa versus Mexico game. They hadn't realised how desperate the situation had become. Like the Mongolian team, they had left the rink pretty soon after the opening ceremony. Frank had sent the two very sick boys to the first aid room to be looked at, with instructions to get on another bus back to Conade when they were finished!

The 10 team representatives talked through the previous night's events and decided on the key points they felt needed to be addressed. Sophie made notes and, as she was apparently now the designated typist, used Brett's laptop to draft the final letter they would present to Friderik Babic, the tournament supervisor. Brett did most of the talking during the meeting. His experience as a business manager, and his engineering expertise, which included work with toxic gases, were certainly paying off. Everyone agreed with the proposals he put forward. When Sophie read back the drafted letter, they were all satisfied. Then, before closing the meeting, they unanimously voted that Brett should be the key spokesman for all four teams. Something needed to be done, and he was the man for the job.

Chapter Twenty-Four

THE FAT CATS SWEAT

At 12.15 p.m., the team manager and appointed medical representative from each team boarded the bus to the Hotel Pedregal Palace. Harry, Benny and Roger stayed back and took the New Zealand players for lunch in the mess hall, then gave them free time at the basketball courts and gym.

This was Sophie's first visit to the Pedregal Palace and she was dying to take a peek inside.

As they drove into the formal entrance way and got off the bus, the contrast between Conade and Pedregal couldn't have been more vast. *Wow!* It was truly breathtaking. Beautiful marble in the entrance way, with waterfalls, extravagant flower arrangements, a luxurious lounge area and their own upmarket bar and café adjacent to the lobby.

Oh, how the other half lived!

A whiteboard in the front entranceway unexpectedly directed them to two separate meetings – one for medical, one for managers. 'Maybe they are working on a divide and conquer principle,' said Sophie. But she and Brett both felt strong enough to tackle anything that came their way. They agreed to meet back in the lobby after the meetings had finished.

Sophie felt nervous but at the same time very bold, as she entered the meeting room. She was fighting for her boys. She took the first seat to the left of the front table. Felix took the seat next to her, then Frank, then Mr Mongolia.

Waiting, waiting, waiting. Still no sign of the tournament officials.

The four did not speak. Sophie sat back in her chair, arms crossed, legs crossed, feeling rather rebellious and defiant. They all knew what they were going to say. And boy, would she let the officials have it! She might be naturally introverted, but when someone or something threatened her cubs, they better watch out!

Felix had a copy of the letter Brett was delivering to Friderik Babic. No one knew which meeting he would show up at, if he dared show his face at all.

Finally, after keeping them waiting for 15 minutes, the same three amigos from their previous medical meeting entered the room. No one stood for them, but they all politely nodded.

The creepy Mexican doctor thanked the medical representatives for coming, and got straight to the topic at hand: The Zamboni had been fixed and CO levels were down to 50 parts per million. This had not been a serious event in any way. They did not want to make a big deal of it and blow it out of proportion. Everyone was here to play hockey. So now that the problem was sorted they could get on with the games…

Sophie was disgusted! Was he serious? People had nearly died! And all this man cared about was to carry on as if nothing had happened! Was there something seriously wrong with his brain?

The Mexican doctor motioned to Sophie, inviting her to begin the discussion. He probably thought he would put the 'little woman' under the spotlight first. She started very calmly.

'First of all, I am not prepared to put my boys back on the ice until I know exactly what caused them to become ill. You say it was carbon monoxide from the Zamboni, and maybe it was, but I'm not so sure because not all their symptoms are in keeping with CO poisoning. Most of my boys were dizzy, nauseous, short of breath, tachycardic, hypotensive and suffering from really bad headaches. But then some had high blood pressure and burning nostrils. And what is that disgusting *smell* in the rink? Carbon monoxide has no smell, so there was something else in the mix. Maybe another gas?

'Secondly, what are you proposing to actually *do* about it? How can you guarantee us it won't happen again? Do you have another Zamboni? Because I don't think any of us believe a do-it-yourself-fix-up-job on such a severely malfunctioning machine is acceptable. How can you guarantee it won't just do the same thing again?'

Sophie was getting into her stride, and emotion was steadily increasing in her voice.

'Thirdly, how are we supposed to monitor the air quality in the rink? And, that's another point. How can you say the rink is now at 50 parts per million? I don't believe that for one second. I've done some research. Out on the streets, the air quality in Mexico City is 200 parts per million, and that's on a good day. So how can you claim that your rink's CO level is now a quarter of what's right outside the doors? That just doesn't make sense.

'Fourth, even if you can correct the problem, put some things into place to ensure it doesn't happen again, like huge fans in one end blowing fresh air in and huge extractor fans at the other end actively sucking it out again (and even then I would want an oxygen saturation machine so I could monitor my players' oxygen levels), most of the boys are now *terrified* to set foot in that rink again. They nearly died, remember? Oh yeah, and thanks for all your help with that, by the way!'

She had become quite passionate by now. The volume of her voice had grown louder and her gestures had become more animated.

'Plus we are all still feeling pretty sick, and I need to make sure exertion isn't going to exacerbate any of the players' symptoms.'

And she wasn't finished yet…

'Essentially, I simply don't trust any of you because you've blatantly lied to us so many times already,' she motioned to the three amigos at the front. 'So until you can guarantee me all of those things and provide answers to *my* satisfaction – as in, I will need to see evidence – I can't see any way these games can *possibly* proceed!'

Sophie concluded her emphatic little speech. She had never felt so bold. She was as mad as all hell. She didn't trust these officials. And boy, had she let them know!

She sat back in her chair, folded her arms again and pinned the creepy little doctor with a fixed gaze, daring him to answer her if he could.

A full 10 seconds ticked by, with him gawking back at Sophie, tapping his pen on the desk, obviously a little dumbfounded about how to respond. And then, his eyes shifted from Sophie to Felix, as he said, 'Thank you New Zealand… South Africa?'

Would he not even address them by their names now? *How rude!* thought Sophie.

'I must agree with what Sophie said. I have nothing to add,' said Felix.

The Mexican doctor motioned to Frank, who simply stated, 'Same,' and then to Mr Mongolia, who nodded once.

The little doctor sat completely still, aside from continuing to tap his pen irritatingly on the desk. He had written nothing down.

'Okay,' he concluded, 'we will discuss with tournament chairman.'

So Friderik Babic will get involved after all? About time!

The Mexican doctor stood to leave and his sidekicks followed suit.

Felix spoke up. 'We would like to call a meeting with Mr Babic. Maybe later today?'

The doctor simply turned and left the room. Without another

word. No acknowledgement of what Felix had just said. No good-byes. And his two amigos followed on behind, firmly shutting the door as they departed.

'Wow, these meetings always go so incredibly well!' Sophie chuckled. Felix and Frank laughed as her sarcastic comment broke the tension in the room. Now she realised she was shaking a little. Adrenaline. It was times like these she wished boldness didn't take so much effort.

'You didn't mince words, Sophie,' said Felix with admiration. 'I think that's the shortest meeting we've had so far! I wonder how Brett's getting on with the management meeting. Shall we go and see?'

The three agreed, and Mr Mongolia followed them as they left the room and made their way to the lobby. There was no sign of the managers, so they took the stairs to the second floor, where the other meeting was being held.

When they arrived at the meeting room, Felix simply reached out, opened the door and waltzed on in. Sophie, Frank and Mr Mongolia glanced at each other then quickly followed his lead.

Friderik Babic was at the centre of the table and speaking. He nodded respectfully to them as they entered, and continued with his speech. Sophie settled herself in an empty chair and looked around the room. Babic was flanked by the Mexican Ice Hockey president and team coach, Juan, as well as several officials and volunteers. The team representatives had definitely been outnumbered.

All the managers, including Brett, had finished putting forth their objections, but Babic was brushing off their opinions and comments as trivial.

The gist of what he was saying in his very boring monotone was similar to what the medical representatives had already heard – that the poisoning incident had not been a serious event, the officials did not want to make a big deal of it and blow it out of all proportion, everyone was here to play hockey, so now that it was all in the past they could get on with the games.

Sophie was astounded. *Holy freaking cow!* People had nearly died, and now it appeared that Babic was joining with the Mexicans in an attempt to sweep the whole thing under the carpet.

Sophie had only been in the room for a few minutes but was already so disgusted she knew she had to speak. She raised her hand and Babic gave her the floor.

Sophie didn't try to reiterate all that she had said in the medical meeting, but instead started by pleading with Juan to ask the Mexican TV news channels to report something about the incident as a service to their own people. She presented directly from the information she had printed off about the dangers of CO poisoning for unborn babies, and pointed out that there could have been pregnant women in the crowd who would now need to consult their obstetricians. And then (loading up her most powerful weapon) she looked directly at Babic and said, 'People with any type of heart condition would immediately need a full check-up with their cardiologist.'

The colour drained from Babic's already rather grey face. With her eyes still fixed on him, she gave a full rundown of all the side effects and ongoing potential complications for those with serious health conditions.

Babic was now listening intently and rubbing his face and head. He was looking more and more clammy and uncomfortable as Sophie continued to speak. When she finished, he stood. Wiping his brow with a handkerchief, he announced a five minute break. Then he loosened his tie as he stepped out onto the outside balcony attached to the room and closed the glass door behind him. He immediately pulled his cell phone from his pocket and proceeded to make a phone call.

Bingo! thought Sophie victoriously. She had made a calculated guess that Babic had a balloon-full of heart attack and stroke risks hanging over him and now, in his mind at least, it was ready to pop! If he didn't care about anyone else's wellbeing, perhaps she would get his attention by pointing out the risk to his own health.

Several officials and Juan joined Babic on the balcony. Meanwhile, Brett gave Sophie a summary of the managers' meeting so far. He had spoken first and had begun by stating his qualifications and experience with health and safety, toxic gases and working environments, before voicing the combined concerns of the four teams. He had concluded by reading from the letter that he had composed, and Sophie had typed, earlier that day.

The minutes passed by. Brett twice ventured out onto the balcony to see how things were progressing, and twice was rudely waved away by Babic. He did, however, manage to overhear some brief snippets of the conversation Babic was having on his cell phone, and confirmed Sophie's suspicion – Babic was talking to his cardiologist in Slovakia!

After 15 minutes, Babic finally ended the call. He then talked for about five minutes with the officials who were still on the balcony with him. Eventually the glass doors opened and they all returned to their seats. The meeting resumed once more, but only so it could be abruptly concluded.

Babic stated they could not replace the Zamboni, but the rink manager was confident the fix-it job should hold. He promised to put in place, over the next two days, all the other things the teams had demanded. This included fans in the walls and supplying Brett with a multi-gas detection meter so that he could monitor the air quality during games. He asked the team managers to meet at the rink at 5 p.m. that afternoon to inspect the work done so far, and for Brett to phone him afterwards to report back their satisfaction. Then they would reconvene the following day at noon to discuss the possibility of recommencing the tournament.

Finally! A solid plan to move forward.

Sophie planned to check in with Dr Nate in New Zealand that evening, mostly to ensure there would be no further health complications if the players skated hard so soon after the poisoning. Then would come the onerous task of convincing the cynics amongst the team that it would be safe to play again.

Chapter Twenty-Five

FOYER FACE OFF

The bus took the team representatives from Hotel Pedregal Palace back to Conade. Once there, they found the New Zealand and South African players still hanging out together in the basketball court area. Sophie checked how each of her boys was feeling. Headaches were at about seven out of ten, and some were still suffering from nausea. She dished out more paracetamol and anti-nausea tablets accordingly. The New Zealand team had become firm friends with the South African players. These boys had nearly died together. *Out of crisis comes camaraderie*, she thought to herself.

Brett made a short and purposely vague announcement to the team about what had been discussed and explained that things were being put into place, but didn't promise that everything would be resolved. Most were pleased, quietly exclaiming, '*Yes!*

But Stephen and his stooges kept their sullen faces. Stephen even muttered under his breath, 'Fuck you, I am still not playing, and you can't make me.' It was clearly aimed at Sophie.

Harry heard him and replied very loudly, 'Well that's your choice Stephen. But that also means you can't be the captain any longer. Take both your shirts to Sophie. Today please.'

Wow! De-throned! What will happen now? thought Sophie. This was unprecedented.

Some of the boys had asked to make a trip to the grocery store.

It didn't seem like the teams were ever going to win the snack and water battle. They had resigned themselves to continue buying their own. Meanwhile, Harry and Benny thought the coaches and managers all deserved a drink, so they intended to buy beer and wine. Sophie suggested that a bit of 'fresh air' and a constructive walk would do the players good.

The defiant cynics didn't want to go. Their loss. But if there was no New Zealand adult there to ensure their safety, they would have to wallow in misery in their rooms.

The remainder of the team had a relaxing, albeit slow stroll to the grocery store and back. It was nice to see these boys being positive again.

Except Kevin. He had something on his mind. On the way to the store, he confessed to Brett that he'd had a problem opening the window in his room the night before. The poor kid had bashed the frame, hoping that would force it open, but the glass had cracked in one corner. He was worried sick about potential repercussions with the armed guards. Brett said, 'Just keep it to yourself for the moment and I'll deal with it if it becomes a problem.'

The walk was missing Kieran to entertain them, as he was one of those who had stayed behind. But Tom and Verne both stepped up and told stories and jokes, making the trip light-hearted and fun.

Sophie was once again bodyguarded in the middle of the team. This time nobody was in uniform. But the workmen on the bridge still stopped, downed tools and stared at her as the team passed by.

Stephen, Kieran, Brad and Matthew had all slept and seemed in slightly better moods when the team returned.

Later in the afternoon, Brett and Sophie boarded the bus with the other managers again. Back to the rink to inspect the work that had been undertaken so far.

The rink still smelled foul, but not as bad as the other days. The managers were pleasantly surprised to find that four huge holes, at least a metre in diameter, had been cut out of the walls near the four corners of the rink. Two blowing fans and two extractor fans had already been installed but had not yet been wired in. The workmanship looked rough, but as long as the fans worked the air flow would be greatly improved.

The tournament doctor's right hand amigo was there, and greeted Brett with a smile, a handshake and a portable gas detection meter. He talked to Brett in broken English about the detector for a couple of minutes. A pleasant surprise to hear him speaking at last!

But what about Sophie's oxygen saturation machine so she could monitor her boys oxygen levels while playing? The man had completely ignored her, so she asked him about it directly.

'No,' replied the amigo, 'doctor say you no need. No point.' At her enquiry, his demeanour had instantly changed. He sounded irritated. He was brushing her off. Then he actually stepped right in front of her, turned his back and cut her out of his conversation with Brett. He was falling all over Brett to help him, but wouldn't lower himself to talk to the little woman on the team.

Sophie saw red, suddenly feeling her blood boil.

There was *every* need for her to know that her boys had safe levels of oxygen! If carbon monoxide poisoning struck again, their oxygen levels would drop very quickly, alerting her to what was happening before they became critical again.

She was under-slept, and over-stressed. And she needed that oxygen monitor!

'Your doctor is a bloody idiot!' she yelled at him, threw her hands up in absolute despair and desperation, and turned away. *Geez, why did everything have to be so difficult!* She was on the brink of having a meltdown.

'Sophie, come on, we need to stay calm here. He's trying to help us,' Brett said quietly. He was once again the voice of reason, having grabbed hold of both her shoulders and taken her aside.

Then even more quietly he said, 'This could get really ugly. We've got to stay on the right side of these guys, cos we still need them to help us. Just let me talk to him for a minute, okay?'

Sophie nodded with tears in her eyes. She knew he was right, but she couldn't bring herself to say anything more to the idiot doctor's amigo. She was fuming mad and her stress levels were exploding out of her brain. She walked away, but stayed within earshot.

The amigo told Brett he had sourced the gas detector from a friend who worked at the National Autonomous University of Mexico (UNAM), and now suddenly thought he might be able to find an oxygen monitor as well. He would bring it to the rink the next day.

Brett passed the good news on to Sophie. He had come through, yet again. Maybe good cop, bad cop had worked again. Even if she had been a little rude.

Okay. A lot rude.

Brett briefly showed her the gas detector, which he had already switched on. It displayed a series of lights on the left side, with a bunch of letters in the middle. It was beeping, and one of the lights and some of the letters were flashing.

'Is it working properly?' Sophie asked. Brett nodded with a frown. He started walking towards the front doors. Sophie didn't want to be any more trouble so she didn't ask any more questions. Maybe he was cross with her because of how she had behaved.

On board the bus back to the sports village, Sophie and Brett both felt cautiously optimistic that things were moving in the right direction to get the tournament back on track. Brett could calculate the cubic feet per minute of air that would need to be displaced to ensure the airflow in the rink was sufficient and, if Sophie could monitor oxygen levels and symptoms, then the games would be good to go.

She sent another text to Dr Nate. If he still didn't answer, she would speak with the toxicology consultant via Bella again later.

Brett and Sophie made it back to Conade in time to catch another terrible dinner of slop. Lumpy mashed potato, overcooked chicken and dried out re-fried beans. Bradley had nicknamed them 're-fried-re-fried beans,' which still wasn't an adequate description of just how disgusting they were.

After dinner, the boys headed back to their rooms. They were all exhausted, and understandably so. The plan was for them to chill out and listen to music or read until they felt ready to sleep. They had moderate headaches, down to about six out of ten, and some mild nausea continued. But everyone reported feeling better than they had that morning.

Apart from its single computer, Conade also 'boasted' a single telephone. On the way back from the mess hall to their rooms, Brett, Sophie and Roger stopped in the lobby so Brett could phone Friderik Babic and update him on progress at the rink.

Standing around in the main reception area was the Mexican coach, Juan, and his assistant coach, Raul, accompanied by the entire Mexican team, dressed in uniform. Amongst them were Carlos and Julio, the New Zealand team hosts, who had mysteriously reappeared, having been conspicuous by their absence all day. All of the Mexican players, including, for some reason, Carlos and Julio, looked hot and sweaty. They had obviously managed to sneak in some sort of training session. Roger walked over to talk to Carlos and Julio.

For a nice change, a pleasant, older Mexican woman was on desk duty and allowed Brett to make the phone call to Babic's room at the Hotel Pedregal Palace.

Brett was obviously struggling to hear, hunched over the desk with a finger stuck in his right ear and the phone glued to his left ear. The Mexican team grew louder and louder in the lobby.

Sophie walked over to Carlos, Julio and Roger. 'Would you mind asking the Mexican boys to keep the noise down a bit?' she

201

politely asked Carlos and Julio. 'Brett's trying to talk to Friderik Babic, to get the games back on track.'

Carlos raised the team's attention, and said something in Spanish. Everyone burst out laughing. Then, low and behold, the noise grew twice as loud as before!

Hmmm. That was a waste of time, Sophie thought. There was no point asking again. She didn't know what Carlos had said, but it clearly wasn't, 'Please keep the noise down.' Carlos and Julio were turning out to be rather unhelpful.

She was watching Brett as he struggled more and more to hear and to be heard.

Just then, the Mexican coach/president stepped in between her and Brett and tapped Brett on the shoulder. Brett excused himself from the phone and turned to see what Juan wanted.

The 196 centimetre tall Mexican towered over Brett, looking like he had steam coming out of both ears and both nostrils. It was a face-off. He was shaking with rage as he shoved Brett.

'*Don't you people talk to my team! How dare you talk to them!*' Juan screamed as he shoved him again.

Brett instinctively coiled, ready to strike. He stood his ground, locked eyes with Juan and stared him down. Juan wisely backed away. Brett slowly put the phone back up to his ear to talk to Babic.

'Are you there Friderik? Terribly sorry about that,' he said calmly, still staring Juan down. 'That was our friend, the Mexican president of ice hockey, screaming at me.'

Juan continued backing away, so Sophie followed him.

'He's talking to Friderik Babic, trying to get the games started again, but he can't hear with all the noise,' Sophie said loudly over the noise. She was mildly amused by the Mexican's outburst, and the fabulous timing, given that it had taken place 'live on air' to the tournament supervisor!

Juan turned to face Sophie. He continued to shake with fury.

Now, standing over her, he put his finger millimetres from her face, hardly able to contain himself.

Don't be intimidated by this thug, she thought to herself, as she put on her best poker face.

'D'you know, people go missing in Mexico, *every day!*' he hissed at her through clenched teeth.

'Like *that!*' he thundered, as he snapped his fingers.

'Oh really?' Sophie's answer sounded suitably disinterested and bored, despite his threat. She was terrified on the inside but was never going to let him see it. She took a few tentative steps back around to where Brett was standing, with his head down now, still talking on the phone. He hadn't heard or seen the exchange, and probably just as well.

Then Sophie spotted four of the New Zealand boys coming down the stairs towards the noisy lobby. *Oh no!* They did not need to get involved in any of this. She made a beeline to them.

'Go back to your rooms, *now!*' she said, 'And don't come down again tonight. We're fine but things are getting a bit heated and I do *not* want you in the middle of it.' It was her bossy mum voice again. They didn't ask questions, but stood and stared at the commotion in the lobby. They must have heard all the noise from their rooms and come down to investigate.

'Yeah, c'mon guys, let's get back up to our rooms.' It was Roger behind her. He too had spotted the boys and now passed her as he swept them back up the stairs.

By then, Brett had finished his phone call and had made his way through the Mexican commotion to Sophie. With one hand gently on the small of her back, he protectively guided her up and away from danger. Ever the gallant bodyguard.

Sophie was still shaky, but kept Juan's threat to herself.

Chapter Twenty-Six

JUST DOING MY JOB

Felix, Frank, Mr Mongolia and their coaches joined the New Zealand managers and coaches for a drink in Harry's room early in the evening. Sophie's first glass of wine went down very smoothly and rather quickly, closely followed by a second, slightly slower glass. Another cork for her corkboard.

On just four hours sleep, Sophie was exhausted anyway, but Juan's little performance in the lobby was getting close to the last straw. With the stress of the last few weeks – her marriage disintegrating, an intruder in her Salt Lake City hotel room, nearly being kidnapped at the airport, carbon monoxide (and whatever else) poisoning at the rink, and now a blatant threat on her life – her nerves were understandably a bit shot!

In the safety of Harry's room, everyone chatted for a couple of hours, mulling over the events of the previous evening and of that day. Benny asked Sophie to elaborate on the ongoing side effects and complications from their CO poisoning. He seemed particularly interested to hear about its effects on the heart. Benny's blood pressure had been just fine on the night and again that morning, and he had minimal symptoms – only a mild headache and mild nausea. Being a big bear of a guy, his body had coped well. She reassured him quietly when she had the chance.

The group went on to discuss plans for the scheduling of the

205

teams' rest days. New Zealand had been due to have their rest day on Thursday, but now that there was confusion about when and if games would be played, everything was up in the air. The Teotihuacan Pyramids north-east of Mexico City had been highly recommended as a must-see, and Brett and Roger had been planning the trip for the boys. Felix and his team were intending to do something similar.

Sophie sat back, sipped her wine and let the men talk. She was exhausted. She let herself be a passenger to the discussions.

At 10.15 p.m., everyone jumped out of their skin when Sophie's cell phone suddenly rang in the back pocket of her jeans. It was a miraculous event, given the issues they'd all had with cell phone coverage and connections. The caller ID showed it was Dr Nate! Just the man Sophie needed to talk to. She excused herself and stepped into the hallway to take the call.

It was reassuring to hear Nate's voice, and incredible to think of it travelling all those kilometres from his home in Queenstown, New Zealand, to Mexico City. He hadn't received Sophie's text messages, but had read the group email sent that morning. He had then phoned a friend who specialised in toxicology, and was satisfied that Sophie had done everything right in responding to the emergency. She might have been 'flying blind,' but she had made all the correct decisions.

Half way through the conversation, an armed security guard appeared from nowhere and started yelling at Sophie in broken English, motioning her back into Harry's room…

'Curfew! Shut up! Go to room! Curfew! Shut up! Go to room!' he kept shouting, over and over again.

Sophie had had enough. She let fly at the man, screaming all the atrocities of the last few days at him, 'We nearly died! We have extremely limited computer time, with only a dial-up internet connection! Only a few of our phones work! Texting is drawn out and limiting! Are you kidding!' She wasn't sure he understood any of it, but her intent and body language were rather obvious.

Several doors opened, including Harry's, as half the New Zealand team as well as Brett and Roger poked their heads out into the hallway to see what was happening. The boys obviously felt Sophie had it in hand – they all closed their doors and left her to it.

Brett stood, ever vigilant at the slightly ajar door of Harry's room, watching Sophie. Bodyguarding her.

'I will finish this very important phone call when I am good and ready! *So, get out!*' Sophie told the guard, and pointed back towards the stairs. '*And, let me talk!*' Sophie did not care that he was armed – she was not to be messed with after all she had been through. To his credit, the guard must have thought better of the situation, and made a hasty retreat.

'Sorry Nate. That was one of the armed guards inside the village,' Sophie continued into her phone, like nothing had happened.

She checked her plan with him for their next few days – monitor, monitor, monitor, and treat symptoms as they arose.

Nate advised Sophie that Matthew had suffered a severe orchard spray poisoning when he was seven years old and was now particularly sensitive to pollution and other chemicals. That made a lot of sense based on what Sophie had observed. Sadly, this meant the poor kid would be out for the remainder of the tournament – not that he was keen on playing at the moment anyway. The rest of the team could continue on and, so long as their vital signs and symptoms stayed stable and if there was no worsening of headaches, dizziness and nausea, then no further harm would be done.

Sophie sought one last piece of reassurance. In her line of work, one silly mistake or omission could lead to a patient's death. She lived in fear of that. Some of the parents' emails to the team management had come across as ungrateful and scathing, questioning Sophie's ability and the appropriateness of her treatment, and particularly her decision not to take the boys to hospital. Though she knew it shouldn't have, this line of personal attack made her question herself and her professional judgement. Had she missed anything? Was there something more she should have, or could have done?

'Absolutely not,' said Nate. 'Sophie, you have gone above and beyond. I believe some of our boys would have died if you weren't there last night. Any time you need a job in Queenstown, you will call me, right?' He laughed to diffuse the seriousness of the situation. Sophie grinned. This was the fourth time in the last three years he had offered her a job.

'Thanks Nate. That means a lot,' she said humbly, 'but I was just doing my job.'

Still standing nearby, Brett opened the door to let her back into Harry's room as she ended the call.

'Everything alright?' he inquired.

'Yep. It is now!' Sophie answered with a smile.

Inside Harry's room, discussions had moved on to the topic of what would happen if the remaining games were cancelled. International Ice Hockey Federation rules stated that any money given by the federation to the host nation would have to be returned. None of them knew exactly how much the Mexican federation had received, but they knew it was in the vicinity of US$150,000.

Wow! thought Sophie. If they had spent that much money on the games, why did the teams not have decent accommodation, enough water and proper food? And why could they not sort out the basic problems at the rink, like laying acceptable ice and sufficient rubber matting? The rules certainly stipulated all of this.

Brett had a potential insight about the situation. When they had first met, Juan, the Mexican coach/president, had boasted to Brett that he had secured use of the rink from the Mexican minister of sports, who happened to be a very close personal friend.

That same close personal friend had also provided funding for the Conade sports village accommodation, so the Mexican Ice Hockey Federation hadn't paid a dime. If the teams' accommodation and the ice time were all free, the only remaining outlay was for the Hotel Pedregal Palace and expenses for the officials.

'So where is all the money going then? Are they pocketing it for their hockey federation?' asked Sophie. 'Because I can kinda live with that, if they put it into junior hockey development. Or… do you think they are just paying themselves?'

Whether it was to dissuade Sophie's line of questioning or because he didn't know, Brett simply shook his head.

Harry had a theory of his own. He'd had a long coaching career and had seen and heard all sorts.

'The 'fat cats' on these tours live like rock stars. You've heard of 'what goes on tour, stays on tour'? Did you ever stop to think about why the meetings involving these guys never start until at least midday? And why hardly any of them ever bring their wives on these trips?' Without getting into explicit detail, he embellished his theory about the activities he believed some of them indulged in.

Sophie was quite disgusted. She knew she was pretty naive on these matters and she wasn't sure if Harry was joking or not, but he spun a good tale either way, and it certainly raised more than a few eyebrows in the room.

Brett mentioned that Juan had also boasted about a new beach house in Acapulco and a new boat. A coincidence?

What if Juan had siphoned funds in the form of an organiser's wage and expenses, or via pure fraud, and what if there was actually no money left in the pot? If the tournament was cancelled, under the IIHF rules, Juan would have to pay it all back. But how?

Suddenly realising the enormity of the situation, Sophie felt sick to the stomach.

'Ah, Juan said something to me earlier…' said Sophie. All eyes were suddenly on her. She sheepishly divulged that Juan had threatened to make her disappear. 'Like *that!*' she said and snapped her fingers, as Juan had.

The men were quiet for a minute. Then Felix connected the dots. 'At the medical meeting this morning, it would have appeared like Sophie was the antagonist, questioning everything, because she was the one who spoke first. She said everything that needed saying, and the rest of us simply agreed with her. That situation probably made its way back to Juan. Then later, at the manager's meeting, Sophie was the one who confronted Babic with the dangerous side effects and complications of CO poisoning.'

So, there it was. Roger let out a low whistle. The implications were obvious.

What if Juan's rage in the lobby that evening had been because he had skin in the game? Sophie was his biggest threat. The person who just might bring him down. A thorn in his side. A troublemaker.

The men looked at each other, but not much more was said. They were all lost in their own thoughts.

Soon enough it was 11.40 p.m. and time for everyone to say their goodnights. They'd had a few laughs. But for Sophie, the evening had mostly been overshadowed by stress and fear, once again.

On the way back to their rooms, Sophie had an idea.

'I wonder if we should be contacting the New Zealand embassy to let them know what's going on. If the Mexicans find themselves in a tight spot over paying back the money, we could be in a whole lot more danger. This could turn into an international incident. Maybe we need to think about an evacuation plan, just in case. We would need a bus and somewhere to hide before our flights. If they can't help, I could contact Aunt Annelise.' She was really just thinking out loud.

'Agreed.' Brett was smiling as he pulled a piece of paper from his pocket and showed it to her. It was a list he had written earlier in the day, before the drama in the lobby had even occurred, and the top item was 'phone NZ embassy'. Once again, Brett was onto it. *Man, he was good!*

Before turning in, Sophie rinsed the day off her in the shower. She was asleep by midnight, but slept fitfully once again. The sound of water pipes banging in the walls and ceiling woke her several times. She tossed and turned with night terrors in between. This time the taxi drivers pulled her towards a black tunnel, stuffed her into the boot of a car, tossed her two suitcases on top of her, then smothered her face and gassed her. At the last moment, her blond knight came to rescue her on his white stallion, wielding a gas detector in his hand. Her phone alarm woke her at 8 a.m.

Chapter Twenty-Seven

TUESDAY, BACK ON TRACK

Tuesday morning had rolled around all too quickly for Sophie. She dragged her sorry self through the same routine again. She showered and dressed in black Capri pants and a red knitted camisole top. She grabbed her backpack, met the team for breakfast slop, then checked the wellbeing of each of the players. No further poisoning symptoms had arisen and the headaches had continued to subside. Nausea had mostly resolved. Just as well, because she was running low on her basic supplies of medication.

Thankfully, the team were looking much improved. Except for the four defiants.

Brad had awoken in a better head space, probably because he was feeling less ill. But he was still a bit antsy and still refusing to play. Kieran's vitals were still not okay and Sophie decided to stand him down for the time being. This suited him, because he was just as surly about playing anyway. Matthew was on edge too, but mostly because Sophie had stood him down on medical grounds for the remainder of the tournament, backed by Dr Nate. The truth was, because he had become so sick and because of his childhood poisoning history, he was actually too afraid to play again. Sophie was merely a convenient scapegoat for his angst.

Part of Stephen's foul mood could be attributed to a long cell phone conversation he'd had with his mother, Carla, after breakfast

213

that morning. Sophie had offered, and then pleaded to speak with her, so she could reassure her that her son's safety and best interests were being taken seriously. But Stephen blankly refused Sophie's request. Carla was a difficult, negative, antagonistic woman at the best of times and often questioned the abilities of management and coaches. The current situation just made things worse.

The boys hung out in the gym, playing on the equipment rather than doing any proper training, and dabbled in a bit more basketball on the outside courts.

Sophie used the time to unpick the C's from Stephen's shirts. There hadn't yet been a vote for who would take over as captain – assuming the games recommenced.

Brett phoned the New Zealand embassy from the lobby. The woman he spoke to was very helpful and gave him her personal cell number in case they should need urgent assistance. It was incredibly reassuring to have a local ally.

The impending meeting at the San Jeronimo Rink with Babic and his Mexican entourage hung over the heads of the team management. Just after 11 a.m., as they waited for the bus to take them there, Brett, Roger, Felix and Frank discussed the work that had been completed at the competition venue and what still needed to be done. Sophie also briefed Felix on what Dr Nate had said the night before.

At the rink, the management meeting proved to be just as tense as the ones that had preceded it. The managers really didn't have much to say. However, Friderik Babic was suitably subdued and humble. It occurred to Sophie that the magnitude of the gas poisoning, and just how sick he personally might have become, had sunken in. He recognised that ventilation was a huge problem. The committee agreed, and in addition to the 1.4 metre blower and extractor fans, they would also place a one metre extractor fan in each of the change rooms. The emergency exit doors at each end of the rink would be opened and guarded throughout the games and trainings, and there would be an oxygen tank on each players' bench and in each changing room, with a further two in the first aid room.

Brett was satisfied with these arrangements and Sophie was able to tell Babic that she was confident most of the players would be well enough to safely play again.

Babic advised them that the extra work on the rink would continue well into the night and begin again early the following morning, to be completed in time to resume the games at 4 p.m. the following afternoon.

The next item on the agenda was drafting a revised schedule for the remainder of the games. This would be confirmed on the proviso that the final rink inspection was approved and accepted by all teams. The schedule would also include team rest days and a function day for the officials and team management.

New Zealand's next game would be against South Africa and was scheduled for the following day at 4 p.m. They would inspect the arena twice more before then to ensure they were happy with progress – at 5 p.m. that afternoon and again the next morning. If they were happy, they could then take the boys onto the ice for a light training before the game if they wished. New Zealand's rest day would be the day after that, and a bus would be available to take the team wherever they wanted to go.

Yippee! Now we're talking! Sophie thought to herself. This was more like it.

The only clash was that the officials' function day had to be scheduled for the same day as the New Zealand team's rest day, so this created a dilemma for Brett. He confided in Sophie that he would far rather stay with the team than socialise with the Mexicans, and Sophie was very relieved. The thought of losing her bodyguard for an entire day did not thrill her. At all!

Sophie was also told she could collect her oxygen saturation monitor from the rink that afternoon at the 5 p.m. inspection. It seemed the Mexican doctor's amigo might follow through on his promise.

Sophie, Brett and Roger headed back to Conade feeling cautiously optimistic. As long as the players' symptoms continued to improve and the rink repairs and upgrades were completed in time for their game against South Africa, all would be well.

Lunch was finishing up when they returned to the sports village. Gabi and her boyfriend Fabian were sitting with the team in the mess hall. Sophie wondered how on earth they had got through the three point security check. The young couple offered to help the team in any way they needed, and Brett and Sophie gladly accepted. It was nice to have friends with local knowledge. Having made an appearance during the lobby commotion the previous night, the team's wayward hosts Carlos and Julio had disappeared again.

As they ate atrocious 're-fried-re-fried' beans, cereal and bananas, Brett and Sophie gave Gabi, Fabian, Harry, Benny and Roger an update on all the news from the management meeting. When Roger heard about the officials' function day, he was as keen as mustard to attend and thought it would be a great opportunity to network with other referees.

Gabi and Fabian arranged to come back to Conade at 8 p.m. that evening and bring Gabi's parents with them for a drink.

That afternoon, the entire team gathered in the lobby before setting out for the shopping mall Gabi and Fabian had recommended. Nobody wanted to stay behind this time. Sophie gave Anton her Spanish phrase book and a few pesos of spending money. She hoped she would find a nice-looking sombrero for Hayden.

They headed off in the same direction as for the grocery store in their familiar sea of black uniforms, with Sophie surrounded in the middle. Just after the bridge where Sophie received her traditional eyeballing, they arrived at the outside of the mall – the graffiti-covered, turquoise brick wall they had walked past on every previous trip.

The team entered the large building not really knowing what to expect. And, wow! It was hard to believe this expensive, chic mall had been hidden behind such a humble-looking exterior!

The air conditioning was the first thing that made an impression on Sophie. It was so lovely and cool. Almost too cold! The first shop they walked through to get to the main atrium was a department store stocked full of beautiful bags and purses, make-up and perfume, shoes and jewellery – all in locked glass cases. It was breathtaking.

Then they were in the atrium of the mall – it was huge! Sophie was in awe.

Brett whispered to her, 'Did you notice? Even the women working in that department store were hypnotised watching you!'

He was looking out for her safety, but she hadn't noticed and wished he hadn't drawn her attention to it. Now she felt like she was being stalked by the public.

'I'm sure it's only because they don't see many blonde women,' Sophie said, uncomfortably brushing it off.

'No. I'm convinced they think you're a supermodel or a movie star or something!' Brett was being completely honest. But Sophie blushed and laughed. She wasn't convinced at all.

Having set a meeting time and place for the team, and having reiterated the buddy system for everyone's safety, the five adults set off to explore the mall. On the ground floor, they found a pharmacy kiosk where Sophie discovered Tylenol (paracetamol), Advil (ibuprofen) and metoclopramide (anti-nausea). She stocked up her supplies. In addition to these medications, the shop had all kinds of antibiotics that could be purchased over the counter without a prescription. Fascinating!

'We can't buy any antibiotics over the counter in New Zealand!' she remarked to Brett.

Brett smiled as he watched her. Just as she had been in the medical supplies shop they had visited in Salt Lake City, Sophie was entranced, like a little kid in a candy store. He waited quietly and patiently for her, while Roger, Harry and Benny went ahead to the Levi's denim store.

At another shop, they bought three bottles of wine for their gathering that night with Gabi and her family. Sophie's search for a sombrero for Hayden was unsuccessful – this flash mall was way too upmarket to stock such a thing.

Then the five of them stopped for coffee and a snack in a little side café on the second floor. They sat chatting, enjoying each other's company and arguably the best coffee they'd had since leaving Salt Lake City. They indulged in idle chit-chat – it was really pleasant and very relaxing. So nice to not have to talk rink stuff for a little while.

Soon enough their hour and a half was up, so they gathered the troops and headed back to Conade Castle. The workmen on the bridge downed tools once more to stare at Sophie as the team passed underneath.

Chapter Twenty-Eight

CHEMICAL COCKTAIL

In the lobby of the sports village, Sophie and Brett met up with Felix and Frank and their managers, just in time to be collected by the bus, which whisked them back to the San Jeronimo Rink for yet another inspection. Brett had placed the gas detector in Sophie's backpack. Hopefully she would soon receive her oxygen saturation monitor.

The rink smelled awful again, but it certainly looked and sounded a bit different. More rubber had been laid on the concrete in the benches to protect the players' skate blades. The four new fans were connected, working and humming loudly. Brett did all his fancy measurements to calculate the airflow and he seemed satisfied. Work on the changing room fans hadn't yet started, but the units were there, sitting along the back wall of the rink. Meanwhile, as usual, five staff were slop-mopping the rubber matting surrounding the ice pad.

The doctor's amigo was waiting to greet them. This time Sophie hung back. She didn't bother trying to talk to him. He handed an oxygen saturations monitor to Brett and showed him how to use it. Brett thanked him profusely. Sophie simply nodded to him as he left, but she couldn't bring herself to smile. Was she being rude? She reconciled this in her mind – the bad cop never smiles.

Brett brought the monitor over to her and she recognised the model immediately. It was basic, but it would definitely do the trick.

Brett carefully put it into Sophie's backpack and drew out his gas detector. As soon as he switched it on it started beeping again, but this time more quickly. Sophie took a closer look. The one light that was flashing was adjacent to the letters 'Cl' and the area beside it showed the number 5.5.

'Cl is chlorine, isn't it?' Sophie remembered from her nursing biochemistry class. 'But where's it coming from?'

'I'd put money on that cleaning product they're mopping the floors with. I was thinking about it last night, but it clicked when we came in and saw the staff mopping again this morning. I'm getting a higher reading than I did yesterday – it's up to 5.5 parts per million.'

Without hesitation, Brett headed straight for the rink's main office and Sophie followed. He asked the rink manager about the product they were using to mop the floors. The rink manager led them to the nearest mop and bucket and picked up the bottle to show Brett.

Under cross-examination, the story unfolded. It transpired that the staff rarely cleaned the floors and were inexperienced at doing so, being that they usually just hosed them down. Making a special effort for the international tournament, they had ordered cleaning bleach but had never used the product before. So they had simply tipped it into their buckets then slop-mopped it all over the floor. Day after day.

Brett read the label on the bottle, which was printed in Spanish and English, and realised the problem immediately. The directions were to mix one part bleach to 20 parts water – they had been using full-strength undiluted industrial bleach. No wonder the monitor was going off!

In his ever-respectful way, Brett pointed out that they could save a considerable amount of money if they watered down the product, because the floors were already so much better now. The rink manager was very appreciative of the advice.

Brett had a new-found friend, and before long the man was chatting about all kinds of things, including some interesting information about the night the carbon monoxide poisoning had occurred.

The television crews that were present to cover the games had brought their own diesel generators to run their equipment. The rink manager had stood near one of the TV crews during the first period of the New Zealand game and said the diesel smell was so overwhelming that he felt like he was going to pass out. He'd had to move away.

Brett realised that this particular generator had been positioned directly in front of the intake for what he had discovered was the 'fresh air' circulation system. Effectively, the diesel fumes were being sucked straight into the intake, then circulated throughout the entire rink.

Sophie was watching Brett in action. He had an amazing way with people and she could see that the rink manager trusted him.

Brett asked the man about all the wonderful painting they had been doing in the rink, complimenting him on all their hard work. Of course the rink manager's chest puffed out and he was only too happy to give Brett and Sophie a guided tour of the amazing make-over. The redecorating had been completed just before the tournament had started.

Brett asked to see the type of paint they had used to obtain such a polished finish. As the rink manager pointed to the paint cans, Brett immediately recognised the symbol on the labels that showed the paint was lead-based. The TV news station in New Zealand that reported poisoning from lead fumes had not been so inaccurate after all!

Brett and Sophie shook the rink manager's hand, thanked him warmly, and went on their way. They didn't breathe a word about any of this newly discovered information until they were safely back on the bus to Conade, then Brett fully debriefed the others.

'So I was right in thinking there was more than one chemical in the mix. It was like inhaling a chemical cocktail!' Sophie exclaimed, after Brett had finished. 'First, carbon monoxide from the Zamboni – the silent killer – odourless, colourless, tasteless. Second, chlorine – from the cleaning bleach – which measured 5.5 parts per million today, even with the new fans going full speed. That would account for the burning nasal passages too. Third, diesel fumes – from the two generators used by the TV crew. And fourth, several fresh coats of lead-based paint. Holy freakin' cow! We really were on thin ice! It's a miracle we survived!'

The team managers sat silently on the bus for the remainder of the trip back to Conade, contemplating just how serious the entire situation had been. They had been lucky to get away with their lives. They each thought of their loved ones back home. Sophie thought of Hayden and her parents, unwillingly picturing their faces and imagining how they would have reacted if they had been told that their beloved mother/daughter and brother/grandson had tragically died.

She didn't think of Charlie.

It was 6.45 p.m. by the time the bus arrived back at Conade. After they had picked at their usual evening meal of atrocious slop, Brett and Sophie went to see about using the computer to do more research on gas poisoning. Rather than the fake-smiling assistant, the pleasant older woman was on duty at the reception desk. They weren't sure if she understood all of what they said, but she simply smiled and held up the key without a word, even though they hadn't booked. Sophie took the key with a big smile and a thank you, before the woman had a chance to reconsider.

According to the World Health Organisation's 'Emergency Exposure Guidance Levels', the safe level for a maximum of 15 minutes chlorine gas exposure was one part per million. The detector had shown over five times that amount. There was no way of knowing for sure, but Sophie wanted to bet it had been at least that same dangerous level on the evening of the gas poisoning – and exposure had been for far longer than 15 minutes! She remembered the staff had been mopping the rubber matting as they entered the rink while the public session was still on. That was four hours before the team had started to get really sick.

Some of the effects of chlorine poisoning were shortness of breath, nausea and vomiting, headaches, dizziness, burning nasal passages and lungs, and body weakness – mostly similar to carbon monoxide, but with a few imperative differences.

Sophie and Brett took the opportunity to check their emails and found one from Jolana, the chef de mission, and Henry, the New Zealand Ice Hockey Federation president. They were both grateful for all Sophie and the management had done so far, but urged them to tread carefully. Confirming Brett and Sophie's fears, they felt that the cancellation of the games might make it difficult for the team to get out of Mexico safely.

There was a bit of backlash from some of the parents, as expected. A few of the parents had initially freaked out and, in desperation, emailed Brett to demand that their kids be put on the next plane home to New Zealand. However, they had then written again, apologetically, having re-evaluated the situation, and were nothing but incredibly appreciative of the care their boys had received.

The most welcome email, which also explained the parents' more appreciative messages, was from Dr Nate to the team and parents, with Sophie copied in – 'As a result of Sophie's timely intervention, in instituting appropriate care and treatment for the players, the situation was handled extremely well. I want to acknowledge her input and congratulate her for a job well done! I feel confident that the players should all make a full recovery, and am confident in Sophie to look after their wellbeing.'

Sophie felt elated. Vindicated. She had made a real difference in these boys' lives. But in the same breath, she also knew she was simply lucky enough to be in the right place at the right time, and doing what she was trained to do.

Scary though, to think she'd had to plead with Charlie to be allowed to go on this trip in the first place. His own son could have died.

Brett and Sophie shut down the computer, locked the room, and took the key back to the lobby.

Just before Gabi and her parents were due to arrive, Sophie caught up with Anton in his room. He was feeling fine. Barely a headache, he reassured her. Steele was also feeling well. As she went about her rounds, she checked on Matthew and Kieran. Although they were still a little surly, answering her with one word answers, they were both doing much better. Their headaches were at about four out of ten and they had no nausea. To their credit, they both said thank you as she left their room.

Brett and Roger had ventured down to the lobby to phone the Pedregal Palace and let Friderik Babic know they were satisfied with progress at the rink. They waited to meet Fabian, Gabi and her parents when they arrived, then led the way up to Sophie's room. Of course there were no chairs, but everyone found a spot somewhere on the two steel-framed beds.

Over wine and beer, Gabi's parents told the New Zealanders that their eight year old son had become very ill during the gas poisoning. He had made a full recovery though and was at home with Gabi's other sister. It was upsetting to hear that someone so young had been affected. The New Zealanders talked about how serious the politics had become and Sophie told the story of how Juan had threatened to make her disappear.

Gabi's parents made a genuine offer for the whole team to stay at their beach house in Acapulco if they needed to find somewhere safe. Sophie and the others were extremely grateful to have that as a backup plan, but they were feeling quietly confident that the worst was over.

The rest of the visit was laughter and friendly chatter, as they learnt about each other's lives. Everyone said their goodbyes just before the 10 p.m. curfew. Best not to tangle with the guards again!

Sophie went to bed that night feeling less of a nagging feeling in her stomach. The games were going to continue. Surely nothing else could possibly go wrong…

She was in bed by 11 p.m. but slept restlessly once again, tossing and turning. Two taxi drivers were chasing her and she was hiding in a cave that had four huge extractor and blower fans. The evil men found her and smothered her face with a mask and were gassing her, only her oxygen monitor wouldn't work.

Water pipes banged loudly in the walls and ceiling above her room, waking her several times in the night. Each time she drifted back to sleep, but the nightmares continued.

Chapter Twenty-Nine

WEDNESDAY, NZ VS. SOUTH AFRICA

Wednesday morning went like clockwork. Up. Shower. Breakfast slop. All the teams were in the mess hall for breakfast. But Mexico had once again separated themselves and didn't interact with anyone.

Sophie raced back to her room with her backpack and collected the gas detector, oxygen monitor, the C's from Stephen's shirts, and her sewing kit. The team met in the lobby at 9.30 a.m. sharp and boarded their bus. When they arrived at the rink, so long as work had progressed as expected, the players could get back on the ice for a light training. Harry assured the boys that nobody was under any pressure to train.

Stephen and Matthew were still saying 'no way' to playing, although Sophie had ruled out Matthew anyway, on health grounds, for the remainder of the tournament. Brett had given them the choice of being confined to their rooms back at Conade or sitting quietly in the grandstand at the rink and watching. He didn't want their negative attitudes affecting the rest of the team.

As for Bradley and Kieran, it was obvious that, although they were trying to be loyal to Stephen, they were both chomping at the bit to get back on the ice. Kieran needed another day or two to recover, but Brad was ready to go. They both seemed to be in pretty good spirits.

Tom and Verne had seamlessly taken over the roles of mentor and big buddy for some of the younger players. They had really stepped up, showing their maturity. And their wicked humour was a welcome breath of fresh air, given the sullen, negative demeanour that Stephen had adopted.

Just before the bus arrived at the rink, Harry announced to the players that they wouldn't need their full gear – just padded shorts, shin guards, helmets and skates. He divided the team in two by standing half way down the centre aisle. The players in the front half of the bus were to wear their away shirts and the back half of the bus would wear their home shirts.

'Touch rugby!' he yelled, and the boys cheered.

This sounds like fun, thought Sophie, smiling. Trust Harry to come up with such an innovative way to ease the team back onto the ice.

Inside the arena, Brett made a point of showing the boys the powerful blower fans at the end of the rink. When Sophie walked past it, her hair blew wildly like a hurricane and the whole team laughed.

In their change room, they discovered a one metre hole had been cut into the wall, but the fan was sitting next to it, not yet installed.

Sophie, Brett and Roger waited in the players' benches. Brett had his gas detector and Sophie's oxygen saturation monitor out of her backpack in no time. He intended to circle the ice pad and take measurements throughout the entire training. Sophie would measure oxygen levels and heart rates each time the boys were subbed off during the training session.

It was wonderful to see the players back on the ice as they threw the rugby ball around, scrambling backwards and forwards on their skates. The game was filled with fun and laughter. Sophie noticed that oxygen levels were remaining low throughout the session. The average was around 90 to 92 percent – 96 and above was considered normal. Levels of 90 to 92 percent were common in people with pneumonia and emphysema. She tested the monitor on herself – 89 percent – but apart from being tired and a little dizzy, she had no other symptoms. And all the boys said they felt fine.

The emergency doors were fully open, guarded as promised, and all four fans were roaring.

Sophie watched the defiants. Stephen wasn't a bundle of joy, sitting in the grandstand on the opposite side of the rink. He had Kieran, Bradley and Matthew with him. Matthew had saved face when other players had asked if he was going to play by saying, 'Sophie won't let me.' Sophie had just smiled and apologised for not wanting him to die. He knew as well as she did that he wouldn't recover the same as the others because of his childhood poisoning. But she didn't mind being the scapegoat.

Kieran was looking keener to play, but was torn between wanting to get back on the ice and wanting to side with Stephen. He was being rebellious for the sake of it. But it was a moot point either way because his vitals weren't yet back to normal. He only had a four out of ten headache but with significant dizziness and low blood pressure, so Sophie wouldn't clear him to get back on the ice.

Brad was a different matter. It was very obvious to Sophie, watching him from the other side of the arena, that he was becoming more and more restless during the touch rugby game, walking around the sides of the rink, watching intently. All good signs.

After the game, Harry gathered the players to vote for a new team captain. They sat in the grandstand opposite the defiants, who would not be eligible to vote this time. Harry gathered up the small pieces of paper, then counted the votes one by one. It was almost unanimous – Tom would be the replacement captain, and Verne would step into Tom's alternate captain position. Dave would of course keep his position as second alternate. Tom and Verne were both surprised, humbled and absolutely rapt. They had shown real leadership and mentoring abilities in the last couple of days and their teammates had rewarded them accordingly.

Tom and Verne fetched their second shirts from the change room and took their playing shirts off, giving both to Sophie to stitch on the C's and A's respectively.

As the boys went to the change room to dress, Harry said to Sophie, 'Can you just tack them on?' He still believed in Stephen and was betting he wouldn't be long out of the captain's position.

The five adults met briefly while the boys were changing and agreed they were satisfied with the conditions of the rink. They felt sure the other teams would be too. Brett would make the phone call to Friderik Babic – the games would officially resume. In just a few hours!

The New Zealand team boarded the bus back to Conade to grab an early lunch. Afterwards they took a quick walk to the grocery store for supplies, workmen staring, as always, as the team passed underneath the bridge. Then back to Conade, and straight on the bus to the rink again, all by 2 p.m. Clockwork organisational precision.

Brett had announced they wouldn't be bothering with the 'take-out dinner slop boxes,' and that they would do 'something much better' instead. Everyone was quietly relieved and a little intrigued.

The New Zealand team arrived at the rink slightly ahead of schedule. In the change room, Brett immediately attempted to turn on the one metre fan, which had now been installed. Hooray! It worked! The boys put on their off-ice gear then began their warm-up outside in the parking lot.

Sophie followed to watch Anton. He had been in good spirits and was fired up to play hockey. *Everything's going to be okay,* thought Sophie as she put on her iPod headphones, pressed shuffle on her three songs, and cranked up the volume. Without realising, she had started singing quietly to herself, 'November Rain', smiling as she watched her darling boy.

Three of the four defiants were starting to thaw out and had even talked to Sophie during the course of the afternoon. Matthew and Brad came and sat quietly by Sophie, watching the off-ice training. Matthew seemed to have forgiven her for standing him down. He was looking forward to watching the game. Harry had asked him if he wanted to be on the benches as the gate opener. He was chuffed. He couldn't play but he could still be a pivotal part of the team. And the boys would benefit from his support.

Bradley was back to his cheerful cheeky self, still siding with Stephen, but to a much lesser extent.

During the warm-up, he tapped her on the arm. He wanted to talk. Sophie duly took off her headphones.

'What if we all get gas poisoned again? Wouldn't we just, like, die next time?' he asked quietly. He obviously wanted to play, but the poor kid was just plain terrified.

'I think we're going to be fine,' Sophie answered back softly. 'The Zamboni is properly fixed. The big doors will be open. The fans will provide ventilation and Brett will be monitoring the air quality. I'll have the oxygen monitor on the benches, and I'll be keeping an eye on everyone throughout the whole game. So if anything does go wrong, this time we'll know about it *waaaay* before we get sick.'

Brad didn't look convinced.

'But, why don't you just wait and see how you feel,' Sophie suggested quietly to him.

'Okay. Thanks, Mum,' he replied, nodding.

Sophie smiled, put her headphones back on, and to lighten the mood, started singing out loud to 'November Rain', then played air-guitar through the riff. Matthew and Brad laughed at her performance.

She was singing the end of the song, 'Don't ya think that you need somebody, Don't ya think that you need someone, Everybody needs somebody, You're not the only one,' and thinking how true that was, when she was suddenly interrupted.

At some point Juan and his off-sider, Raul, had appeared in the parking lot and were now engaged in a heated discussion with Brett and Roger. Friderik Babic appeared to be refereeing the conversation. Apparently Juan was trying to have the New Zealand team expelled from the tournament on the grounds that they had played on-ice touch rugby without wearing their full protective gear. This man was a piece of work! Babic shut down the line of attack and ordered Juan and Raul to remove themselves from the New Zealand team's warm-up area.

Kieran and Stephen had stayed at the other end of the parking lot during the warm-up, but now followed the team back into the arena and sat in the grandstand while the players changed into their full hockey gear. Kieran was noticeably quiet. Sophie wondered if he, too, was having second thoughts about boycotting the game.

Sophie waited on the benches after collecting snow to make her ice packs with Roger in tow. So far, the players' vital signs had been normal enough. The chlorine smell had diminished. She assumed the cleaners had stopped their usual routine after Brett's input the previous day, or had at least watered down the bleach.

Brett ducked in and out of the changing room, gas detector in hand, checking the time on the scoreboard as it counted down.

Someone called out Sophie's name from the grandstand and she turned to see Fabian and Gabi with her parents and little brother. They were all smiling and waving. Sophie cheerfully waved back.

She scanned the crowd, wondering where Carlos and Julio were. There was no sign of them. *Great hosts,* she thought sarcastically.

The scoreboard clock continued to tick down and soon the boys entered the playing area for their brief on-ice warm-up, before retreating to their change room again.

As the Zamboni cleaned the ice, Brett lapped the rink with the gas detector. It didn't beep and no lights flashed. So far, so good.

The buzzer sounded and the boys made their way back into the arena to line up for the national anthems of New Zealand and South Africa. The announcer called out the players' names, just as badly pronounced as the first game, then Tom and the South African captain swapped souvenir pennants and badges.

New Zealand performed their haka, with more passion than their first game, and finished with a resounding 'Heee!' The crowd clapped tamely, except for the small contingent of black-jacket-wearing New Zealand fans, who whistled and cheered.

The referee's whistle blew. Game on. The first period was a flurry of activity and New Zealand's passing was smooth and accurate. Anton scored two goals and Nigel even assisted one from his own goal mouth.

Sophie was kept busy monitoring each player as they came off the ice. All oxygen levels were steady at 90 to 92 percent, including Matthew as he opened the bench gate, and heart rates were only as fast as she would expect, considering how hard they were skating. Players reported no symptoms. The gas detector remained silent.

When the buzzer sounded for the end of first period, the score was 5–0 to New Zealand. The players, Harry, Benny and Sophie with her medical bag all retreated to the change room. After unlocking the change room door, Brett went back out to lap the ice pad, monitoring the air quality while the Zamboni cleaned the playing surface. Roger guarded the players' bench. Harry and Benny talked strategy, passing and shooting to the team.

Sophie suddenly realised Brad was standing beside her. He had fire in his eyes.

'Harry, I'm ready! I wanna play!' he burst out.

'Well, you better get a move on and gear up then!' Harry answered back.

Brett came in and gave them the two minute warning. As the rest of the team left the change room, Brad hurriedly scrambled to get into his gear. He made it onto the ice about five minutes into the second period, and skated his socks off! Sophie had never seen him play so well. She paid extra attention to monitoring him – only because she knew how worried he had been – but his vitals stayed stable throughout.

Near the end of each of the three periods, Sophie raced up into the grandstand to measure Stephen, Kieran and Matthew's vitals. She knew they would be fine because if the players breathing in the gases closest to the Zamboni were okay, those in the grandstand would be even safer. Her reason for checking the boys was purely for their own reassurance. They thanked her each time.

The buzzer sounded for the end of the game and New Zealand had triumphed by ten goals to three. It had been a tougher game than the one against Mongolia. Nigel had played the first two periods and only let two goals through. Beauden played the last period and his defences were only breached once. Having arrived on the ice in the second period, Brad had played his fiercest game ever, although as a result, he'd spent 14 minutes of it in the penalty bin!

It had been a high-quality, competitive, fast game but without any animosity between the teams. The refereeing was fair and consistent.

There had been no need for the oxygen on the benches or in the change rooms. Sophie chatted briefly to Felix, who reported that his boys were also fit and well. Everyone had come through unscathed and the playing conditions hadn't created any ill-effects.

Sophie gave Anton a quick hug as he passed by on his way to the change room.

'Great goals, bud!' she said. Of course, she had to follow it up with the traditional line, 'Pooh, you stink!' Anton laughed.

'Thanks Mum!' he answered, beaming from ear to ear.

Fabian, Gabi and her family came down from the grandstand to congratulate the team on their win. They were almost more excited about the result than Sophie was!

As she said her goodbyes, Gabi said, 'We see you there.' Sophie was perplexed. She didn't know what this meant, but politely agreed, 'Okay.' Maybe something had been lost in translation.

Stephen, Kieran and Matthew had followed their teammates into the change room and were congratulating them on the win as Sophie arrived.

Sophie detected a degree of remorse on Stephen and Kieran's faces.

The players were feeling great. They had survived the game and nothing had gone wrong.

Brett handed out the game pucks. It was tradition that when a player scored his first ever goal at world championship level, he would receive the puck he scored it with.

Anton received his lucky puck and passed it to his mother for safekeeping. Sophie was nearly exploding with pride!

The boys changed quickly, then, without staying to watch the next game, Brett led the whole team on a 'short walk to dinner'. Everyone was once again chatting, laughing, smiling and telling stories and jokes. But it was dark outside and Sophie was nervous.

As they walked along the pavement, Brett suddenly lurched to one side as he stepped into a pot hole, rolling his ankle. He nearly fell, but quickly recovered his balance on his agile karate feet. Sophie just about leapt through her skin and had screamed out loud when she saw him stumble.

'Are you okay? Did you hurt yourself?' she asked Brett, forcing her voice to sound calm. She was trying hard not to fuss over him, but realised her scream hadn't gone unnoticed. Brett's ankle was fine – no damage done – but Sophie's heart was beating through her chest. The situation had startled her, proving that her nervous system was still very much on high alert.

Two blocks later, Sophie's heart-rate still hadn't returned to normal as they arrived outside an Italian restaurant. Gabi and family were there to meet them. So that was what Gabi had meant by 'We see you there'! Brett had arranged for them all to join the team for dinner. What a lovely surprise.

The boys found their seats across five tables within the restaurant. Sophie's stress-response slowly lessened as she enjoyed a beautiful, relaxing meal and great company with their Mexican friends.

Gabi and Fabian arranged to accompany the team on their rest day activities. They were excited to be able to show the New Zealanders the good side of their city – the beautiful landmarks, buildings, markets, and lots of sights along the way, with the highlight being the Teotihuacan Pyramids. The team bus would leave at 10 a.m. the next morning, and they had the whole day free.

Yahoo! Sophie was getting excited now and couldn't wait.

There still had been no sign of Carlos or Julio all day. Sophie wished Gabi and Fabian could be their hosts instead.

Back at Conade Castle, the players all headed for the showers, then straight to bed. It had turned out to be a lovely day, but it was after 10 p.m., and nobody wanted to have a run-in with the guards. 'Pooh, you still smell!' Sophie said to Anton again, smiling, as she hugged him goodnight outside his room.

Chapter Thirty

THURSDAY, DOUBLE-CROSS DAY

The alarm on Sophie's phone jolted her awake. She stretched, replaying the night's instalment of nightmares. This time, two evil cartoonish taxi drivers had hauled her through a blackened cave, gassing her via a face mask. She had kept standing in pot holes and twisting her ankles. There was no knight in shining armour.

She dragged herself out of bed. Brett's room was empty, and Roger was outside guarding the door. She showered, and washed and styled her hair. It felt good to know that the team didn't have to go to the rink that day. At all.

Today was their official rest day. Their trip to the pyramids. She dressed in a denim mini skirt, a white t-shirt and little black kitten heels, and carefully applied a little mascara and lip gloss. Then, with backpack on, she walked with Roger and met some of the team in the lobby.

At the mess hall, Sophie checked over all the players. Everyone was now feeling pretty good, except Kieran. He was the only player who had any real symptoms. His headache was a dull three out of ten and he was still a little dizzy when he stood up too quickly. Sophie had said, 'Nope, still not ready to play,' much to his relief. This meant he could keep up the facade of being a bit surly and stay loyal to Stephen.

By then, the team had given up trying to convince the remaining two defiants to play. The boys were determined to enjoy their fun day, then get on with what they had come to Mexico to do – play hockey.

Sophie and Brett said goodbye to Roger as he left to attend the officials' function then, just before 10 a.m., the team piled out of the gates of Conade Concentration Camp and down through the three point security check on foot.

The bus for their day out was a bigger, more luxurious coach with air conditioning. Their instructions were to meet the driver in a little side alley outside the sports village.

Gabi and Fabian were waiting there to greet them, and Carlos and Julio had turned up as well. Their hosts had been noticeably absent the whole of the day before. Even for their game against South Africa. How convenient that they would turn up now, for the fun day! But of course, in true New Zealand style, the team happily welcomed them.

The bus was waiting with its engine running, so they all clambered on board.

While waiting in the coach, Stephen was mouthing off to anyone who would listen. He was still negative about playing and it occurred to Sophie he was trying to recruit followers. Didn't he realise he was fighting a losing battle? Matthew had become rather neutral, choosing not to comment but was still sitting by Stephen. Kieran was rather quiet and contemplative. As for Bradley, he was completely over the whole situation and had now distanced himself from the others.

Tom and Verne continued to be great leaders and role models, and their wicked humour was still a welcome breath of fresh air that helped offset Stephen's sullen, obstructive demeanour.

Most of the boys were excitedly chatting about the day ahead and the remainder of the games to come. Sophie was three rows back from her normal spot at the front of the coach, so she could sit near Gabi and Fabian. She was chatting to Gabi about her studies in Mexico City. Brett was standing just inside the doorway of the bus, talking to Carlos and Julio, who were relaying messages to their same non-English speaking driver. The engine was running, but nobody seemed to know what or who they were waiting for. Twenty minutes had gone by as they sat there.

'What exactly are we waiting for?' Sophie overheard Roger ask Brett.

'Apparently, the driver has to wait for some instruction from his boss before we can go. I don't understand what the problem is,' Brett answered, shaking his head, sounding unimpressed.

So everyone patiently carried on chatting, feeling sure the situation would sort itself out. Gabi was quite tearful as she recounted the story of how her little brother had lost consciousness then vomited relentlessly the night of the gas poisoning. She had thought he was going to die. To reassure Gabi, Sophie regaled her with the full medical details of everything she had found out about the chemical cocktail they had all endured, focussing on details about how carboxyhaemoglobin leaves the body within four to five hours, meaning that Gabi's little brother shouldn't experience any ongoing complications.

Another 15 minutes had passed and the engine was still running. Brett appeared to be getting nowhere with the driver. The man was getting more and more agitated. Carlos phoned someone and talked to Julio and the driver. Sophie couldn't make out anything Brett was saying over the noisy engine and the chatter in the coach, but she was sure he would have it under control.

Gabi and Fabian went on to tell Sophie about their plans to visit New Zealand after Gabi had finished her study. They wanted to get work visas so they could stay with Gabi's sister, Brigid, for a year or two. Gabi's English was okay but she struggled to remember words and sometimes put her phrases together wrongly. Whereas Fabian was quite fluent. He had learned in school, he told Sophie. As the conversation continued, Fabian got up from his seat and stood in the aisle a little closer to the front of the bus, listening intently.

Five more minutes passed, then suddenly Fabian turned and started yelling at Carlos and Julio in Spanish, waving his arms above his head. Carlos and Julio yelled back at him with their own set of gestures. The driver stood up and joined in, then Gabi also joined the fray.

What on earth was going on?

Fabian started to translate to Brett what Carlos and Julio had been saying in Spanish. They had been caught out because Fabian had overheard their private conversation. That was why he'd gotten out of his seat – so that he could listen more closely.

Brett was under the impression the delay was because the coach company hadn't received payment for the day trip, and therefore, the coach driver was awaiting the green light from his boss to say they had now been paid. The Mexican Ice Hockey Federation, with the money they received to host the tournament, and according to the rule book, were to pay for each coach and driver for the teams' rest days.

Carlos was supposed to be phoning Juan the Mexican coach/president to sort the issue out. But instead, he had faked the call. Carlos, Julio and the driver had plotted to make the team wait for another 10 or 15 minutes, then tell them the trip was cancelled.

Brett was extremely annoyed that Carlos and Julio had tried to double-cross them. This was absolute betrayal. And it was sabotage. They were planning to ruin the New Zealand team's rest day! Was it part of their ploy to help Mexico win the tournament, by first putting them up in shabby accommodation, not feed them decent food, not supply enough water, poison them with a chemical cocktail of gases, then ruin the one proper outing they were supposed to have?

After ordering Carlos and Julio to either take their seats or get off the coach, and after a good 10 minutes of hard, heated bargaining between Brett and the driver, with Fabian translating this time, Brett finally agreed to pay the driver US$1000. He would give the man half now, but would not hand over the other half until the end of the day, when the team were safely delivered back to Conade.

The situation was criminal. But the driver essentially had them over a barrel. It was already 10.50 a.m. – there wasn't time to organise another bus, and this was the team's only day off. There was no way of verifying whether the payment story was true, and even if Brett could have reached Juan by phone, he wouldn't trust him to tell him the truth anyway. The whole thing stunk of corruption and it seemed as if almost everyone was 'on the take'.

The boys heard some of the commotion. But only the adults would ever know the full story. They had to protect their players from these kinds of distractions and anxieties.

Sophie didn't understand why Brett had allowed Carlos and Julio to stay on the bus. 'It's like the old adage says,' he would tell her later, 'keep your friends close, and your enemies closer.' During the coach trip, he managed to get around every player and quietly tell them, 'Carlos and Julio tried to double-cross us. Do *not* tell them any team secrets. Do *not* trust them at all.'

None of players questioned this instruction.

Chapter Thirty-One

THE PYRAMID OF THE MOON

Finally, almost an hour late, the coach carrying the New Zealand team was en route to the Teotihuacan Pyramids. With fascination, the boys took in the scenery and buildings they passed along the way. Mexico City was a colourful mix of palatial homes, with shanty town corrugated iron shacks barely standing up in between. The road systems were just as bad as on previous days, as the traffic swerved and dodged around them with its usual chaotic confusion, horns blaring endlessly. Their driver only had two speeds – flat out, or stopped.

Even sitting near the front of the bus, Sophie felt incredibly motion sick by the time they reached their destination an hour and a quarter later. She thought of Hayden and was glad for his sake that he wasn't there. He had unfortunately inherited his mother's vulnerability to motion sickness, having become infamous, when he was nine years old, for getting off a team bus on a Friendship Ice Hockey Tour in Canada and puking right in front of the bus steps… Sophie was very grateful not to have done the same!

Brett had put the same buddy system rules in place for exploring the area around the pyramids. The team was to meet at 1 p.m. at El Jaguar, the Mexican restaurant on the north-east corner of the grounds.

Everyone got off the coach, then Brett, Harry, Benny, Gabi,

243

Fabian and Sophie set off together. They wandered through the markets on their way towards the restaurant. The souvenirs were all beautiful, colourful and very cheap.

Sophie was on the lookout for the perfect sombrero for Hayden. She spotted a stunning big, black and silver sombrero that she thought was an absolute beauty and immediately bought it. It was only NZ$20, and Hayden would love it! She still hadn't figured out how she was going to get it safely home to New Zealand, but she would worry about that later. For now, she would wear it. At least she didn't have to worry about getting sunburnt!

The market stands offered an abundance of handmade silver jewellery, bags, clothing, shoes and trinkets. Some of the boys bought gifts for their parents, siblings and girlfriends. Sophie bought four silver bangles for herself that had detailed, traditional Aztec markings engraved on them. She had fallen in love with them at first sight. They were incredibly cheap at only NZ$3 each. Anton and some of the other boys bought traditional green, white and red Mexican ponchos and wore them for the rest of the day. Others bought themselves sombreros. Beauden was wandering around in a magnificent black and gold one.

'Maybe when Beauden and Hayden's club teams play each other next time, they could wear their sombreros on top of their goalie helmets!' Sophie joked to Brett who laughed with her.

They picked up brochures on their walk through the grounds. Sophie learnt a range of impressive facts: The pyramids had taken 350 years to build, starting in 100BC; because Teotihuacan City was so large, it became the centre of the entire Mesoamerican region; Teotihuacan means, 'The place where the gods were born'; the city had flourished with jewellers, potters and craftsmen who helped create artefacts that are still being uncovered today; the 'Pyramid of the Sun' is the third largest pyramid in the world, stands 200 feet high, has 248 steps to the top, is built over a cave, and is still considered extremely sacred; it is located east of the 'Avenue of the Dead'; the Aztecs worshipped a number of gods – the Great Goddess, the Storm God, the Old God, the Feathered Serpent, the War Serpent, the Netted Jaguar, the Fat God and the Pulque God (pulque is a traditional Mexican alcoholic drink made from fermented agave sap).

With the positive effects of fresh air away from the pollution of Mexico City, and a good walk through the markets, Sophie was starting to feel much more relaxed and content. By the time the team met at the restaurant, she realised she was famished. She was hoping like crazy that the food here was nothing like Conade's slop. What she wanted was real vegetables, or some fruit, and maybe even some delicious, fresh, warm corn tortillas.

Brett had organised 'two long tables for 28, please'. Thankfully, because the area was a tourist hotspot, there were English menus and English-speaking wait staff. Sophie ordered a vegetable dish, baked in a traditional earthenware pot, with a mild traditional Mexican sauce. Just what she was craving, and it sounded divine!

Their four waiters brought out plenty of fresh, warm corn tortillas for everyone to nibble on while they were waiting for the main course. A three-man Mariachi band, wearing huge sombreros, embroidered waistcoats and enormous moustaches, played their Mexican guitars and a trumpet, singing jovially as they wandered from table to table.

Before long, lunch was served. Sophie admired the handmade, glazed, terracotta pot with matching lid that her meal arrived in. If she could have bought the dish to take home, she would have. It was filled to the brim, and she struggled to finish it but was determined not to leave behind a single morsel of food. She almost always lost weight on these trips and this one hadn't turned out to be any different so far.

Part way through the meal, the Mariachis arrived at the New

Zealanders' table and stood directly behind Sophie, serenading her. It was quite lovely and all the boys were cheering them on, clapping in time to the music and singing some of the words to the one tune everyone recognised – 'La Cucaracha'.

Sophie sat back and watched all the boys. Every single player was smiling, laughing, chatting to others and genuinely enjoying themselves. She realised she hadn't stopped smiling since getting off the coach when they had arrived. Their day off had turned out to be exactly what everyone needed – fun, laughter, camaraderie, and a really good start towards healing some of the emotional wounds of the last few days.

Sophie felt sure this would be the day that would turn the trip around.

Brett tipped the band as they finished their performance. Then he paid the bill for the meal and the team headed back out to the pyramid grounds. They explored some of the archaeological sites where Aztec artefacts had been discovered, looked at two of the smaller pyramids – the Pyramid of the Moon and the Pyramid of the Feathered Serpent – then finally arrived at the main attraction – the Pyramid of the Sun. This was the pyramid they all wanted to climb.

It was slow progress up the large, uneven, steep steps – no mean feat considering the combined residual effects of high altitude and gas poisoning. A handful of the team had reached the top of the pyramid and were already on their way back down, passing Sophie and the other adults near the top of the third tier.

It was about 10 minutes before the closing time of 5 p.m., and they needed to return to the bus soon. They were taking their time to look around at the incredible architectural structure and the views, before tackling the last, steepest and most difficult tier of the pyramid. It would only take them a few minutes.

Suddenly, they heard large vehicles roaring towards the pyramid with their horns blasting. They turned to see three army trucks, each carrying about 20 armed military police. Some of the team thought the MPs were coming to escort them out of the grounds, so with Brett giving the rallying call, 'C'mon boys, it's now or never!' they shimmied up the last part of the pyramid on their hands and feet, so they could say they had made it to the top. They weren't going to give up when they had gotten so close.

However, Sophie, whose legs went wobbly and turned to jelly at the merest thought of heights, was already well outside her comfort zone and was definitely not going to shimmy up the last tier in a mini skirt, backpack, sombrero and kitten heels!

As the trucks lurched to a halt at the base of the pyramids, they could hear the MPs yelling, '*Arrestado! Arrestado!*' as they started running in lines towards the steep steps.

'Hurry up boys! I think they want to arrest us!' Sophie yelled out, giggling at the sight. It was like something out of a movie.

Soon enough they had made their way back down to the bottom of the pyramid where the MPs were now positioned only 20 metres away, surrounding them, all hand guns and assault rifles pointing in their direction. The team stood with their arms raised. Sophie had stopped giggling. Were they being arrested because they were five minutes late exiting the grounds? It was crazy.

'Guys, I think we need to cooperate here. I seriously do *not* want to end up in a Mexican prison tonight,' Sophie said out loud to anyone who was listening.

Fabian frantically yelled something to the MPs in Spanish, who in turn, slowly lowered their guns. The MP's commanding officer yelled something back to Fabian, who yelled a bit more, then turned to the boys and yelled,

'Did anyone "moon" the public from the top?'

The situation seemed to be getting more farcical by the moment. Every single member of the team tried very hard not to laugh out loud. They furiously shook their heads and yelled back, 'No, wasn't us.'

'I think it was some German tourists,' Brad called out loudly with an expressionless face, pointing towards his left.

The head MP yelled something to his men, who then ran off in their lines in the direction Brad had pointed.

'We gotta get out of here, now!' Fabian said quietly to Brett.

They hastily rounded up the boys and the team walked briskly back towards the coach.

Once safely aboard, Fabian laughed as he recounted the full story, filling in the bits that had been lost in translation. Because the pyramids are considered sacred ground, allegations of mooning were taken extremely seriously. The MPs had a warrant for the perpetrator's arrest and this perpetrator was allegedly amongst the New Zealand team.

The truth was, Fabian had been standing right beside Brad when Brad had gotten out his bare butt in public, but both were playing the super cool innocent. Ever the joker, while mooning at the top of the pyramid Brad had announced, 'The Pyramid of the Sun is hereby the Pyramid of my moon!' He now repeated his line on the bus.

Everyone was having a good laugh about it, until Fabian told them the head MP had said it was two tall Mexican boys who had dobbed Bradley in. It was immediately obvious that Carlos and Julio fitted the description.

Sophie hadn't noticed until then that their two hosts hadn't got back on the coach. They had apparently made the excuse that they had met some girls and weren't coming back with the team. No one believed that was true, especially as no one had seen them with any girls during the day.

Luckily, the coach driver genuinely did not speak any English, so the team was safe to talk around him.

Brett walked to the front of the coach, pulled out the microphone from beside the driver and announced, '*This did not happen, okay?*' The boys burst into laughter again. But Brett continued, 'I'm deadly serious guys, we *cannot, ever,* admit to this incident. We need to stick together. Brad could get arrested and we could get expelled from the games. We are going to absolutely stick to Brad's story that it was German tourists.' Brett had seen the funny side, but had also immediately seen the potentially serious ramifications.

Everyone understood and immediately agreed to keep the mooning incident secret. Sophie realised that, in a strange twist, this situation might prove to be the very thing that would restore team unity. Whatever the outcome, it was certainly a unique bonding experience!

Ripples of laughter and chatter slowly resumed throughout the coach and stayed with them all the way back to Conade. Despite two serious betrayals by Carlos and Julio, everyone had thoroughly enjoyed an amazing day.

The mooning incident played over and over in Sophie's mind. Like everyone else, she had thought it was a bit of light entertainment – except for the part where 60 military police had pointed hand guns and assault rifles at them! And except for the part where she'd had the terrifying thought she might end up alone in a Mexican prison.

Having had her eyes opened to the level of corruption they had already encountered in this country, and having very nearly been kidnapped at the airport, she realised that if she ended up in a Mexican prison, she might never again see the light of day. And how would her bodyguards protect her in there? So while she laughed along with everyone else, the incident had added another layer of anxiety to her already shattered nerves. A timely reminder that, under the surface of calm waters, she was a quietly bubbling, blithering mess.

The rush hour traffic on the journey to Conade was slower, so the coach driver was forced to drive a little less maniacally. Sophie didn't feel as ill as she had on the morning trip. Eventually they pulled into the little side alley, outside the sports village, and the team poured out of the coach, still wearing their ponchos and sombreros. After arranging to take Brett and Sophie to the markets the next day after lunch, Gabi and Fabian said their goodbyes and headed home.

Sophie was pleased and thankful that the young couple had come along on the outing. It would have been a disastrous day without them, on several accounts. She felt a lot of comfort knowing the team could trust them both.

As the boys trudged up the hill to Conade, through the three point security checks, Sophie noticed a marked change in their demeanour. The further into the sports village they trudged, the darker their moods became.

Everyone took their souvenirs and bags back to their rooms, then made their way down to the mess hall to catch what was left of dinner. Sophie looked at the slim pickings – some dried meat, jerky perhaps, that smelled disgusting, cereal, rehydrated, lumpy, cold mashed potato, water-logged soggy peas and dried out macaroni with plastic looking pale cheese. *Hmmm.* Sophie took cereal, potato, peas and macaroni, peeling off the plastic cheese and putting it to one side. It was a far cry from the delicious meal she'd had at El Jaguar.

After dinner, everyone turned in early. Brett and Sophie were in their rooms with their doors open, each quietly doing their own thing. Both heard a knock at the door and came to the entranceway to find Roger, returned from the officials' function, holding a half empty can of beer in one hand and a full one in the other. Sophie thought he might have come to share a beer with Brett. But he continued to hold onto the unopened can as he told them about his day.

The officials had had an amazing time. Roger didn't go into detail about the activities they had participated in, but they had finished with a very posh and expensive restaurant dinner. He had obviously been plied with copious amounts of alcohol because he was very jolly and was slurring his words. Sophie had never seen him so sloshed! He commented that the Mexicans were 'really, really cool blokes,' and 'we all need to be much more respectful of them.'

Hmmm, thought Sophie.

Apparently Carlos and Julio had wasted no time getting on the phone to Juan about the mooning incident at the pyramids. All the officials were at the posh restaurant by then, including Juan and Babic. Juan immediately and gleefully reported the incident to Babic, greatly exaggerated, no doubt. Then Juan had again demanded Babic expel New Zealand from the tournament, this time for its 'disgraceful behaviour'. He was indeed a piece of work!

Babic had then pulled Roger aside, who insisted that none of his players would ever conduct themselves in such a disrespectful manner. Of course, this was normally very true. Historically, New Zealand players always conducted themselves with grace and good behaviour because they knew they were ambassadors for their country. But in Sophie's opinion, given how abysmally they had been treated and everything they had been through thus far, it was a surprise that only one player had mooned in public that day! Luckily, Roger hadn't been at the pyramids to know any differently and Brett wasn't about to enlighten him.

Once Roger had toddled off to his room, Sophie rinsed in the shower, took herself to bed and read the second to last chapter of Katie's book to distract her overworked mind. She hadn't had time to pick it up since the flight into Mexico City.

Having met by chance in a café in Paris, the girl in the story and the older brother of her first lost love went to the La Louvre together. They had a perfect day. They talked and laughed – it felt so natural. There was undeniable electricity between them, but neither commented or acknowledged their feelings. For now, they were kept apart by the guilt of potentially betraying the memory of the man they had in common, and they were both wary of falling in love, given their recent divorces.

On the last page of the chapter, Sophie's mind started to drift, so she finished the page and put down the book.

As she floated off into sleep, she felt a happy glimmer of hope for the characters in the story, then entered a twilight zone as the water pipes banged in the walls and ceiling above her bed. Suddenly, she found herself in a cheap, nasty, backstreet hotel in Paris, and someone was breaking into her room. They kidnapped her, gassed her with a mask forced over her face. Then, as she tried to escape, 60 military police surrounded her, pointing their assault rifles. She tried to scream. Then, at the last moment, the brother of the lost love came to save her. She awoke suddenly with a deep gasping breath and her heart racing.

She felt like she had been dragged backwards through a tornado. Emotionally and physically. Sleep deprivation was torture in itself. Let alone the feeling of terror that stayed with her for some time after waking. When would it end?

Chapter Thirty-Two

FRIDAY, NZ VS. CHINESE TAIPEI

Sophie once again forced herself through the shower and, despite the shocking sleep she'd had, put on her best game face. She dressed in a pale yellow tank top and knee-length, black linen shorts. Brett was waiting for her in the entranceway of their rooms and they headed down for the monotonous breakfast slop of dried meat from the night before, more rehydrated, lumpy, cold mashed potato, water-logged soggy peas and dried out macaroni with plastic-looking cheese.

'Oh look, they added cold watery porridge!' she said sarcastically, to no one in particular. She took porridge and cereal.

The South African, Mongolian and Chinese Taipei teams were all there, and the boys mingled with each other. It was nice to see them all getting along.

Mexico were notable for their absence. They had definitely distanced themselves from the other teams since the night of the gas poisoning.

Sophie made a point of checking in with all the members of the New Zealand team. Everyone was feeling good. No headaches, no nausea, no dizziness. Even Kieran said he was feeling well again. He had a slight headache but no dizziness.

After breakfast, the team boarded the bus to the San Jeronimo Rink for their light on-ice training.

Stephen and Matthew were the only players who didn't gear-up and train. Kieran announced to Sophie he really did feel fine and asked if he could do the light training to see how he felt. Sophie checked his vitals and gave him the green light. The team was almost back to full strength.

Training went like clockwork. Kieran was focused, like he had something to prove, and worked harder than Sophie had anticipated. But his vitals stayed stable throughout the session.

Stephen sat in the grandstand next to Matthew. Both watched the training. Stephen looked absolutely miserable. Matthew had his headphones on, listening to his iPod, and his body language showed that he was ignoring Stephen.

Meanwhile, Brett periodically lapped the rink with the gas detector, which didn't beep or light up.

After training, Harry gathered the boys at the side of the ice for a pep talk. He purposefully positioned them directly under where Stephen and Matthew were sitting in the grandstand. Sophie was hovering, measuring oxygen levels on the players.

Stephen came down to the boards.

'Excuse me, Harry,' he said, then spoke quietly to his coach. Sophie watched with bated breath. She thought she knew what was about to take place…

'Team, Stephen has something to say,' said Harry as he stepped aside so everyone could see and hear their former captain.

Stephen suddenly looked like a respectable young man, instead of a surly, angsty teenager. 'I just want to apologise. To you all. I'm really, really sorry for my behaviour. I have been an absolute dick, and I want to make it up to you all. I want to play. If you will have me back.' His speech was straight from the heart. Really genuine. And he was almost in tears by the end.

The team immediately rallied around, some patting him on the shoulder or the back, voicing their approval, accompanied with fist-bumps, handshakes, man hugs and high fives all round.

Sophie had a lump in her throat. She was so proud of Stephen, taking responsibility for his actions, facing up to his team and apologising like a man. That took a lot of guts. She couldn't speak when he came up with open arms and hugged her.

'Sorry, Mum.' And that was all he needed to say. Just like that, all had been forgiven. The real Stephen was back!

Harry asked Sophie to sew the C's back onto Stephen's shirts. Everyone agreed, including Tom and Verne, that in the spirit of true sportsmanship, he should be reinstated as captain.

'Let's *do it!*' shouted Harry, as all hands went in for the end of training cheer.

'*Do it!*' The team echoed Harry, uttering their menacing, double base growl.

Sophie felt a shiver go all the way down her spine. Full unity had returned to the team.

Tonight, they would play Chinese Taipei at 7 p.m. The full team, apart from poor Matthew. He was in great spirits though. He knew the situation was out of his hands and accepted his predicament. He would stay with the players on the benches and operate the gate again.

Back at Conade, the team joined South Africa, Mongolia and Chinese Taipei in the mess hall, where everyone picked at smelly, dried meat, cereal, rehydrated, lumpy, cold mashed potato, waterlogged peas and dried out macaroni. The watery porridge from breakfast was still there too.

Mexico were once again absent. Sophie was beginning to wonder where they were disappearing to for their meals.

This lunch, of course, begged another walk to the grocery store for supplies, so the team set out under the supervision of Roger, Harry and Benny. Benny was again in charge of buying wine and beer for evening drinks.

Meanwhile, Gabi and Fabian collected Sophie and Brett for

their prearranged trip to some local markets. Their taxi was waiting outside the lobby.

Sophie climbed into the back, with Brett on her left and Gabi on her right. Fabian sat in the front to direct the driver. Sophie felt even sicker in the taxi than she had in the bus. It didn't help that the driver appeared to have a death wish, dodging in and out of cars and trucks across all four lanes. It was a disorganised chaotic mess, but everyone expected the unexpected so no one seemed to crash.

At 37 degrees, it was the hottest day they had encountered in Mexico City so far. The air conditioning in the taxi didn't work, so the windows were all down and Sophie's hair was blowing around wildly. She asked Gabi what the speed limit was. Gabi didn't know, but commented that it didn't matter because if the police pulled you over, you just gave them money. Cash could buy you out of any offence, whether the offence was real or fabricated.

Sophie had become a bag of nerves in this dangerous, corrupt city. Now she just wanted to make it to the markets in one piece. Brett had picked up on her anxiety. He reached across and squeezed her hand tightly. Sophie looked up at him and smiled gratefully. He had a way of calming and reassuring her without saying a word. Always looking out for her. Ever the gentleman.

He held her hand for the remainder of the taxi ride. Sophie momentarily worried what Gabi would think if she noticed. But Brett didn't seem to be concerned at all. It was, after all, a perfectly innocent gesture.

There weren't many people at the markets. However, Sophie remained on high alert and Brett stuck to her side. It would be too easy for someone to drag her into the back of a shop unnoticed. Despite her not so irrational fears, the markets proved to be a lot of fun. The four of them had three hours of exploring every shop and stall without having to worry about keeping an eye on a hoard of teenage boys.

Sophie admired one particularly gorgeous silver and turquoise Aztec sun necklace, but couldn't justify buying anything more. Due to the problems with their food and water supply, she had already spent more money than she'd budgeted for the trip. Plus she had treated herself by buying the silver bangles at the pyramids.

She fleetingly thought of Charlie, but made the decision not to buy him anything. After telling him she didn't love him any more, it would just feel awkward and hypocritical to give him a gift. Anyway, she had learnt her lesson the previous year when she'd given him a gift from her hockey trip to Canada. She had found a sports cap for him that she thought he'd really like. Only, Charlie had been incredibly rude and ungrateful, constantly referring back to how much the trip had cost. 'This is all I got,' he'd say to anyone who would listen. 'This cap cost me $13,000.' Sophie wasn't going to make that mistake again!

Brett bought presents for his wife, Kristine, and their daughter, Nicole. And Gabi insisted on buying tiny lapel pins of Mexican sombreros for all the players. They were a cute souvenir and the boys would love them.

Sophie was still feeling a bit nauseous from the taxi ride and faint from the heat. She told Brett she needed to sit down for a while, so they stopped for a cold drink and snack. While Sophie chatted with Gabi and Fabian, Brett wandered off for a while. He said he wanted to go back and buy something he'd seen in one of the stores.

Sophie felt vulnerable and worried while he was gone. She felt so silly about it, but she was more than relieved when he returned a few minutes later.

They caught another taxi back to Conade. This driver was just as insane as the first one and Sophie felt even more nauseous by the time they arrived at the sports village.

It was almost time to gather the troops for their evening game.

Brett and Sophie went back to their rooms so Sophie could stitch the C's and A's back onto Stephen and Tom's shirts. She felt a pang of sadness for Tom and Verne who had been nothing but mature and gracious about being demoted.

Brett did the rounds, making sure that the boys were all sorted for the game. Once everyone was changed into team uniform, Sophie quickly changed too, grabbed her medical bag, met Brett in the foyer of their rooms, then headed down to the lobby.

The team were well-rested, fed and watered, and ready to play. Mostly.

On the bus to the rink, four of the boys, including Stephen and Tom, approached Sophie to say they were feeling a bit queasy. *Hmmm.* The bus trip wasn't that rough, even for Sophie, although she did still feel a little nauseous herself. Maybe it hadn't been the taxi ride that had made her feel off colour. Luckily, she had stocked up her supplies of metoclopramide anti-nausea tablets at the mall. She gave the boys one each, and took one herself.

'Man, I hope we're not all coming down with a tummy bug now too!' she joked to Brett and Roger who were seated behind her, but she was genuinely a little concerned.

The bus arrived at the ice rink and the team headed towards their change room. Friderik Babic intercepted Brett and pulled him aside. Sophie instinctively knew it would be about the notorious mooning incident. She couldn't lie to save herself and would blush profusely for sure if asked for her testimony, so she steered clear of the conversation.

Later that evening, over drinks, Brett regaled them with what transpired. Babic commenced by retelling the story as told to him by Juan. Brett managed to maintain a poker face throughout, then reassured the IIHF chairman that there was no way in the world his team would ever behave in such a disgraceful and disrespectful manner, and that the boys believed it was some young German tourists nearby. Babic was persistent, pushing and pushing the matter.

Finally, Brett politely asked him to challenge Juan to produce any eye witnesses that could verify it was one of the New Zealand team – but not Carlos or Julio. He explained the trick the hosts had pulled to postpone the bus trip the day before. Babic simply smiled politely, thanked Brett for his help, shook his hand and made a hasty retreat. It seemed the matter was now closed.

Once in the change room, Brett immediately switched on the ventilation fan. All the boys, except Matthew, changed and headed outside to the parking lot for their warm-up. Sophie and Roger gathered snow for her ice bags. The early evening game between Mongolia and South Africa was in its second period and the score was 7–1 to South Africa. Brett lapped the rink with his gas detector and nothing beeped or lit up.

Soon enough, the boys were back inside, changing into their ice gear. Two more players came to get anti-nausea medication. *Hmmm.* Sophie was even more concerned. But everyone's vitals remained stable.

The buzzer sounded on the South Africa versus Mongolia game, and South Africa were victorious, 12–2. The New Zealand boys congratulated their new South African mates with gloved fist-bumps as the South Africans exited the bench area.

After warming up on the ice, the Chinese Taipei and New Zealand teams lined up for their national anthems, presentations and the New Zealand haka.

The players took their positions, the whistle blew and the puck dropped.

Nigel started in goal and was replaced during the game by Beauden. Both played well, and the teams were locked in an even game. The refereeing seemed mostly fair and reasonably consistent. But there was something missing from the game. The New Zealand players lacked a sense of drive, determination or urgency. It was like they had lost their mojo. At the final buzzer, the scoreboard showed 8–6. New Zealand had lost, and everyone felt deflated.

Chapter Thirty-Three

CONADE INFIRMARY

It hurt, but losing to Chinese Taipei wasn't the end of world. In the change room after the game, as the players quietly changed out of their gear, Harry did the maths and worked out that if they beat Mexico well the next day, they could still win the tournament. They had gone into the competition as the top-ranked team, so it was definitely achievable.

Sophie chatted to Gabi and Fabian in the grandstand, then Frank came by to say hello. He mentioned that some of his Chinese Taipei boys had been feeling nauseous. Sophie confided that six of her boys had been feeling unwell too.

By the time the New Zealand team boarded the bus at 10 p.m., they were starving. Everyone had snacked prior to the game, but not on anything substantial. Brett had promised them another surprise destination for dinner and, after driving for a block and a half, the bus stopped outside a McDonald's restaurant. The boys, who had been more subdued than usual, were suddenly very excited. They piled out onto the sidewalk, much noisier than when they had boarded.

Their joy was short-lived. The doors to the restaurant were locked and the lights were dimmed. There were definitely people inside, but when Brett looked closely, he realised they were only staff. Damn!

Then he spotted that the drive-through was still open. He headed towards the window on foot, which is always a strict no-no and, like a flock of seagulls, the entire team followed him.

Sophie didn't hear what Brett said to the drive-through attendant, but he soon turned around to the team and commanded, 'Go *now*, and wait by the bus.' The hoard of strapping youths had probably scared the living daylights out of the McDonald's employee.

Brett paid the staff US$200 to make 25 burgers, 25 large fries and 25 soft drinks. He'd made it worth their while to break the rules and serve the team, even though it cost him a significant corruption fee (yet again) to do so. Gabi was so right. Money could buy anything in this country.

Without exception, everyone devoured their burgers and fries in the bus on the way back to Conade.

No one complained about any part of their meal. The usual comments such as, 'I don't like pickles/tomatoes/cheese,' 'My fries are soggy/cold/unsalted,' 'My drink is flat/warm/has too much ice,' disappeared in favour of concentrated munching. The junk food fix had definitely improved the team's spirits after their mediocre game.

The bus drove up the long driveway into Conade, past the three-point security check, to the front of the lobby. The boys quietly made their way upstairs and headed straight for the showers. It was well past curfew and the guards were already agitated. Even though Sophie's room contained Benny's acquisition of a dozen beer cans, sitting in a plastic bucket on ice, and two bottles of wine, the adults weren't going to risk having drinks that night. Brett and Sophie followed their well-oiled bedtime routine, said their goodnights, and drifted off to sleep. The beer and wine would keep for the following evening.

Their last night in Mexico.

In Sophie's night terrors, two strange, cartoonish Mexican men wearing huge black and silver sombreros, colourful ponchos and enormous moustaches, dragged her onto a military police truck. She was kicking and fighting, screaming '*No…! No…! No…!*' as someone tapped her on her shoulder.

Suddenly awake, she sat bolt upright as she yelled her final '*No…!*' then breathed a sigh of relief. It was only Brett. But her heart was racing.

'Oh my God, you scared me!' she exclaimed.

'Sorry Sophie. I did knock but you didn't hear. I think you were having a nightmare,' Brett said softly. 'Hugh and Verne have been vomiting. Can you come and see them?'

Sophie quickly jumped out of bed, pulled a sweater over her pink sleep t-shirt, climbed into some jeans, grabbed her medical bag and followed Brett. Neither Hugh nor Verne had complained of feeling nauseous that evening. She checked their vitals and took a quick history of how their symptoms had started, then gave them each a metoclopramide tablet. If they could keep the medication down for long enough, it would take the edge off the nausea and hopefully stop the vomiting.

Unfortunately, they weren't the only ones to succumb to illness that night. Almost the entire team, including the adults, were up with varying degrees of nausea, vomiting, abdominal cramps and/or diarrhoea. Sophie couldn't do much about the latter but advise them to let it take its natural course.

There was also audible activity in the other teams' rooms. Sophie wondered if they had been woken up by the commotion the New Zealanders had caused or were sick as well. By 7 a.m., she calculated she'd had about three hours of very broken sleep. She had seen every team player and adult over the duration of the night, including Anton, who was suffering with bad nausea.

Brett had initially concluded it was either food poisoning from their burgers or a contagious tummy bug, but Sophie had engaged her medical mind to work through all the possibilities.

She deduced that it wasn't a highly contagious norovirus-type gastro bug – although something like that would whip through the team very quickly, they would drop like dominoes one at a time, passing it on to each other. This illness was affecting everybody at the same time. It wasn't the burgers, because some had been nauseous before the game. And besides, she was nauseous too and she'd had a salad burger. And Frank's Taipei boys had also felt nauseous.

Brett and Sophie racked their brains to think what foods or drinks they had consumed that could make everyone sick. The only thing she could come up with was the water in the porridge or the mushy peas. It could be accidental food poisoning, but there was no real pattern… What if it was deliberate poisoning?

In the mess hall later that morning, they discovered that almost all the South African and Mongolian boys were also suffering from vomiting and diarrhoea. In general, they were sicker than the New Zealand and Taipei players. Almost everyone was looking a bit green around the gills.

This time the entire Mexico team were present and, funnily enough, seemed to be fighting fit. No signs of vomiting or diarrhoea, and very healthy appetites. Sophie remembered they had been absent from breakfast and lunch the day before. Felix commented that they had been absent from dinner as well. *Hmmm.*

'I don't think this is a coincidence,' Sophie declared to the adults. Nobody spoke too loudly about their suspicions but everyone agreed. It was just too convenient for the Mexican team.

Conade had turned into an infirmary. Everyone suffered. Every manager, every coach and every player. Some only had mild nausea, but some suffered relentless vomiting and explosive, watery diarrhoea. Not ideal when each room configuration had four boys to one bathroom!

Luckily, Sophie only had moderate nausea, so she was able to do her rounds all day. By midday that day, it seemed the worst had passed and all four teams had stopped vomiting. The fact that the onset and curtailing of the illness had occurred almost simultaneously for everyone further fuelled suspicions about deliberate poisoning. Everyone must have been contaminated at exactly the same time.

Harry asked the team if they should forfeit their evening game to Mexico.

The players were unanimous. '*Hell no!*'

If they could stand up, they could skate. And if they could skate, they would play. There was no way they were going to let the Mexicans get the better of them!

Chapter Thirty-Four

SATURDAY, THE FINAL SABOTAGE

The New Zealand team boarded their bus, behind schedule but determined, bound for their final showdown at the San Jeronimo Rink.

The third period of the Chinese Taipei versus Mongolia game was just beginning as the boys walked into the arena. They glanced up at the scoreboard – 10–0 to Taipei.

The New Zealanders had crossed paths with the Mexicans in the carpark, where their opposition had been completing their pre-game warm-up. The players' faces were steely and they avoided eye contact.

As the team changed, Sophie dished out a few more metoclopramide tablets, then the boys made their way outside for their own warm-up. They wouldn't have much time, but even then, Harry cut the session short because most of the players didn't feel well enough to be running sprints. Back inside, they took their time to change into their ice gear, taking as many urgent bathroom stops as possible prior to heading out onto the ice.

The Taipei versus Mongolia game came to an end and the score stood at 13–4 to Taipei. Despite all the players feeling ill, Mongolia had showed their fighting spirit and made a minor come back in the last period.

Roger went with Sophie to gather snow for her ice bags as the Zamboni cleaned the ice. The teams made their way to their benches.

Sophie spotted Gabi and Fabian sitting with the New Zealand supporters and waved. They had arranged to come to Conade after the game to celebrate with the managers and coaches, win or lose.

The whistle blew, and New Zealand and Mexico lined up on the ice. The national anthems played and the team captains swapped souvenir pennants and badges.

Then New Zealand commenced their haka.

If it hadn't already been obvious, it soon became clear that the boys were in hostile territory. Brett, Roger, Sophie, Harry and Benny watched in utter disbelief and disgust as the crowd booed loudly and the Mexican team turned their backs on the New Zealand challenge.

The disrespect shown by the Mexican crowd and their team only served to add fire to the New Zealand players' determination as the first line readied themselves for the face-off. The referee blew his whistle and the puck dropped.

From that moment on, the game became a chaotic blur in Sophie's memory.

Afterwards, she would remember recoiling at every relentless and brutal hit that was dished out against her boys.

She would remember Harry incredulously questioning the first few penalties against New Zealand, and being told by the referee that he would penalise the team harshly because 'the noise of the New Zealand hits on the opposition made him nervous'.

What?

She would remember the refereeing being unbelievably inconsistent and overtly biased toward the Mexican team.

She would remember throwing her hands up in despair at the blatantly bogus penalties against them.

She would remember the referee warning her, 'If you do that again, I will call a bench penalty against you and expel you from the rink.' Her! Little old Sophie!

She would remember New Zealand's one goal being conveniently disallowed under the pretence of an exceptionally questionable high stick penalty.

She would remember the players making emergency trips to the toilet as cramps seized their stomachs.

She would remember having to *beg* the referee to release Stephen from the penalty bench during yet another bogus (10 minute) penalty, so he could make a very urgent bathroom stop.

She would remember saying to Brett, 'I don't care if we lose 50–0. I just want to get these boys out of this game in one piece.'

Sophie had never been so relieved to hear a final whistle. Her boys were sick as dogs, bruised, battered, and they had lost the game 7–0.

The only silver lining was that there were no serious injuries. And tomorrow they could leave this God-forsaken country.

Meanwhile the Mexican team, including Juan and Raul, celebrated jubilantly. Did it not matter to them that they hadn't won the game fair and square? They had won by refereeing assistance, food poisoning, four types of gas poisoning, double-crossing and their opposition's lack of decent nutrition and sufficient water.

The game had barely finished when the closing ceremony started.

Mexico, gold.

Chinese Taipei, silver.

New Zealand, bronze.

South Africa, fourth – and Mongolia, fifth.

Then came an astonishing announcement from the music booth…

'*Armed police* will be at Conade, *all night*,' said the voice. 'There will be *no* parties. There will be *no* alcohol. Anyone found with alcohol, *will be arrested*. There will be *no* noise after curfew. Anyone breaking these rules *will be arrested!*

'Jesus F.C!' exclaimed Harry. 'Talk about concentration camp!

After all we've been through, we're not even allowed to have drink! Unbelievable! Let's get out of this shit hole!'

Sophie looked at Brett with a worried expression on her face. In her room, she still had a dozen beer cans sitting in a plastic bucket of slightly icy water, and two bottles of wine. They would have to come up with a plan en route to Conade.

The boys changed in lightning time, making several urgent trips to the toilet while packing their hockey bags. They loaded their gear onto the bus and climbed aboard. The mood was dark. One of undeserved defeat. They weren't sore losers. It was just unbelievably unjust. They absolutely had the players, the skills and the ability to have won the tournament and become the World Division III champions. Instead they had been stripped of their chance to have a fair run at the title through a series of despicable events that were completely out of their control.

It was after curfew and there were armed police everywhere as the team walked through the lobby of Conade Castle. The boys made their way to their rooms, and the adults, including Gabi and Fabian, tailed closely behind. Everyone was silent. Nobody was questioned by the guards.

Roger had come up with a plan to get rid of their contraband without pouring it all down the sink. The adults headed straight to Sophie's room. If the five men sculled two beers each, and Sophie and Gabi sculled one each, when the guards came in, all that remained would be a dozen empty cans. No actual evidence. Gabi would take the wine. The police would never question a Mexican girl and would never search her bag. Only the gringos would come under suspicion. These were two corks Sophie would not get for her corkboard.

Shortly afterwards, there was a knock on the hallway door outside Brett and Sophie's rooms. Sophie's eyes widened as she quickly sculled the bottom third of her beer and tossed the empty into the plastic bucket of icy water. The others did the same. On the second knock, she opened the door. Two large armed policemen immediately barged in, without so much as an 'Hola', straight past her into the room where Brett, Roger, Harry, Benny, Gabi and Fabian were seated across Sophie's two single beds. No wine bottles in sight. No beer cans in hands. Just a bucket full of icy water and empties.

The guards smiled at Gabi and Fabian.

'Hola. Está todo bien?' ('Hello. Is everything okay?') the larger policeman asked Fabian jovially.

'Sí. Todo está bien, gracias, señor,' ('Yes, everything is good, thank you, sir') Fabian courteously replied with a big smile.

The policemen turned and left without looking around, let alone checking any bags. They didn't acknowledge the gringos.

Whew! Thank goodness Gabi and Fabian were there! Somehow, the New Zealanders knew that things might have otherwise gone very differently.

The five bid a fond farewell to Gabi and Fabian at the end of their short visit. It was well past 10 p.m. and the whole team would be up at 7 o'clock the next morning to shower, pack, get to breakfast at 9 a.m., meet in the lobby to formally check out at 9.30, then depart by bus from Conade at 10 to be at Terminal 1 by 11 for their 2.45 p.m. flight to Los Angeles.

Sophie's flight would leave three hours later from Terminal 2. She had been fretting about getting to her terminal and being there alone. So Brett had asked Gabi if she would take Sophie out for a couple of hours sight-seeing before her departure. Basically, it was just his way of having her looked after. He hated to leave her unattended. Sophie didn't argue. She was relieved to have a trustworthy companion in Gabi.

Sophie and Brett said their goodnights, then Sophie set out her flight clothes and packed her bags in her room. She crawled into bed feeling cautiously relieved. Their Mexican nightmare was almost over. They were on the brink of escaping this terrifying place. And almost in one piece. Not unscathed, that's for sure!

But nothing they wouldn't recover from…

Eventually…

She slept fitfully again, as the night's horror film played on the screen of her mind. She dreamed she had woken up in a nasty, backstreet hotel in Paris. This time she was endlessly vomiting as the same two evil men with black and silver sombreros, colourful ponchos and enormous moustaches gassed her. Then 100 armed military police pointed assault rifles at her as they uncovered the hidden wine bottles she had in her backpack.

LET'S GET OUT OF HERE!

Brett was missing when Sophie awoke at 7 a.m. His bedroom door was open and his suitcases were sitting packed on his bed, but he wasn't there. Sophie reassured herself that he was probably just organising the team.

She sped through the shower, dressed, styled her hair, and carefully applied mascara and lip gloss. She was retrieving her passport out of the pile that had been buried deep in her backpack all that time, just as Brett came back into the foyer of their rooms.

Oh good, he's back, she thought. *Nothing to worry about.*

Breakfast was the same slop as usual. But, the boys hung back from the serveries, reluctant to touch the food after their probable poisoning. Sophie bravely led the way by taking dry cereal and black coffee. That would get her through until she could find something safer to eat at the airport. The team followed suit, and they all found something that they hoped would be reasonably safe.

Nobody had vomited since midday the day before, but many still had grumbly stomachs and were still rushing to the bathroom from time to time. It would make for an interesting couple of plane rides home for the team!

After breakfast finished, the boys were under strict instructions to fetch their bags to formally check out at 9.30 a.m.

To their surprise, when the team arrived at the lobby they were greeted by an armed policemen who announced in broken English that all their rooms were to be inspected before they could check out. Armed guards stood at either side of the front doors. Sophie wondered how much money would be involved this time!

Brett insisted on being present during the inspection.

Even so, having conducted their investigation, the police demanded a payment of US$1500 for damage. Brett admitted the team's responsibility for Kevin's broken window. But the broken drawers, missing drawers, broken handles, holes in walls, broken and leaking water pipes, rips in the curtains and broken springs on beds? All these had been damaged before they arrived.

The policemen knew that. Brett knew that. Everyone knew that. But despite arguing back and forth, it was clear that the team wouldn't be allowed to leave until the matter was settled to the Mexicans' satisfaction. It wasn't a matter of *whether* the New Zealanders would have to pay, but rather *how much* they would have to pay. At the end of the negotiations, Brett reluctantly parted with yet another US$500 out of his own pocket, just so the team could get out the door and onto the bus.

Due to the inspection fiasco, the bus arrived at Terminal 1, Benito Juarez International Airport, around 45 minutes later than Brett had planned. Gabi and her parents had come to see off the team and collect Sophie for a short tour of their favourite sights. The team checked in, painfully slowly. With very little time to spare, Sophie said a tearful fond farewell to her beloved Anton. She hugged him tightly, and he rested his chin on her head.

'I love you more than all the stars in the sky,' she told him, with tears rolling down her cheeks, her voice choking up. 'See you soon.'

It broke her heart to say goodbye to him, especially after all they had been through these last three weeks. Her precious angel. But he would be in Brett's capable and safe hands.

'Love you too, Mum. Be safe,' Anton answered.

Then every single player in the team lined up to hug her. 'Bye, Mum,' 'Thanks for saving my life, Mum,' 'See you soon, Mum.'

Roger, Harry and Benny were next, and her tears continued to flow.

The last person to say goodbye was Brett. He bear-hugged her tightly. They had become firmer friends, developing a remarkable bond because of this crazy, treacherous trip. She was going to miss having him around 24/7.

'You gonna be alright?' he asked, when the hug ended. They were both aware the whole team were watching, including both their sons.

'Yep.' Sob. Was all she could squeak out. Then once she had pulled herself together a little more, 'Thanks… For everything. You saved this trip, you know.'

'No, actually, you saved the trip!' Brett reflected back to her. 'And you saved my son's life!'

'Team effort. I couldn't have done it without you. We did good!' Sophie laughed, trying to dab away her tears with her fingertips without giving herself raccoon eyes.

Just before the team went through the departures gate, Brett gave her a small paper bag and told her not to open it until she was on the plane. Sophie placed it safely into her jacket pocket.

Sophie waved goodbye to the team, blowing masses of extravagant kisses to Anton as the boys passed out of sight.

Gabi and her parents led Sophie to their car in the parking lot. Sophie thanked them in advance for looking after her until her flight.

With Gabi's father in the driver's seat, the four of them drove around Mexico City for the next two hours. Sophie was so incredibly sleep-deprived and worn out, and the car was such a warm, safe place, that she drifted off to sleep.

She awoke as they arrived at the drop off zone at Terminal 2.

Embarrassed, she apologised to her hosts but they understood. Then she started crying again as she said her emotional goodbyes to these wonderful people.

Gabi walked Sophie through the same glass doors she had nearly been kidnapped through just days before, then along the corridor to the departures check-in area.

She stayed with her until they reached the front of the queue, then Sophie bid a tearful farewell to her beautiful Mexican friend and thanked her profusely for everything she and Fabian had done for the team.

Then Sophie was by herself – quite possibly the only blonde person in the terminal. Once again she was stared at, but she didn't blink an eyelid this time, having now become almost completely desensitised to the attention.

Besides, she didn't have to put up with it for much longer – she was getting the hell out of there!

After receiving her boarding pass, she was instructed to take her bags to the security counter. And for the first time during the whole trip, an officer searched her medical bag. He demanded to see the scissors he thought he had seen on his x-ray machine. Sophie pulled out her NZ$300 suturing kit and showed him the needle holder forceps that were in it. He threatened to take the forceps, until she broke open the sterile pack and showed him that they had no sharp edges.

But he was in the mood to confiscate something. Anything!

He kept searching the bag until he gleefully discovered her NZ$10 gel heat pack and stated, 'Aha! You can't take this!'

She pointed out that it was clearly labelled, and 'just a heat pack'.

He was adamant. 'After 9/11, no gel allowed.'

She was tired of arguing, so she gave in. 'Fine. Take it.'

The man was satisfied and she was allowed to go.

The irony was that she was also carrying a pair of very sturdy plaster scissors, very sharp surgical scissors and a multitude of needles and syringes. But thankfully, the officer hadn't noticed them on his machine.

Once Sophie had off-loaded her cases, she made her way straight to the final checkpoint. She would feel much safer on the other side. So, with her backpack firmly strapped over her shoulders, and the enormous black and silver sombrero on her head, she passed through the immigration check with no further issues.

She found a little café, bought a cup of black coffee, a very large salad and some dark chocolate, then wiled away the time, people-watching, until her flight was due to board. No matter how hard she tried, she couldn't stop her brain from thinking through the events of the trip, over and over again.

She tried to distract herself by imagining what the team would be doing at that moment. They would be at Los Angeles International Airport, awaiting their Air New Zealand direct flight back to Auckland. She wondered how their stomachs were feeling and how their emotions were holding up.

She thought about Hayden and hoped he had coped okay without her for three weeks. And she guarded herself from feeling too safe just yet. She wouldn't allow that feeling to seep through until she was safely out of Mexico, out of America, and on her way home.

Her flight boarded half an hour late, then the plane sat on the tarmac for another half an hour. It felt like half a day to Sophie. She dared not even look out of the window. She was terrified that, at any moment, there would be an announcement to say the flight had been cancelled, or that her name would be called out and she would be hauled off the plane for some crazy reason.

She remembered the little paper bag Brett had given her and pulled it out of her jacket pocket. Inside was the turquoise and silver Aztec sun necklace she had seen at the markets! 'A present from the team,' said the note in the bag. She would treasure it forever.

At last the plane took off, touching down at LAX an hour late. She would need to hurry if she was going to make her next flight, but she was out of Mexico and she was going home.

Chapter Thirty-Six

THE AFTERMATH

Sophie finally drifted peacefully off to sleep, curled up in her window seat with her backpack stowed under the seat in front and Hayden's sombrero now safely draped over it at her feet.

She had a massive headache from retelling her three-week nightmare to Josh, the total stranger sitting in the seat beside. He had listened intently, asking questions and constantly exclaiming 'Wow!' and 'Oh my God!' and 'Unbelievable!' throughout the story. Sophie had held back no details. And actually, it had been hugely cathartic and therapeutic for her.

Having off-loaded the contents of her exploding mind, she then slept for seven hours straight as the plane winged its way to Melbourne, her final stopover on the way home. Poor Josh was wide awake. He was so blown away by her incredible tale that he didn't sleep for one second of the 16-hour flight. He was still wide-eyed when she shook his hand and said goodbye in Melbourne.

Sophie enjoyed her four-hour stopover and three-hour flight to Auckland. She finished Katie's book on the last flight. The woman and man in the story had promised to keep in touch after their amazing day together in Paris, but were both still wary of betraying the memory of their lost love/brother. Some three months later, the woman was the guest speaker at a conference, and at the end of her speech, she spotted the man across the crowded room, walking towards her. As their eyes met, the sparks flew once again, and any possible sense of guilt finally melted away for them both. They had been stupid to have denied themselves the love and happiness they both deserved. The book finished with the couple marrying and starting a family. Their first child, a boy, was named after the lost love/brother. And they lived happily ever after.

Sophie closed the book with a contented smile. She was a sucker for a happy ending. Katie was right. It was a gorgeous story. Sophie felt an overwhelming sense of hope that one day she would find her own fairy tale ending.

Though she felt shaken and emotionally drained, she also felt an incredible strength that she had never really experienced before. If she could survive this trip and all the things that had happened to her, she could survive almost anything.

Charlie had collected Anton from Auckland International Airport at 7.15 on Tuesday morning, New Zealand time, then trekked back to collect Sophie at 3.10 that same afternoon. By then, Anton had told his father some of what had happened on the trip. On the car trip home, Sophie told him a little more, but she didn't feel like opening up and telling him everything. He was suitably surprised by what she did tell him, but he was hardly the loving, protective husband. All he could say in response was, 'That doesn't sound very good.'

Charlie tried to make an effort in their relationship over the next few weeks, but Sophie still felt numb, completely detached. His efforts were far too little, far too late.

A month passed before Sophie gathered the courage to finally sit down and tell him their marriage was over. He left quietly, without a fuss, finally realising she was right.

One week after that, Sophie officially changed back to her maiden name, Elliot, and happily exclaimed, 'I'm me again!'

As the months rolled by, Sophie recognised that separating was singularly the hardest thing she would *ever* do in her entire life. It had taken more courage to separate than it had to stay and keep the status quo all those years. She had never wanted her boys to come from a broken marriage and, for a long time, she had sacrificed her own happiness for their sake. But she had no regrets.

Ironically, Anton and Hayden seemed to take the separation in their stride and adjusted quickly. The night she and Charlie told them they were separating, Hayden had quietly said to his mother, 'Once everything settles down, I think you're going to be a lot, lot happier. And so will Dad when he gets over it.'

With her back turned to her son as she stood at the stove, Sophie wept silently, the tears rolling down her face and into the pan as she cooked dinner. She had tried so hard to keep it all from her boys for so long, but now she realised how truly wise and balanced they were.

Charlie would initially claim that Sophie had ruined his life, but he met someone else four months later. He learned a lot from the separation. He became a more involved father and, when he had Anton and Hayden at his house, he made an effort to take them places and do things with them. The boys now had a better relation-ship with their father than when their parents had been together.

On the surface, Sophie felt like she had coped with the emo-tional aftermath of the hockey trip, but her night terrors continued.

She finally made her corkboard, and the Chilean corks from the wine she'd drunk in Salt Lake City and Mexico formed the centrepiece. She would think of her perilous adventure every time she tacked up a note.

One day, at work in the accident and emergency clinic, she tended to a patient from Mexico. As she put his broken hand into a cast, she gave him a well-rehearsed five minute summary of her journey to Mexico City. He was able to shed some light on why the Mexicans had stared at her so much.

'It's because you look so much like Phoebe!' he said. 'You know? Off *Friends*! The TV show!'

She laughed at the connection, but this was a dark side that possibly explained why she had nearly been kidnapped. The Mexican patient told her that blonde women fetch a high price as sex slaves on the black market. Being a look-a-like of a famous actress would only increase her value. This was the stuff her nightmares were made of.

Then six months after the trip, late one evening at the clinic, she was caught up in an armed robbery. She wasn't harmed but she was very shaken.

She finally admitted to herself and others that she had turned into a bag of nerves. She no longer went out by herself in the evening. She slept with a weapon under her pillow. She awoke several times each night to random noises. And the night terrors persisted for many years to come.

Her happy baseline disposition was still intact but Sophie knew a small part of her had been lost. She had become wiser, more wary, more jumpy and less naive. Her willingness to trust strangers had been replaced by a healthy respect and fear for her own safety.

As for the boys on the New Zealand hockey team, the ripples of their treacherous adventure in Mexico were felt in a number of significant ways. Matthew experienced symptoms on and off for another year after the chemical cocktail gas poisoning. Theo, one of the bigger and less physically affected players, suffered quite severe post-traumatic stress disorder. He needed ongoing counselling and was unable to work for the next year as a consequence. Having dodged death, Kieran realised his family meant everything to him and, at the tender age of 16, with his parents' permission, he got a poignant tattoo on his arm – 'Family' inked in Japanese kanji.

The team shared an extraordinary bond following the trip that would never be forgotten. They had skated on thin ice together and survived. For years to come, whenever Sophie saw any of the boys at various tournaments, they would always stop and talk, give her a big bear-hug, and call her 'Mum'.

Chapter Thirty-Seven

SOPHIE'S FINALE

There is something about surviving life-threatening situations that causes people to re-evaluate their lives and make changes they might not have otherwise made.

Benny's marriage became stronger than ever. Harry flew home to Canada to help his newly widowed mother run the family farm. And no one was surprised when Roger left his wife later that year.

Sophie began to put the demons of the trip to rest and bloomed into a more confident person, eventually becoming a much respected charge nurse of another busy accident and emergency centre. And she did all this through the love and support of a very special person who came into her life 18 months after separating from Charlie…

On the evening of Sophie's parents' fiftieth wedding anniversary, at an ice hockey tournament in Auckland, Sophie was covering first aid, stationed down behind the players' benches, when she received a text out of the blue that went something like this…

'Good evening Ms Elliot. Would you like to go for dinner and dancing tonight after this game?'

Her best friend, Maree, who was also an official at the tournament, was standing beside her. Sophie's face lit up like a Christmas tree.

'Brett's here, at the rink!' she said. 'And I think he just asked me out on a date!'

Sophie was frozen to the spot, knowing he was probably watching from somewhere behind her, up in the grandstand. She was excited, and her eyes were dancing wildly as she gave Maree her phone to read the message.

Eight months after the trip to Mexico, Brett had also separated from his wife. He and Sophie were firm friends but they only saw each other at hockey, so his invitation had come out of the blue.

'That's so romantic!' said Maree as she handed the cellphone back with a knowing smile. 'You would be perfect together.'

Sophie typed in her answer and pressed send. 'Good evening Mr Evans. Yes, I would love to!'

She raced home after the game and changed out of her rink clothes into a cute little purple cocktail dress. She was incredibly nervous and had wild butterflies in her stomach for the first time since she was a teenager and dating Chad, her first love.

Brett collected her, and they had a magical evening. When he dropped her home, he kissed her on the doorstep, and Sophie thought she would surely melt. He had swept her off her feet!

Because of their four teenage children, Brett and Sophie agreed to take it slowly. There was an incredible friendship at stake here too. So while they still saw each other a few times at the rink, they didn't go on another date for several weeks. At the end of year 'Auckland Ice Ball', Brett asked Sophie to dance. They danced inseparably for the entire evening, and the electric sparks of attraction were undeniable.

They were inseparable, forever, from that moment.

Three years later, down on one knee, Brett presented Sophie with a perfect, princess cut diamond ring and asked her to marry him.

She burst into tears and, once she could breathe again, whispered, 'Yes, of course!'

Brett and Sophie were married at a small ceremony with their close friends and family present. Beauden was Brett's best man,

Maree was Sophie's maid of honour, and Anton and Hayden walked the bride down the aisle.

Anton and Hayden had already known Beauden and Nicole for years and they all got along famously, with a lot of fun and laughter.

As time went by, Brett and Sophie would say they were more in love with each other every day. They would never take each other, or their fairytale love, for granted. They were the happiest they had ever been in their lives.

Like a phoenix from the fire, their love had risen out of an amazing friendship and an extraordinarily precious bond forged in difficult times. No couple they knew could ever match it.

Sophie had found her fairytale ending.

She was his princess, and he was her knight in shining armour.

Chapter Thirty-Eight

EPILOGUE

Nine years later, Brett and Sophie were sitting in the grandstand of Paradise Ice Rink in Botany, Auckland, when New Zealand's senior men's ice hockey team, the Ice Blacks, beat Mexico 4–2. Anton was with them watching the game, and Kieran, Steele, Craig and Dave were all on the ice.

Sophie raced down to the benches at the end of the game to congratulate the players on their avenging win. 'And *we* didn't have to poison anyone!' she exclaimed jubilantly.

As Brett and Sophie left the arena, hand in hand, Brett stopped to talk to a friend by the entrance. Sophie stood back.

Then she saw Juan at the score bench. It was the first time she had clapped eyes on him since their infamous trip to Mexico. As he turned to walk in her direction, his eyes locked with Sophie's.

She stood her ground.

He stopped dead in his tracks.

She held his gaze.

The instant flicker of recognition and shame in his eyes were unmistakable.

She – avenged.

He – defeated.

Closure.

Sophie simply smiled.
Then walked away.

THE END
(Inspired by true events)